and the Year-Round Christmas Mysteries

"Delightful. . . . [A] humorous tinsel-covered tale that made me laugh out loud even while keeping me guessing."
—*New York Times* bestselling author Jenn McKinlay

"Delany has given us a story full of holiday cheer, an exciting mystery, [and] wondrous characters all in a place I would love to really visit. Its charm just lit up my day. This is one mystery you shouldn't miss this holiday season."
—Escape with Dollycas into a Good Book

"[A] smartly funny series."   —Kings River Life Magazine

"I delved right into this story—it grabbed me in and wouldn't let me go."   —Socrates' Book Reviews

"Vicki Delany does a masterful job of creating an inviting fictional small town that is all about Christmas."
—Open Book Society

"The dynamic characters in this series really are what stand out most. . . . Compelling and kept me guessing. A great holiday read."   —A Cup of Tea and a Cozy Mystery

"A cozy mystery filled with murder, mayhem, warmth, and Christmas cheer. What more could you want?"
—Carstairs Considers

BERKLEY PRIME CRIME TITLES
BY VICKI DELANY

The Catskill Summer Resort Mysteries

DEADLY SUMMER NIGHTS
DEADLY DIRECTOR'S CUT

The Year-Round Christmas Mysteries

REST YE MURDERED GENTLEMEN
WE WISH YOU A MURDEROUS CHRISTMAS
HARK THE HERALD ANGELS SLAY
SILENT NIGHT, DEADLY NIGHT
DYING IN A WINTER WONDERLAND

Deadly Director's Cut

~

VICKI DELANY

BERKLEY PRIME CRIME
New York

BERKLEY PRIME CRIME
Published by Berkley
An imprint of Penguin Random House LLC
penguinrandomhouse.com

Copyright © 2022 by Vicki Delany
Excerpt from *Rest Ye Murdered Gentlemen* copyright © 2015 by Vicki Delany
Penguin Random House supports copyright. Copyright fuels creativity, encourages
diverse voices, promotes free speech, and creates a vibrant culture. Thank you for buying
an authorized edition of this book and for complying with copyright laws by not
reproducing, scanning, or distributing any part of it in any form without permission.
You are supporting writers and allowing Penguin Random House to continue to
publish books for every reader.

BERKLEY and the BERKLEY & B colophon are registered trademarks and
BERKLEY PRIME CRIME is a trademark of Penguin Random House LLC.

ISBN: 9780593334393

First Edition: March 2022

Printed in the United States of America
1 3 5 7 9 10 8 6 4 2

Book design by George Towne

To all the cozy readers

Chapter 1

"LIGHTS. CAMERA. ACTION!"

Velvet McNally clapped her hands. "This is so exciting, Elizabeth. I can't believe I'm watching a real-life movie shoot."

"Quiet!" a clipboard-bearing man bellowed. "Or I'll have the set closed." He gave us a furious glare, his right cheek bulging with chewing gum, and Velvet dipped her head and mumbled, "Sorry."

"Quite all right, Gary. Enthusiasm does get the better of attractive young women sometimes." The director turned in his chair and gave my friend a smile and a slow wink. "Which is why we love them so."

Velvet giggled and blushed to the roots of her sleek blond hair. I refrained from rolling my eyes. As the manager of a Catskills resort, I've learned not to let my feelings show on my face. Not too much, anyway.

"Now, shall we try again?" the director said. "Miss Grant, when you are ready. Which I sincerely hope is this very moment."

The woman in front of the camera lifted her arms, and the emerald-green silk of her dress flared around her. It was a hot day, and the sun was strong, but she appeared cool and composed, hair and makeup flawless, dress unwrinkled. She cried, "This is a mistake, Reginald. You'll regret it for the rest of your life."

"I have to take a chance, Grandmama," the heartbreakingly handsome man facing her said. "Surely you, of all people, can understand that." A light wind blew off the lake and rustled his slightly-too-long black hair. He wore perfectly tailored casual beige slacks, an open-necked shirt, and his accent was direct from the Upper East Side.

The camera, mounted on a tripod of legs on a wooden plank, closed in on her. One man stood behind it, peering through the lens, while another crouched alongside, guiding the big wheels. Two canisters containing film were mounted on the top. A box, which I'd been told held sound recorders, dangled from a boom held above the actors' heads. Even though it was full daylight, giant lamps poured light onto the actors' faces. "I've made mistakes, Reginald," the woman said, her own aristocratic voice breaking with emotion. "Dreadful mistakes. I don't want to see—"

I touched Velvet lightly on the arm to get her attention, and when I had it I raised my eyebrows and tapped my watch.

She shook her head and mouthed, "Nothing."

I nodded, gave her a wiggle of my fingers to say goodbye, and turned my back on the lake and the movie shoot. I couldn't get over the number of people and the amount of equipment needed to film one short scene in one Hollywood movie. A great many of the people seemed to do nothing but hang around in the background, looking bored and smoking one cigarette after another.

I carefully negotiated my way past catering tables laden with lunch and cold drinks and around the maze of thick black cables crisscrossing the lawn, up the small hill toward the main hotel building. We employ our own security staff, of course, but the movie had brought theirs, who were keeping an eye on the crowd. This was a well-heeled, well-behaved bunch, and the guards didn't have much to do.

I could understand why Velvet, the outdoor activities coordinator at Haggerman's Catskills Resort, had nothing to do today. Almost every one of our guests was gathered on the hillside watching movie magic being made. Who would want to do calisthenics on the dock, take a paddleboat out for a slow tour of the lake, or play rounds of tennis when the great Gloria Grant was being directed by the equally great Elias T. Theropodous.

Not only guests were entranced by the movie production. At the sight of me rapidly crossing the lawn and rounding the flower beds, hotel staff scurried inside, where they would pretend to be hard at work.

Various paths meet in front of the hotel at a circular flower bed, into which a tall pole filled with brightly painted direction signs points to the swimming pool, the beach, the boat dock, the tennis and handball courts, the cabins, and the parking lot. Something had been nibbling at the flowers at the base of the sign, and the earth was disturbed as though tunnels were being dug beneath. As it was unlikely to be anything that would threaten the foundations of the hotel, I simply made a mental note to ask the head gardener about it.

In the circular driveway that sweeps around the front entrance, a group of bellhops were clustered around Mr. Theropodous's shiny baby-blue 1953 Buick Skylark while cars tried to edge past it. Another bunch of my male employees peered into the back of the equipment van pulled onto the verge and chatted to the movie technician.

"Excuse me," I said to Mr. Theropodous's chauffeur, a tall, thin, scraggy-faced Black man in his late sixties, dressed in a plain dark uniform. "I'm sorry, but you can't park here. You're blocking the driveway."

He touched his uniform cap. "Apologizes, ma'am. Mr. Theropodous instructed me to remain here with the car."

"Perhaps he did, but this is my resort, and I'm instructing you to park around the back. With the exception of that one truck in case something's urgently needed, we agreed that your cars, equipment trucks, and trailers use our staff parking lot. I need you to park there with them."

He lowered his eyes and shifted his feet. "Mr. Theropodous insists that the car be available the instant he's ready to leave. He's staying at Kennelwood, ma'am."

"Yes, I know that."

The director and most of the major cast had rooms at Kennelwood Hotel, a resort considerably larger and more famous than us. The crew and lower-ranking actors were stuck in an assortment of bungalow colonies or cheap hotels near the town of Summervale. Only Gloria Grant herself was staying at Haggerman's, and that's because she'd taken my room in the house I share with my mother, Olivia Peters, the resort owner. To the delight of our guests, Gloria didn't tuck herself away but used the pool or enjoyed walks along the lakeside and woodland paths. Most people kept their distance, but if anyone approached her for an autograph she was always polite and signed cheerfully. I'd told my security guards to keep an eye out and if they thought anyone seemed to be bothering her to send them on their way, but their intervention had not been necessary.

I was bunking in with Velvet. By bunking, I mean sleeping on the floor on a reed-thin mattress, which had been taken out of service long ago.

I gave the chauffeur a bright smile, to show him how reasonable I was being. "Guests will be arriving throughout the day, and they have to be able to unload. I can't have the driveway blocked."

He twisted his hat in his hands. He looked genuinely concerned, and I felt awful. The man had his orders from his employer, but I had 350 guests to think about.

"Is there a problem here?" A man stepped off the veranda, flicking his half-smoked cigarette into a flower bed. I was glad the geraniums had been watered this morning. We hadn't had a drop of rain for more than a week, despite the constant humidity, and the temperatures remained in the high eighties. The surrounding woods were dry and brittle.

The chauffeur let out a sigh of relief at the sight of the new arrival. "Lady needs me to move the car, Mr. Oswald."

Mr. Oswald smiled at me and thrust out his right hand. He was also in his sixties, dressed in a dark suit and blue tie, close-shaven with thick silver hair, of average height, and the bearer of a round belly that might have been a basketball stuffed under his starched white shirt. "I'm sorry, but I don't think we've met. Matthew Oswald. I'm one of the producers of *Catskill Dreams*."

I took his hand in mine, and we shook. His grip was strong but not excessively so, and his hand smooth. "Elizabeth Grady, resort manager. My mother's Olivia Peters."

"Darling Olivia," he drawled. Louisiana, I guessed. "It's been years since I had the pleasure. I'd like to have a chance to catch up. Is she around, do you know?"

"Probably. But this car has to be moved. Either that or the truck."

"The truck's needed if a light bulb blows or another piece of equipment's called for in a hurry."

"Then move the car. Please."

Matthew studied my face for a moment. The bellhops, dressed in their red-and-blue uniform with the Haggerman's logo—two pine trees forming an *H* silhouetted against an orange sun rising over the lake—on the breast pocket, watched us. The chauffeur twisted his hat in his hands.

Oswald snapped his fingers in the direction of a hovering bellhop. "You. You'll be my runner."

The man—a decorated World War II veteran in his thirties—blinked. "Me?"

"You. Go with Freemont here and see where he parks the car. Then wait by Mr. Theropodous's side. The moment he looks like he's ready to call it a day or take a break, run and get Freemont and the car. That should work. You'll be back with the car," he said to the chauffeur, "and he won't need to know you moved it."

"Good plan. Thanks, Mr. Oswald," Freemont said.

"My staff work for me," I said. "I need Gordon here. We have a substantial number of new guests arriving this afternoon."

"What you don't need, Miss Grady, is an angry movie director."

"It's Mrs. Grady, and I guess not. Okay, Gordon, you can do as the man asks."

Gordon gave the watching bellhops an enormous grin. "Sounds like I'm in for a tough day, fellas. Standing around in the sun by the lake watching a movie being made. Better than unloading suitcases and trying to mollify guests tired and disgruntled after the long drive. Have fun, guys." He rounded the car and opened the door. "I don't suppose you can take the long way around and show me what this baby can do?" he said to the chauffeur.

"Not on your life," Freemont said.

We watched the Skylark drive slowly away. The bellhops returned to their jobs, and the technician clambered back inside his truck, leaving me alone with Matthew Oswald.

"You'll find," he said, "that Elias is demanding. He expects nothing but the best of everyone around him. That's why he's got three Academy Awards under his belt."

"At Haggerman's Catskills Resort," I said, "we give our best. To every one of our guests at all times. Unfortunately, that occasionally means some individuals can't have their pet needs accommodated. Not if it inconveniences others."

"I like you, Mrs. Grady," he said. "You've got spunk."

I tightened my lips rather than express what I was thinking.

"How much are we paying you to let us film here? Never mind answering, I can look it up fast enough. A great deal, I'd guess." He slowly looked around him, taking in the white four-storied main hotel shining in the sun, the spacious veranda dotted with tables and chairs, the line of cabins by the lake, the manicured lawns and perfectly maintained flower beds, the tennis and handball courts, the swimming pool, the small sandy beach. The lush green hills curving down to the sparkling waters of Delayed Lake. "Nice place you got here. Your mother inherited it last year, meaning this is your second season. You've got, what, two months, three at most, to earn enough to see you through the year, never mind maintain the place all year-round. You need the revenue; it's no secret Olivia Peters doesn't have any money of her own to put into the place."

"Do you have a point?"

"My point, Mrs. Grady, is you need us. You need Elias and WolfeBright Pictures. They're filming only a couple of scenes here, but they're important ones. After this one, there'll be more movies. Folks love the Catskills, and folks love seeing places they've been, or hope to go to one day, on the big screen. Because Elias is a perfectionist he insisted on coming all the way out here, rather than using a swimming pool and plastic pine trees on a Hollywood back lot to stand in for your mountain paradise. Make Elias happy and word will get around. He might even come back with another picture."

"I'm not entirely sure what you mean by making Elias happy," I said.

"Probably not what you're thinking," he chuckled. "We're having dinner here tomorrow, right?"

"Yes. Your group's dining in one of our private dining rooms and later staying for the evening's entertainment in the ballroom. Mr. Theropodous is hosting the dinner in my mother's honor."

"Good. Those old-time stars have a lot of appeal to Elias."

"He's older than she is."

"Not professionally, not by a long shot. Elias is on the top, and he's determined to stay there. Olivia Peters is finished."

I bristled at his comment and bit back a retort. What he said might be true, in one way, but he could have phrased it better. Her career might be finished, but that was only one part of my mother's life. I like to think her relationship with me, her only child, was growing stronger now that we were living and working together.

"Because I like you, Mrs. Grady, I'll give you a tip for nothing: don't worry too much about the food tomorrow night. Elias doesn't care. He'll eat anything. And everything. But make sure your waitstaff and bartenders are the best you have and that they're on the ball. When Elias orders something he expects it to be in front of him before the last words of the sentence are out of his mouth."

I wasn't sure if this man was giving me kindly advice or trying to frighten me. Probably even he didn't know.

"I'll be around most of the week, keeping an eye on my investment. I'm also staying at Kennelwood. Call me there if you need any advice on handling Elias. His secretary's been delayed and should be arriving on tomorrow's train." Matthew Oswald walked away without another word, pulling a cigarette packet out of his jacket pocket.

I watched him go. He'd been right about one thing: this hotel is all Olivia has left in the world, and it provides the livelihood of me and my aunt Tatiana. So far we're squeaking by and even running a small profit, but the hotel business is high-risk, and a seasonal resort even more so.

Richard Kennelwood, son of the owner of the neighboring hotel, had suggested the film crew work here, and I was more than grateful.

The substantial fee WolfeBright Pictures was giving us in order to film on our property would give us a comfortable amount of breathing room. Aside from the direct fee, word had quickly spread that we had movie people here, and reservations were pouring in from outside for our restaurant and ballroom as people hoped to get a glimpse of the stars. First thing this morning, I'd been told all seats at dinner were taken for the rest of the week, and we'd be squeezing them into the early-evening cocktail hour and the late-night entertainment.

Income was good, but a full hotel meant more work for me, and I'd better get back at it. I turned around quickly, in time to see rows of faces peering out the front windows. Some of the staff didn't duck fast enough, and they got the full force of my disapproving stare.

The door leading to the business offices and the kitchen areas are on one side of the lobby, tucked under the sweeping staircase leading to the grand ballroom and the more intimate dining and reception rooms. I crossed the lobby as fast as I could, dodging suitcase-laden bellhops, overexcited children, activities coordinators trying to corral overly excited children, gossiping women ("They say she's been seen . . ."), gossiping men ("Not for me to say, but I heard . . ."), complaining teenagers, couples arguing over whether they wanted to play handball or attend the dance classes, and all the cacophony of weekend arrival and departure in the Catskills.

As I passed the bell desk, the man behind it was saying into the phone, "But I don't have anyone." He saw me, and a look of sheer relief crossed his face. "Okay. Got it." He hung up and waved me down. "Mrs. Grady. A moment."

"Yes?"

"Switchboard has a long-distance call for Mr. Th—Th . . . The movie guy."

"Mr. Theropodous, what of it?"

"We've turned off the loudspeakers down by the dock. You said that was okay, right?"

"While they're filming there, yes."

"So switchboard can't call him to the phone. They want

me to send a page, but . . ." He looked around him and shrugged. "I haven't got anyone right now."

"Can't the switchboard tell them Mr. Theropodous will call them back?"

"Caller says, 'Right now. And make it snappy. Time is money, and so is a call from Hollywood.' I was wondering if you . . ."

"Okay. I'll run down and get him." I turned and headed back across the lobby. I'd already lost one bellhop to be Elias Theropodous's personal runner, and now I was expected to play message boy.

Time might be money, and the Hollywood executives might not be happy at holding on the phone line, but I didn't think Elias would be any happier at being interrupted in the middle of a scene. I was going to whisper the message to the gum-chomping assistant director, standing close, but not too close, to the great man, but I found myself momentarily mesmerized by the activity. There truly is something captivating about seeing movie magic being made. The cameras were rolling, Elias leaning forward in his chair, his hands on his knees, watching intently.

Gloria Grant lifted her arms, and the emerald-green silk of her dress flared around her. She cried, "This is a mistake, Reginald. You'll regret it for the rest of your life."

Hadn't I heard that very same line a while ago?

"I have to take a chance, Grandmama," the young man exclaimed. "Surely you, of all people, can understand that."

"I've made mistakes, Reginald," Gloria declared. "Dreadful mistakes. I don't want to see—"

"Stop. Stop." Elias leapt to his feet. He was a large man, tall and heavyset, with a formidable presence.

"Gloria, I have told you and I have told you. You're sounding regretful at having to tell him no. I don't want regret. I want rage!"

Gloria's eyes flared. "And I have told you and told you, Elias. This character's a woman of depth, of years lived.

She needs to bring her full range of human experience to dealing with her wayward grandson. She herself—"

"I don't want her life history, Gloria. I want you to do what I'm telling you to do." He swore loudly and heartily.

Some of the onlookers gasped in shock. A woman covered her son's ears. Too late, I thought.

I stepped forward and cleared my throat. "Mr. Theropodous?"

He swung around and glared at me. "Who are you, and what do you want?" His brown eyes were small and close together, his prominent nose lined with rosacea. His fleshy jowls wobbled when he talked, making me think, for one brief moment, of Winston, my aunt Tatiana's bulldog.

"Uh . . . I'm Elizabeth Grady? Manager of Haggerman's? Olivia Peters's daughter? We met when you arrived?"

"Can't you see I'm busy?"

"You have a phone call. From Hollywood. They say it's urgent and don't want to wait until you have a chance to call back. They're still on the line."

"Always something. Very well. We'll take a break. Fifteen minutes, people. And you"—he stabbed a finger at Gloria—"think about what I said. We do things my way here, and if that's not okay with you . . . you aren't the only old broad in Hollywood."

Gloria's face tightened with such anger I feared her makeup would crack. "Good luck finding someone else to step in at this point in time, Elias. How long do we have the use of this nice hotel for our filming? Less than a week, and then we're back to a sound stage."

Rather than reply, Elias snapped at me. "Where's the nearest phone?"

"I'll show you to the writing room. It's usually quiet in there at this time of day."

"It had better be. I'm not broadcasting my business to everyone in the mountains. Gary, get this scene rearranged. The sun's moving. I hate filming on location."

He stalked off, and I scurried along behind. Gordon, the bellhop assigned to be the director's runner, scurried after me.

I showed Elias to the writing room. As expected it was empty. On rainy days guests come here to play cards or board games or to write letters. I picked up the phone and pressed the button and told the switchboard operator I had Mr. Theropodous on the line. Then I handed him the receiver and left the room.

"This better be important," I heard him growl.

I shut the door behind me. "How's it going down there?" I asked Gordon.

"As Shakespeare says, 'Much ado about nothing.'" He shrugged. "I studied for a degree in English lit before the war. I wanted to be a college professor. But, well, the war happened."

It happened to all of us, I thought. Some far worse than others. I didn't ask him why he hadn't gone back to finish college.

"The lady says her lines. The director yells at her and says she did it wrong, so she says them again, exactly the same as before. Then the guy says his lines, and the director tells him he did it wrong, so he says them again, and the director says that's much better, even though I didn't see any difference."

"Outrageous!" Elias's voice leaked through the solid wooden door to the writing room. "Impossible! Do you want an Academy Award–worthy production or a high school play on film?"

A moment later the door flew open and Elias stormed out. He pushed past Gordon and me without a word. He shouted at two women fresh from the beauty salon, chatting happily and walking slowly, to get out of his way. They leapt aside and clutched their purses to their chests in terror.

Chapter 2

MY MOTHER, OLIVIA PETERS, HAD BEEN A BROADWAY and Hollywood dance star. The professional life of a dancer isn't long, and after one injury too many she'd been forced to retire. When she unexpectedly inherited Haggerman's Catskills Resort from an unknown admirer, she managed to convince me to move to the Catskills with her and run the hotel for her.

I'd been raised above a corner shop in Brooklyn and spent most of my adult life living in Manhattan walk-ups. I'd moved to the mountains with a great deal of trepidation, but I soon found that I like it here. I like it a lot. When I can get time to enjoy it, which over the summer isn't often.

I left my office at five thirty and went upstairs to check on preparations for this evening's cocktail party. Rosemary Sullivan, our manager of food service, was putting the finishing touches on the bar supplies as I came in. I popped a green olive in my mouth and asked, "All under control?"

"Need you ask?" she said.

"No. But I'm asking anyway. Where's the food?"

At that moment, the doors flew open and waiters carried in platters piled high. Tonight guests would munch on pigs in blankets, smoked oysters on toast, deviled eggs, small tomatoes with mayonnaise in the center and a shrimp placed on top, celery filled with a line of Cheez Whiz, fruit on skewers, squares of cheese stuck into a pineapple, and plenty of pickle trays. The cocktails would be as served in the most fashionable nightclubs of New York City. As well as managing the dining rooms and everything to do with the serving of food, outside of the realms of the chef and saladman, Rosemary worked as a bartender because she liked doing it and was good at it.

"Look at that," she said with a laugh. "All you have to do is say the word and things happen around here."

"Don't I wish. Have a good night."

"Are you coming back?"

"I don't intend to. I'm having dinner with Olivia and her guest, and I'd like to get what passes for an early night after that. Not that I get much sleep on Velvet's floor."

"I'd invite you to share my room, but I have even less space than Velvet."

Next I stopped in the main kitchen to check on dinner preparation. The scene of total and complete chaos told me everything was proceeding as normal. Chef Leonardo, aka Leon Lebowski, bellowed at me and waved a meat cleaver in my general direction. "You! Have you come to chop vegetables? To gently stir the roux until it is at the perfect consistency? To wash the pots and pans?"

"No."

"Are you here to finally fire that useless saladman?"

"No."

"Then get out!"

I did so. In the main dining room the waitstaff was laying the tables. They didn't need any help from me either, so I walked across the big room, through the closed doors, and into the busy lobby. On a Sunday evening weary guests were checking in amid piles of luggage, excited children, and overly tired babies.

"We have a lake view, right? We specifically asked for a lake view."

"Yes, Mrs. Cohen. Room 328 is one of our best suites, with a gorgeous view."

Of course all our rooms were "one of our best," and sometimes the "gorgeous view" was of a patch of trees.

"I want extra towels in our room. Last year there were not nearly enough."

"I'll instruct housekeeping, Mrs. Fitzpatrick."

"We expect Jenny to be caring for the children on our stay. She did a good job last year."

"I have a note on your registration card to that effect, Mr. D'Angelo."

I kept walking and managed to get out the door before anyone called for my help.

Outside, bellhops were unloading cars and ferrying mountains of luggage into the lobby or down the path to the lakeside cabins. The movie crew had packed up for the day, and the guests were once again going about their regular activities. On the lake, orange paddleboats steered for shore and rowboats headed out to try their luck at catching a fish. Mothers or hotel-provided nannies gathered the last of the children out of the pool or the lake. A handball game was underway, and next to the tennis court two elderly men were bent over a game of chess. I'd swear those two never moved, except to come in for meals. Their conversation never changed either.

"McCarthy's got the commies on the run," one said.

"He's gone too far," the other replied.

"Check," said the first.

I chuckled and carried on my way.

As I passed cabin four, I heard the sharp growl of my head gardener and stopped to see what was happening.

Mario's a big guy, and he loomed over Francis Monahan, garden assistant.

"Is something the matter?" I asked.

They both turned. At the sight of me, Francis released most of the tension in his neck and shoulders.

Francis is a shy, nervous man with a stutter, still traumatized by his wartime experiences and subject to bullying by some of the other staff. Not entirely willingly, I'd taken him under my wing, and I tried to look out for him without stepping on the toes of his immediate supervisor. He'd originally been employed as a dishwasher. After one catastrophe too many Rosemary had wanted to fire him outright, but I intervened to move him to a position that had less contact with fragile crockery and glassware.

"If there's a problem, Mario," I said, "you don't discuss it with the staff within possible hearing of our guests."

Mario looked around. "Don't see no guests."

"You know what I mean. What's the problem?"

"The garden shed was left off the latch this afternoon." Francis mumbled something about not him.

"Is it secure now?" I asked.

"Yeah," Mario said.

"Then we're okay, aren't we? Francis will remember to shut it properly next time. Was anything taken?"

"Weren't me," Francis muttered.

"Not that I can see," Mario said in answer to my question. "But we can't have people, guests or staff, wandering in willy-nilly." He pointed to the fierce set of garden shears in Francis's hand. "Dangerous places, gardens. Saws, scissors, axes, fertilizer, rodent traps, poison."

"We definitely don't want the guests hearing that we have a rodent problem," I said. "Do we? Have a rodent problem?"

"Squirrels climb in open windows and chew the wiring, mice get in the flour bins in the kitchen and into the bathroom in guests' rooms. Guests don't like seeing mouse droppings."

"I'm sure they don't. I noticed disturbed earth in the flower beds earlier, as though something had been tunneling beneath the soil. Do you know what caused that?"

"Moles. We've laid down poison. Like I said, dangerous places gardens, and we can't have people poking around where they're not wanted."

"Francis says he didn't leave the door unlatched, so please don't accuse him if you don't have proof. Do you?"

Mario glanced at the younger man. "No."

"You can carry on with what you were doing, Francis," I said.

"Yes, m'm." He bolted before I could change my mind.

"I'm sure a reminder notice posted on the inside of the door will help the problem," I said. "Otherwise, how's Francis working out?"

Mario took off his cap and rubbed at the top of his head. "Okay. He's a good worker, Francis, tries hard, but he needs a lot of direction. No initiative, you know. Before you say it, I shouldn't have assumed he's the one who left the door off the latch. Any one of the guys could have done it, but they've all left for the day, so I had no one else to yell at."

"You can't lock it?"

"We lock it overnight, but I can't have assistant gardeners wasting time trying to find me because they forgot their watering can." He grumbled and started to walk away. He didn't get far before he stopped at a pot of geraniums and plucked off yellowing leaves and dying blooms.

Y

MY MOTHER AND I LIVE IN A SMALL HOUSE NESTLED IN the woods at the edge of the property. It gives us some privacy, but it's close enough that I can get to the hotel in minutes in case of an emergency. I turned at the end of the lakeside path and headed up the hill toward home, looking forward to a relaxing evening for a change. The path narrowed when it reached cabin nineteen and the sign clearly marked STAFF ONLY. The dark woods closed in around me. The sounds of the lake and the busy resort fell away, and I breathed deeply, enjoying the scent of pine needles, thick undergrowth, pure clean air, and fresh water.

As I approached the house a furious chorus of barks began, and a woman's sharp voice said, "Calm down, Winston. It's only Elizabeth."

"Only Elizabeth," I said, as I climbed the steps to the porch. "What a greeting."

My mother and her guests smiled at me, and my aunt Tatiana said, "You know what I mean, *lastachka*." She's always called me her little swallow.

"I hope that empty glass is for me," I said.

"It is." My mother reached for the pitcher of martinis and poured me a generous amount, and Aunt Tatiana added two plump olives. I accepted the glass and dropped into a vacant chair with a sigh. Olivia was dressed in white pedal pushers and a blue-and-white-checked blouse with the collar turned up to frame her beautiful face. Her black hair was swept back into a chignon, her dark eyes rimmed with mascara, her lipstick a pale pink matching the polish on her fingers. Tatiana had dressed to have dinner with her sister's guest in a blue housedress that might have been new before America joined the war, thick dark stockings, and heavy-soled brown shoes. As usual she wore no makeup and her only jewelry was the thin gold wedding band she never took off.

I don't think Aunt Tatiana has worn lipstick since her wedding day.

"Miss Grant was telling me about the hours and hours she has to spend in makeup to look natural for a single minute in front of the camera," Velvet said. She'd changed into slim-fitting pink slacks and a pale green shirt. She looked cool and comfortable, unlike me with my girdle and stockings sticking to my hips and legs, sweat soaking into my bra, and my poodle haircut badly in need of refreshing, if I can ever find time to get to the hotel's beauty salon. Like Lucille Ball, I have curly red hair, thus I've copied her hairstyle. It looks better on Miss Ball.

Gloria Grant, legend of the silver screen, smiled at me in greeting and sipped her own drink. She might be a legend, but she hadn't made the effort to look like one tonight, dressed in a simple yellow shirtwaist with a thin belt, sensible shoes, dark brown hair pulled back, no makeup, and jewelry nothing but a pair of square gold earrings clipped to her small ears. But her pale skin was so fine, her eyes so blue, her bone structure so good, her smile so sparkling, I could see why she'd been a star.

A tray of canapés, samples of the food that would be served at this evening's cocktail party, rested on the table. The food was untouched, and I mumbled, "Sorry. I'm famished. I never did get lunch," as I grabbed a pastry-wrapped sausage.

"Tatiana said we had to wait for you." Velvet plucked at a square of orange cheese impaled to a pineapple by a toothpick.

"Is only polite," my aunt said through a cloud of cigarette smoke. Aunt Tatiana is in charge of the housekeeping department at Haggerman's.

"I was telling your mother and your aunt how lucky they are to have this marvelous place," Gloria Grant said. "I'm so pleased I was able to come. The setting is gorgeous, everything is immaculate, the food is wonderful, and your gardens in particular are a delight."

I felt a flush of pride. We'd worked long and hard to whip Haggerman's back into shape after years of genteel neglect by the previous owner. "Like in the movies, it takes a lot of work behind the scenes to make everything look so effortless."

"That is certainly true."

"How did today's filming go?" I asked when I had food in one hand and a full martini glass in the other.

"Well enough, I think. I have not worked with Mr. Thompson before, and I was unsure about him. Those ever-so-handsome young men can rarely act, but he seems to be . . . adequate."

"Sooo handsome is right," Velvet sighed.

Gloria's look was surprisingly stony. "Beware, dear. They're all alike, those ones. Are you coming to the dinner tomorrow?"

Velvet shot me a pleading glance, which Olivia interpreted. "You'd be welcome, Velvet."

"Oh, gosh. Thanks. That will be so great. Not just to meet Todd Thompson, but all the rest of you."

"I was surprised to hear Todd call you Grandmama when you were filming," I said. "Are you playing his grandmother? Surely—"

Gloria's face twisted. "I'm twenty years older than him. Barely old enough to be his mother, never mind his grandmother. But my glory days are behind me, and at my age I'm lucky to get any roles at all, so I don't complain."

"I've been told," I said, "that the director Mr. Theropodous can be somewhat . . . demanding."

"Gloria was married to Elias Theropodous at one time," Olivia interrupted quickly.

"Oh," I said, "Sorry."

Gloria snorted. "Don't apologize, Elizabeth. Elias's temperament is legendary, and his moods didn't lessen one bit once we closed the door of our apartment. Which, I have to add, is why we are no longer married. I've worked with a lot of directors over the years, and none of them are easy, but Elias takes it to a whole new level. He has won three Academy Awards, so as far as the industry's concerned, he can do whatever he wants, although word is . . . never mind that. At least he hasn't assaulted a member of the cast. Not yet. Not

publicly, at any rate." She smiled at my mother. "Do you remember, Olivia, when we were doing that film with Esther
Williams and that awful director, I forget his name now,
threw the young dancer into the pool in a fit of rage because
she went right when everyone else went left? She couldn't
swim, and no one noticed until she'd almost drowned."

"Oh, yes," Olivia said. "Good times."

They laughed. Tatiana shook her head and slipped a piece
of cheese to Winston.

"Is acting something you can learn?" Velvet said in a
soft voice. "Or do you have to be born to it? Like dancing.
I wanted to be a dancer, like Olivia, but . . . sometimes I
have two left feet."

That was an understatement. Velvet could trip over a
speck of dust.

Gloria studied my friend's face and said nothing for a
long time. Velvet turned beet red under the other woman's
scrutiny. "You're beautiful, dear, and in the movies acting
skill is sometimes only secondary. But, I think, you're better off where you are. It's a hard life. Hard and ultimately
disappointing. Particularly for a woman. How old are you?"

"Twenty-seven. Same as Elizabeth."

"Too old," Gloria said bluntly, "to be starting out. I was
at the top of the marquee once, and not so long ago. My part
in this movie is small. Insultingly small, and I'm reduced
to playing an adult man's grandmother and taking orders
from my ex-husband. But they are paying me well because
my name is not yet forgotten and the producers know that."
She shrugged and sipped her drink. "Thus, here I am. Not
entirely because of the money, but because the attention of
the camera is like a drug. Once it bites you, you have to
have it. No, Velvet, better you stay well away."

Velvet smiled politely and chose a deviled egg. She didn't
look all that convinced.

I glanced at my mother, staring vacantly into the trees.
It wasn't the camera she'd loved but the applause. She'd ap-

peared in some movies, but Broadway was Olivia's first love. It had been hard on her when she had to step away from the limelight. She could have gone on to teach dance or become the artistic director of a small dance company, but it wasn't in her nature to take a behind-the-scenes role. She quit show business altogether in favor of becoming a patron of the arts. Then her third husband stole all her money . . . and here we are.

Winston leapt to his feet and set up another chorus of barking. Gloria started and clutched her chest. "Goodness, that frightened me."

We heard the snap of dead branches, the squeak of wheels, a grunt of effort, a minor amount of swearing, and then Randy Fontaine, our head lifeguard and supervisor of water-based activities, rounded the corner, pushing a cart laden with room service dishes. A waiter followed him with a second cart.

"Hey there!" Randy called. "I ran into a couple of busboys heading this way, and I said I'd give them a hand so one of them could get back to work. Hi, Velvet. How you doing?"

"Fine, thanks, Randy," she said.

I threw her a quick glance. Her tone was surprisingly frosty. I'd thought she and Randy were . . . if not exactly dating at least getting close.

Apparently not.

The men reached the bottom of the stairs and began unloading the carts. Delicious smells wafted out from beneath the covered dishes. I put down my glass, grabbed another pastry-wrapped sausage, popped it in my mouth, and hurried to help carry dishes.

"You've brought six sets of plates and cutlery," I said to Randy. "We're only five for dinner."

"Will you look at that," he said. "What a silly mistake. I bet there's enough food for six people here too."

"Oh, all right," I said. "You can join us."

"If you must," Velvet mumbled.

Chapter 3

MONDAY MORNING THE FILM CREW WERE ON SITE AND set up early, wanting to get the morning light as the sun rose over the lake. Todd Thompson, today wearing a perfectly cut white blazer and tailored dark slacks, was on the dock with an older man, who I guessed was playing his father. They yelled at each other a lot and waved their hands in the air while the camera rolled, and Gary alternately shouted "Action" or "Cut." Gloria wore her own clothes, and she and my mother had been given chairs in pride of place next to the director.

Later in the day, they moved everything up the hill to film on the porch of cabin one, the largest and most expensive private cabin we have, situated next to the main building, facing the lake, close to the beach, the courts, and the swimming pool. Fortunately, the occupants of cabin one were big film fans and thrilled to turn over their porch for the day provided they were allowed to get close to the excitement.

Over dinner last night, Gloria had described the movie to us. It was set in 1942, and Todd played Reginald Vandross, scion of a New York family making money hand over fist now that their household-appliance factories had been converted to manufacturing armaments for the war effort. Reginald had decided to join the army rather than take advantage of his father's political connections to stay safe at home in America, helping to run the business. He came to his family's regular vacation retreat in the Catskills to say goodbye to his beloved grandmother, played by Gloria, who is determined to make him change his mind. Gloria is also determined that Reginald will not marry the beautiful but impoverished Esmeralda Sanchez, who labors at a menial job in one of those factories. The woman playing Esmeralda, a new face in Hollywood named Rebecca Marsden, was due to arrive tomorrow for her scenes in which Reginald would visit her in the bungalow colony where he'd hidden her prior to their secret wedding the night before he leaves to join his unit.

"And then what happens?" a wide-eyed Velvet had asked breathlessly. "You can tell us. Does he come back from the war bitter and maimed, or proudly facing the future? Does he still love her? Do they live happily ever after? Please say yes."

Gloria smiled at her. "This movie is already being talked about as an Oscar contender. I won't say I have my own hopes for another nomination, but mine is a powerful, although small, role. I couldn't tell you how it ends even if I wanted to, dear. I haven't seen any of the script other than my own part and of that only the early bits. I appear again at the end, in a scene at my luxury apartment overlooking Central Park when young Reginald returns from the war." Her face twisted. "It's supposed to be four years later, and I fear they'll attempt to age me twenty years. I haven't seen my portion of that part of the script. Elias runs a very tight ship."

"Why's it called *Catskill Dreams*?" Velvet asked.

"When Reginald is away at the war, he dreams of his favorite place on earth—the resort where the family spends their summers," Gloria had told her. "Elias himself grew up close to here, near Summervale, I believe. He left after his parents died when he was young, and as far as I know he never came back. He's anything but a sentimental man, but in the movie he wanted the character, off at war, to have powerful memories of a beloved childhood vacation spot, and he remembered the Catskills."

AS USUAL, I SPENT MOST OF THE GORGEOUS SUMMER DAY inside my dark office, bent over the account books or trying to solve numerous problems. The department heads are good, and I generally leave them to run their departments, but one crisis or another is always popping up, and streams of people come in and out of my office expecting me to solve them.

Velvet stuck her head in around lunchtime to tell me that most of her daily programs were back on track. "It's the second day of filming, so some of our guests have lost interest. Movie people do seem to spend a lot of time standing around doing nothing. I'm looking forward to hearing more about it at dinner tonight." She sighed happily.

I leaned back in my chair, grateful for the chance to take a break. "What's happening with you and Randy?"

Her eyes narrowed. "Why do you ask?"

"I got the impression you two were coming to a . . . shall we say understanding. But last night you were so cold you were almost rude to the poor guy. I considered putting the fire on."

"We never had any *understanding*, Elizabeth. That was your imagination."

I shrugged and picked up my pencil. Break over. "Okay."

"I mean, Randy's nice enough and all, but . . . a Catskills summer romance? How common is that?"

"Nothing wrong with common."

"A girl needs some adventure in her life."

"Romantic adventure is vastly overrated."

"Says you, who's been married. Life with Ron was an adventure, wasn't it?"

I hesitated and then forced out a smile. My brief marriage had not been an adventure. More like being trapped in a horror story. Of that, I never spoke. Not even to Velvet, although she and I had been the best of friends ever since we were very young, back in Brooklyn. Aunt Tatiana knew, I suspected, that I had not mourned the man. I sometimes thought she could read my mind. But she never said anything.

"You heard Gloria invite Randy to dinner tonight," I said. "So be nice."

"I can be nice," Velvet said. "When I want to."

She flounced out, and I picked up the phone and asked to be put through to the kitchen. I should have saved myself some time and walked over. When Chef Leonardo had finally been tracked down, I said, "I'm checking on tonight's private dinner. Is everything going to be ready?"

"You think I wouldn't tell you if I had a problem?"

"Yes, I think exactly that."

He huffed.

"Please go over the menu with me," I asked as politely and patiently as I could manage.

"I sent you a copy yesterday."

"Humor me," I said. Leon was a great cook but a terrible manager, and he had a mind of his own. If he'd decided fish would be a better main course than the chicken we'd decided on, he might not bother to tell me.

"Mushroom soup or beet salad. Stuffed breast of veal with roast potatoes or chicken à la king with rice. Daily vegetables. Chiffon cake or coconut cream pie."

"Juices and pickles and bread rolls?"

"What do you take me for, Mrs. Grady? A short-order cook in a Bronx diner?"

"Just checking. Thank you. If you see Rosemary, will you ask her to come to my office?"

"I am not your messenger boy." He hung up.

I next asked the switchboard to summon Rosemary to my office.

She arrived only minutes later, bearing a tray with a bowl of soup and a sandwich. "I was passing through the kitchen, so I said I'd bring your lunch. It was getting cold waiting for someone to get someone to tell someone to bring it to you." She shoved a stack of papers aside with her elbow and put the tray on a side table.

I eyed it. "Not tuna fish again! I loathe tuna fish. The kitchen knows I loathe tuna fish. Why do they always give me a tuna fish sandwich?"

Rosemary chuckled. "Probably because no one else wants it. Try the soup. It's mushroom, and it's very good. Leon changed the recipe. What's up?"

"About the private dinner for the movie people tonight. I want your best staff working it."

"I can arrange that. Okay if I send Luke?"

"The ladies in the dining room will have to miss him for one night." Luke Robinson had a reputation among what's known throughout the Catskills as "Weekday Widows": women who spend the season at the resorts while their husbands commute up from the city on weekends.

"As you want the best," Rosemary continued, "I'll take the bar myself. Is Olivia going to be okay with that?"

"She's coming around."

Olivia had initially refused to allow Rosemary to work as a bartender, believing that was a man's job. Rosemary had stepped in to cover an emergency and done such a good job, Olivia tactfully never mentioned her objection again. So now Rosemary worked as a bartender as well as the manager of food service. That didn't seem like a good deal to me, but she considered it to be a victory.

"I checked with Leon about the dinner, but my courage

failed me when I was about to ask him to call Nick to the phone."

Nick Timmins was our saladman, in charge of cold foods. He could be as difficult and temperamental as the head chef. "Predinner canapés are under control?"

"I'll make sure they are. With a touch extra."

"Thanks, Rosemary," I said, and she left.

The soup was delicious, and I ate the soggy bread of the sandwich after I'd scraped off most of the tuna fish, trying not to breathe in the odor. After lunch I kept my eye on the clock. The business office closes at five, and I was determined to leave work precisely on time. Our special guests were due to arrive at six thirty for cocktails and sit down to dinner at seven. They would join the rest of the guests in the ballroom after dinner for dancing and to enjoy the evening's entertainment.

At quarter to five the phone on my desk rang. I crossed my fingers, hoping not to hear that the kitchen caught fire, the railings supporting the porch on one of the cabins collapsed, or someone got food poisoning at lunch.

"A lady here to see you, Mrs. Grady," said one of the office clerks.

"What about?"

"She says she's with the film crew."

I sighed. "Send her in."

I straightened in my chair, folded my hands on the desk in front of me, composed my face, and tried to look professional and competent.

A light tap on my door. I called, "Come in," and the door edged open.

A woman slipped in. She was tall and thin to the point of scrawny, with a sharply pointed chin, prominent nose, and washed-out blue eyes that darted around the room, not settling on anything, even me. She wore a dress the color of snow after a pack of wild dogs has crossed over it, which did nothing for her sallow complexion, and her brown hair, streaked with premature gray, was scraped back so tightly it pulled at the edges of her eyes.

"I'm sorry to bother you," she mumbled.

"Not at all. What can I do for you?"

She slipped into the room. "I'm Mary-Alice Renzetti. Mr. Theropodous's secretary."

I stood up and extended my hand. "Elizabeth Grady. Nice to meet you."

She took my hand. Hers felt like three-day-old fish, but she met my eyes and gave me an appraising glance. "They tell me you're the manager here. Of the entire place. That's unusual for a woman."

"My mother owns Haggerman's, but it's not at all uncommon in the Catskills to have women in positions of authority. So many of the places are family-owned. Mothers, daughters, wives simply do what they do best to make their businesses work."

A smile touched the edges of her mouth. "I wanted to check that everything's in order for tonight?"

"Very much," I said. "I'm looking forward to the evening."

"I'm sorry I wasn't here when we arrived but . . . I had a family emergency."

"I hope everything's okay now?"

"My mother had a fall, but she'll be fine. Thank you for asking. Mr. T. likes things to be done properly."

"Let me assure you, so do I and the entire staff at Haggerman's."

"Mr. T. expects . . . efficient service."

"Miss Renzetti, why are you telling me this? The nature of our business here is ensuring our guests have the best of everything."

"Thank you. Thank you. I just . . . well if anything goes wrong, Mr. T. won't be happy."

I assumed that meant he'd take out his anger on his secretary.

"It won't." I sat down. "I'll see you this evening, then."

She mumbled her thanks and left.

Poor woman. I've had bullying bosses myself. We all have. I'd learned that the only way to survive was to grow a backbone and stand up for yourself.

No one needed to come here and ask me to ensure everything went well. It was an important night. Not only for the reputation of Haggerman's but also for Olivia personally, and I was determined it would be a success.

Chapter 4

AT SIX FIFTEEN I WAS IN ONE OF THE SMALL RECEPTION rooms on the second floor. We'd be offering canapés before dinner, and they'd be the same as served for the regular cocktail party but with an added extra touch. A larger shrimp on the cucumber squares, more stuffing in the mushrooms, more clams in the dip. The bar was set up and ready, and Rosemary stood behind it, neat and smart in a stiffly ironed black skirt and white blouse with a black bow tie. Next door in the private dining room the linens on the table were starched, the good silver cutlery polished, the glasses sparkling, the plates shining. I never join hotel guests for dinner, but this was a private party put on by Mr. Theropodous in honor of Olivia, and she wanted me to attend. So here I was.

I'd managed to carve a few minutes out of my day to pop into the beauty parlor and have them tidy up my poodle cut. I wore my best dress, a soft shade of green with a tight bodice, thin straps, and a swing skirt that flared around my knees, with two-inch heels. I'd applied an extra touch of lipstick and rouge; my earnings were gold squares, and my necklace was my sixteenth-birthday gift from my father, a real (although small) diamond on a gold chain.

Velvet was the first to arrive. She looked stunning in a dress of polka dots draped over layers of pink tulle, with a deep square neckline and a huge dark red bow pinned to a thin shoulder strap. She'd arranged her long blond hair to fall over her right shoulder in a golden wave. Her lipstick was the exact shade of the bow on her dress.

"Do you think I've overdressed for dinner?" she asked me. "It's not too much, is it?"

"You look fine, Velvet. It's not only dinner, remember. We'll be dancing in the ballroom after."

"We? You mean you're going to dance?"

"By we, I mean you." Dancing with guests who might otherwise not have a partner is part of Randy's and Velvet's duties here.

I wasn't entirely surprised that Mary-Alice was the next to arrive. She slipped nervously into the room and looked around the dining room. It must have met her expectations, as something relaxed in her shoulders. "This all looks . . . nice."

"Thanks," I said. "Are you"—I tried not to notice that she was in the same dress she'd been wearing earlier— "going to be joining us?"

"Oh, yes. I'll sit next to Mr. T."

"Hi," Velvet said. "I'm Velvet McNally. I work here."

"That must be so nice." Mary-Alice gave Velvet a genuine smile. "This is a beautiful hotel. I love the Catskills. When I was a girl we came to a small hotel near Liberty every year. Such happy times."

Footsteps sounded on the stairs and voices came from the hallway, and we had no time to talk over happy times. I gave Rosemary a thumbs-up, and Velvet and I went to the door to greet our guests.

Ellis Theropodous came in with Matthew Oswald and Richard Kennelwood, son of the owner of the hotel on the neighboring lake, where many of the moviemakers were staying. Mary-Alice hurried to the bar and got her boss a bourbon on the rocks, without asking what he'd like. Richard joined Velvet and me.

"Nice dress," he said. "Dresses, I mean. You both look great."

"Thanks," my friend and I chorused.

"I see someone I want to talk to. Catch you later, alligators." Velvet hurried away. The person she seemed to need to talk to all of a sudden was Rosemary, too busy behind the bar to chat to anyone.

"Can I get you a drink, Elizabeth?" Richard's thickly lashed hazel eyes smiled down at me. His freshly washed dark hair curled slightly at the nape of his neck; he was closely shaven and smelled of spicy aftershave. He'd dressed for the evening in a perfectly tailored dark blue suit and thin red tie.

I felt myself blushing, for no reason whatsoever. "Thank you. Ask Rosemary to make me something light and frothy. But first, I haven't had the chance to thank you in person for . . ." I tipped my head in the direction of Elias Theropodous and Matthew Oswald.

"I should thank you for taking them off our hands," Richard said. "Dad sometimes forgets he isn't running the show anymore."

Kennelwood Hotel had been established by Richard's grandfather and run for many years by Richard's father, Jerome. Jerome's business ethics had occasionally veered onto the shadier side, and after one too many clashes with his father, Richard left for New York City. This past winter Jerome suffered a serious health crisis and Richard returned to take over the running of Kennelwood. The deal had been that Jerome would continue to be the face of the hotel, greeting guests, playing the gregarious host, while

Richard controlled everything. Jerome occasionally forgot his side of the deal, and he'd arranged for WolfeBright Pictures to film their movie at Kennelwood. He hadn't bothered to tell his son about that, or that the movie shoot was scheduled for the same week as a major boat race on their lake. You couldn't have 1953-era powerboats zipping back and forth in the background of a movie set during the war, nor have the actors shouting over the noise of the powerful engines while pretending nothing was going on behind them. Delayed Lake is smaller than the one at Kennelwood, so we couldn't accommodate the boats. Instead, Richard asked me if we could handle the movie shoot, although the major actors would stay at Kennelwood for the duration of the filming.

Gloria Grant contacted Olivia to say she was going to be in the area, and Olivia invited her friend to stay with her. Catering for the cast and crew on set would still be taken care of by the Kennelwood kitchens, all Haggerman's had to do was provide space on our property, the view of the background, and try to keep autograph hunters at bay.

The actors began to arrive for dinner, and Richard went for our drinks. The table in the private dining room had been set at its capacity of twenty, and I hoped that was enough. Last night, although she wasn't the host and she wasn't paying the bill, Gloria had impulsively invited Velvet and Randy to join the group, and I feared what would happen if she'd continued doing that throughout the day.

Richard handed me my drink. It was served in a champagne coupe, pale orange liquid with a frothy surface topped with a red cherry.

"What's this called?" I asked.

"Whiskey sour. A classic. Rosemary says it's hugely popular in the clubs of Manhattan these days."

I took a cautious sip and moaned with pleasure.

"Jerome Kennelwood and I go a long way back." Elias's loud voice boomed across the room. "So, naturally, when I thought of the Catskills, I remembered Jerome. He was unable to join us tonight, so his son, Richard, came in his place. Richard, here's someone you need to meet. Mary-Alice, get Richard over here."

Richard waggled his eyebrows at me and went to join the men. Velvet took his place next to me, champagne cocktail in hand. "Where's Olivia?"

"Waiting to make an entrance, I expect."

"Is Tatiana coming?"

"Heavens no. She was invited, but this sort of formal shindig isn't exactly Aunt Tatiana's thing. Even if she wanted to come, I doubt she'd have something she'd consider suitable to wear, and she won't exactly fit in Olivia's clothes."

"No kidding. Is there any way in which Tatiana and Olivia are similar?"

"Not a single thing I can think of." It would be hard to find two sisters more different than Olivia and Tatiana. Olivia Peters isn't even my mother's real name. She was christened Olga Petrovia, daughter of working-class Russian immigrants. Although her mother claimed, as almost every working-class Russian immigrant did, to be aristocracy who'd lost everything but their lives in the revolution. (When we'd been learning about the Russian Revolution and the first war in school, I did the math. I came home and asked my grandmother how they could have escaped from the Bolsheviks, as they'd been in America prior to 1917. She'd snapped at me to go and set the table.) A long-ago-star of the Bolshoi Ballet (or so she claimed) who lived upstairs from the family recognized Olivia's talent and encouraged it. From then on my mother was trained for the stage, while her older sister learned to be a proper Russian housewife and later took on the responsibly of raising her sister's child. I never thought Tatiana believed she got the worst of the arrangement. She and her husband, Rudolph, didn't have children of their own, but they'd loved each other deeply and had been very happy together until his death three years ago. It had been a good family to grow up in.

"I've seen you around, but we haven't been introduced," a deep voice said. "Let's correct that now, shall we?" The lead actor was looking at Velvet. His smile was so broad, his teeth so white, I almost needed my sunglasses. Up close, he was even more handsome than as seen from a distance. Dark hair worn slightly too long across his forehead, deep California tan, razor-sharp cheekbones, cleft chin, shoulders bulging under his perfectly cut dinner jacket. "I'm Todd Thompson."

Velvet's eyes popped out of her head. "V-V-Velvet Mc-Nally."

Todd took her hand in his and raised it to his lips. At five foot seven, he was shorter than she, but he didn't seem to notice, or care. "I'd offer to get you a drink, but you have one. Let me know when you need another, will you?"

"Uh—uh . . . okay."

"I hope you've been seated next to me at dinner, Velvet." He said her name as though he were caressing the cloth after which she'd been named.

Velvet's eyes flew to me.

I shrugged. "I didn't check the seating arrangements."

Todd didn't take his eyes from Velvet's face. He reached behind him and snapped his fingers. "Mary-Alice."

The woman popped up next to him as though in a puff of smoke. "Yes, Todd?"

"See that Miss McNally's seated next to me at dinner, will you? There's a good girl."

Another puff of smoke and Mary-Alice disappeared.

"Is Mary-Alice your secretary also?" I asked.

Slowly Todd turned to me. He smiled, but it wasn't the same all-encompassing, you're-the-center-of-the-world smile he gave Velvet. "Mary-Alice knows Elias likes me to be happy. I like me to be happy." Back to Velvet. "What about you, Velvet? Do you like to be happy?"

Oh for heaven's sake. I'd always considered Velvet to be a practical, down-to-earth woman, and here she was gushing and giggling as though she were a high school freshman and the quarterback of the football team had stopped to talk to her. There really was something about that Hollywood magic.

I turned to see Randy standing in the doorway. He also was a good-looking man: blond, tall, and muscular, strong facial features, but he didn't radiate charm as though the sun had come out from behind a cloud after days of rain. He certainly didn't radiate charm right now, not with that look on his face.

"Cheer up," I whispered to him. "They'll be gone in a few days."

"What? Oh, sorry, Elizabeth. I was just thinking about—about . . . a problem child in the pool today. Poor thing, scared out of his wits and his dad yelling at him not to act like a girl. Although, considering his sister was racing across the water, perhaps he should have acted more like a girl."

The small room was filling up. Rosemary was hard at work behind the bar, flipping bottles and scooping ice, and the waiters were bringing in fresh canapés and clearing dirty platters and glasses. I didn't recognize several of the guests, and I assumed they were actors, senior crew, or financial backers of the picture.

Richard was still talking to Elias and Gary, the assistant director. Or I should say being talked to by Elias and Gary, the assistant director. His eyes darted around the room, seeking escape. Mary-Alice handed Elias another drink, and he took it without so much as a glance toward her.

Two women came in, and Elias stopped talking midsentence and rushed to greet them.

Behind me, I heard Todd say, "Here she is. Let the

drama begin. I have to go and act happy to see her. Don't
go away, Velvet, I'll be back soon as I can. Rebecca! You're
here! How marvelous!" He strode across the room and
greeted the younger of the newcomers with a kiss on both
cheeks.

She was in her early twenties and stunningly beautiful.
Her golden hair was gathered in a French twist behind her
pale heart-shaped face, her eyebrows were plucked to two
fine black lines, her plump lips a slash of the deepest red.
She wore a floor-length crimson gown that left her white
shoulders bare and clung to every one of the ample curves
in her body. Above-the-elbow gloves matched the dress.

As everyone's attention turned to the two women, Matthew Oswald wandered over to me. "Talentless hack."

"I beg your pardon?"

"I could have used a stronger word than *hack*, but not in
the presence of ladies."

We watched as Todd and the new arrival fussed over
each other, while Elias and the woman who'd come with
the beauty watched approvingly. "That's Rebecca Marsden.
The female lead for the first half of the movie, before the
action moves to Europe. I didn't want her in this picture.
She's got the looks, I'll give her that, but she can't act her
way out of a paper bag. She would have been bearable in
the days of silent films. Voice like chalk on a blackboard."

"She's playing a character named Esmeralda Sanchez?"

"Yeah. I wanted Rita Moreno, but she was busy. At least
this one comes cheap. In more ways than one." He chuckled.

"Who's the woman with her?"

"Nancy Littlejohn. Great character actress. She plays the
supervisor at the factory where the girl works. Came up to
the Catskills to try to talk her out of running away with
Todd's character."

Nancy was a short woman in her thirties, verging on
plump, with a square face and a mop of black curls. She
wore a knee-length blue dress with matching jacket that was

attractive but didn't have the glamour of the other women's clothes.

"The whole darn casting—pardon my language, Mrs. Grady—of this flick is a disaster, except for Nancy and Gloria. Gotta give it to those old broads. They know how to give a producer his money's worth."

"Nancy can't be that much older than me," I protested. "I'm twenty-seven."

"Honey, if her name's not Elizabeth Taylor or Lauren Bacall, a woman's old in Hollywood if she's college age." He nodded to Velvet, watching Todd and Rebecca with wide eyes. "Your friend over there? Looking like she wants nothing more than to be in the pictures? Gorgeous as the best of them, more beautiful than most. Another year or two and she'll be about ready to play the mother parts. Time for another drink, I'd say." He wandered away, leaving me with a sour taste in my mouth, and not from my cocktail.

Nancy and Rebecca melted into the crowd, exchanging air-kisses with people they knew and being introduced to those they didn't. Todd returned to charming Velvet.

I glanced at my watch. It was two minutes to seven. Where was Olivia?

At that moment, I felt the air move. Conversation died mid-sentence, and everyone froze in place. I turned to see Olivia and Gloria entering the room.

Now, that was star power. Doubled.

They didn't pose dramatically. They didn't try to draw every eye. They simply knew they'd get it.

Gloria looked stunning in floor-length white satin with a sequined black bodice. The dress had short sleeves, and she matched it with long black gloves, a heavy diamond-and-gold bracelet, and earrings of cascading diamonds. To my considerable surprise, my mother was understated this evening, her perfect dancer's body wrapped in in a black knee-length dress with a high neckline, a long strand of pearls around her neck, and discreet pearl earrings. The pearls were fake, but you'd have to be a jeweler to recognize them as such. Her black hair was twisted behind her in a loose chignon, her makeup subtle, and her lipstick a soft pink.

She had, I realized, wanted to let her friend be the center of attention this evening. I felt a rush of affection for my mother. She caught me looking at her and gave me a startled smile.

At that moment, the doors to the dining room opened.

Elias dipped his head to Olivia and Gloria. "It would be my honor to escort the two most beautiful women in the Catskills, no, on the entire East Coast, to dinner."

They murmured politely, slipped their arms through his, and went through. The rest of the party followed them, like a couple of small pops after the firework show ended.

Rebecca Marsden's eyebrows were drawn together, and her mouth formed a tight line.

"Careful, dear," Nancy chuckled. "That expression will give you wrinkles. More wrinkles, I should say."

"Hi, Velvet," Randy said. "You look nice this evening."

Todd grabbed Randy's hand and pumped it. "I'm Todd Thompson. I have a small role in this movie. Velvet tells me you're the lifeguard. That must be . . . interesting."

"Elizabeth," Richard said, "can I show you to your seat?"

I turned to him with a genuine smile. "I'd be delighted."

EVERYTHING AT THE DINNER WAS PERFECT, BUT I WAS too anxious that it be so to appreciate it.

The food was excellent and plentiful; the drinks flowed freely. The waiters were attentive. Maybe slightly too attentive, as when Luke bent over Rebecca and gave her a long penetrating look she was happy to return. We served wine with the meal, the best we had, but Elias stuck to bourbon, and Mary-Alice spent most of the time hopping up and down fetching his drinks, because apparently he couldn't wait long enough for a waiter to bring them.

On the surface the conversation was lively and friendly, but there were strong undercurrents swirling around, and I realized that outside this movie shoot, most of these people wouldn't want to have anything to do with one another.

Matthew regaled Richard with the ups and downs (mostly downs, according to him) of being a movie producer, and Gary chomped gum between courses, while he grumbled about the difficulties of filming on location rather than in a studio. Todd dropped names to Velvet of all the stars he was friends with and all the fabulous parties he'd attended lately, and Elias interrupted to say that maybe Todd should spend more time learning his craft and less time at parties. Todd's mouth tightened, but he pretended not to hear. Randy told anyone who'd listen about his time in Hollywood and tried to make it sound as though he'd left the acting life because it bored him rather than because he couldn't make a go of it. Rebecca laughed at everything her dinner companions had to say, but the tightness of her grip on her fork or glass told me she was not having a particularly good time. She barely touched her food, but Luke was constantly topping up her wineglass.

Olivia, by contrast, was having a great time. She was back in her element. She told everyone about her new life at Haggerman's, which, according to her, was nothing but one long glorious vacation. I could have told them about the time the septic tank between cabins nine and ten overflowed, or when I'd stepped between two waiters fighting over tips and got a punch in the face for my trouble, or when a husband had arrived unexpectedly from the city to find Luke in his wife's bedroom, or . . . But no one was interested in what went on behind the scenes (or in the case of Luke and Mr. and Mrs. Berkwowitz, in full view of the entire hotel) at a Catskills resort. Like the movies, they wanted to see the glamour of it and to know nothing about the hard work that made it all happen.

Gloria and Elias chatted about mutual friends and laughed together about the old days when they'd been married. Rebecca gnawed on lettuce leaves and celery sticks and drank so much water as well as wine, she had to keep excusing herself. Olivia and Nancy discovered they knew quite a few of the same people, and they exchanged their news.

I'd been introduced to two other actors. Glenn was young and handsome, although not as handsome as Todd, and he played the best buddy of Reginald, our hero. Roger was an older man who would portray Reginald's father. I couldn't help but notice that he was older than Gloria, who was supposed to be his mother. He was seated next to me, went through our wine at a rapid rate, and told me he'd appear only twice in the movie, both scenes to be filmed at Haggerman's. In one he'd try to talk Todd's character out of joining the army, and later he'd threaten to disinherit Reginald if he marries that "unsuitable" woman. They fight, while Gloria attempts to intervene. Reginald is pushed off the dock and into the lake, and he then storms off to a quick marriage and war. After making sure I knew about all the other movies he'd been in, Roger leered down the front of my dress and said, "Will Mr. Grady be joining us later?"

Before I could answer, Olivia said, "My daughter is a widow. A war widow. Her husband served in the US Army and never returned from Europe."

A hush settled over the table. Gloria gave me a soft, kind smile. A flash of pain crossed Matthew's face, and I assumed he was remembering his own wartime losses. Nancy said, "Such a tragedy," and Elias lifted his glass.

"A toast. To Mr. Grady and all our heroes," Elias said.

Richard, seated on my other side, touched my arm lightly.

I smiled stiffly. Ron Grady had been no hero. He hadn't died charging German fortifications or trying to save a wounded comrade. He'd been in a bar brawl with a fellow GI and struck his head when he went down.

When I'd heard the news that he wouldn't be coming home, I'd not gone into mourning. I'd celebrated.

I picked up my nearly full glass of wine and lifted it. "Thank you," I said.

Everyone drank. I put down my glass, untouched.

Gloria sucked on her half-finished cigarette and then ground it out in her dessert plate. Luke immediately appeared to whip it away, and I surreptitiously slid the ashtray closer to her.

"That was absolutely delicious. Olivia, do send my compliments to your chef," Gloria said. "Now, I believe someone said something about dancing?"

"Our house orchestra is playing tonight," I said. "Judy Rae has come up from New York to sing with them."

"Judy Rae!" Nancy said. "I adore her. Didn't you direct her in a grand musical a few years ago, Elias?"

The director nodded. "Not for long, I'm sorry to say. She had to go. She's a great singer, but her acting skills are barely above the level of Rebecca's, without the youth and the looks."

Rebecca glared at him. Nancy chuckled.

Gloria said, "Elias, that was uncalled for."

"What?" he said, "I said she was a great singer. And she is. I'm looking forward to the show."

"Shortly before midnight we'll be serving a dessert buffet," I added quickly.

Roger patted his stomach. "Can't wait."

"Do I have to dance?" Rebecca said to Elias.

"Yes," he said. "And if you don't wipe that look off your face you're fired."

She grunted and pulled a pack of cigarettes out of her bag. Luke, who, like any good Catskills waiter, could be in two places at once, hurried to light it. She gave him a radiant smile.

"We want Catskills buzz around this picture," Elias said. "And that means we want Catskills people talking about nothing else when they're here, and when they head back to their boring, mundane lives in the five boroughs we want them to tell all their friends about it. Richard, your dad's taking care of that over at Kennelwood."

"He talks about nothing else," Richard said.

"We're having dinner at the Concord tomorrow," Elias continued. "Command performance. You got that, Todd, Rebecca?"

"I never mind going to the Concord," Todd said. "Velvet, would you like to come with me?"

Velvet gasped. Rebecca mumbled something that sounded like "yeah," through a cloud of smoke.

"Glenn? Roger?"

"We get the point, Elias," Roger said.

"I'll be there," Nancy said.

"As will I. If I must," Gloria said.

"Goes without saying," Elias said. "You two never have to be told twice what to do."

"This is the first I've heard of dinner at the Concord," Matthew said. "Who's paying for it?"

"The picture, of course," Elias replied.

"You mean the studio?"

"Take it out of the publicity budget."

"The budget's stretched as it is."

"It'll be worth it. Like tonight."

"Tonight? I thought you were paying for tonight." Matthew's Louisiana accent got stronger the more agitated he became.

"I am. Out of the publicity budget."

"Elias," Matthew said, "this isn't—"

"Business talk is so tedious." Gloria dabbed her lips with her napkin. "Take it outside, gentlemen."

"Rebecca, Todd," Elias said. "I want to see you dancing

with the old geezers and the awkward kids here with their parents. Those people go to movies."

"Do I have to?" Rebecca moaned. "I'm tired. It was a long drive up from the city."

"Tired?" Elias said. "If you're getting too old to give me what I expect, I can find another pretty young thing fast enough."

Rebecca pouted prettily. "I'll dance."

"Glad to hear it. You'll dance tonight, and tomorrow I want you spending all day studying your lines for the big scene with Todd. Meet with me tonight when we get back to Kennelwood, and we can go over what I want from your scenes."

The pout died, and Rebecca's eyes narrowed, but she forced out a smile. "Okay."

Gloria stood in a river of white silk, and the men leapt to their feet. "I'm going dancing. Olivia, I expect to see you tripping the light fantastic."

"I might," my mother said.

"Then we are all in for a treat," Gloria said.

I caught Mary-Alice's eye, and she flushed and dipped her head. *Someone* had better be paying for this dinner.

Chapter 5

A LARGE ROUND TABLE HAD BEEN RESERVED IN THE CENTER of the ballroom at the edge of the dance floor. Word that the movie people would be coming in had gotten around, and the room was packed. The house orchestra was playing "Dancing in the Dark," and the dance floor was full of couples engaging in a gentle foxtrot when the doors flew open and my group entered. Dancers stopped dancing, everyone turned, guests stood up to see better, excited whispers grew. Elias Theropodous walked through the room, Olivia on one arm, Gloria on the other, the very picture of Hollywood elegance and glamour. Todd escorted both Velvet and Rebecca. Nancy, Glenn, and Roger followed them, and Mary-Alice and the rest tagged along behind, unrecognized and forgotten. Richard and Randy brought up the rear, while I hurried ahead to show Elias to their table.

Mary-Alice spotted the bar and broke off, heading straight for it. Matthew and Gary joined her, while Elias made a great fuss of settling Olivia and Gloria in their seats. Todd asked Velvet for a dance.

"No," Elias said.

"What do you mean, no?" Todd said.

"You'll dance the first dance with Rebecca."

"What if I don't want to?"

"I don't care what you want, sonny. Dance with Rebecca."

"I'm as keen as you are," Rebecca muttered.

She smiled brightly and held out her right hand. Todd bowed deeply over it, took it in his, and they walked onto the dance floor. Everyone stood back in awe to watch the new arrivals take the floor. Rebecca threw back her head and laughed delightedly at something Todd said. He gazed at her adoringly. Yup, actors the both of them.

The orchestra swung into Gershwin's "They Can't Take That Away from Me," and Todd and Rebecca stepped into the music. They weren't exceptional dancers, but they knew what they were doing and clearly they'd danced together before. Probably at "publicity" events like this one. Elias and Gloria were next to take the floor, and gradually the other guests fell into step alongside them.

"Work," I whispered to Randy.

"What?"

"You work here, remember? Mrs. Levenson from cabin eight needs a partner. Her husband sprained his ankle at tennis yesterday."

"I was hoping to dance with Velvet."

"Mrs. Levenson." I jerked my head at Velvet, telling her to also find a partner among the guests. She made a face at me but left the center table.

Along with the two professional dancers we have on staff, some of the younger waiters and the girls who mind the children during the day or lead sports activities are expected to attend the dances. Not to dance with one another or their friends but to provide partners for those guests who either don't have a partner of their own or want a turn around the floor with a lively young person.

Olivia rarely, as in never, dances with the guests. The old injury to her leg isn't obvious: I can pretend not to notice if she grimaces with sudden pain on standing up quickly, or has to stop in the path to give her leg a rest. On the dance floor, if her bad leg falters, a nonprofessional dancer might not even realize, but she would, and Olivia never gives anything but her best. She hesitated when Matthew leaned over her and spoke quietly to her, but eventually she gave him her hand. A fresh twitter of excitement passed through the room. More than a few guests came to Haggerman's rather than one of the better known resorts in hopes of getting a glimpse of Olivia.

Olivia had danced since she was a little girl. Olivia had danced on Broadway stages and Hollywood sets. Olivia Peters had partnered with Fred Astaire. Matthew Oswald . . . hadn't. He was clumsy and awkward, but neither her smile nor her leg failed her, and she led him through the steps while appearing to be following his lead.

Mary-Alice put a glass of bourbon at Elias's place and then went to stand against the wall. Glenn, Roger, and Gary found themselves seats in a dark corner and settled in for an evening of serious drinking. Gary took his gum out of his mouth and stuck it under the table. My stomach rolled over. I hate it when they do that.

After two lively dance tunes, the bandleader stepped up to the microphone. "And now, without further ado, let's give a big Haggerman's Catskills Resort welcome to Miss Judy Rae!"

The lady herself, olive-skinned, dark-eyed, dressed all in white with a large white flower arranged in her thick black hair crossed the stage, gave the bandleader a light hug, and the band began to play.

I went back to work, which in the evening consists mostly of keeping an eye on everything.

Olivia danced the next dance with Matthew, and then they left the floor. Olivia took her seat next to Gloria while Matthew headed for the bar. Rebecca and Todd didn't dance together again, and Todd monopolized Velvet more than I (or Randy, judging by the look on his face) liked. A few of the braver male guests cautiously approached Rebecca, and she graciously accepted every one. Elias partnered Gloria a few times and then had a couple of turns with Rebecca. He held the younger woman closer than he had his ex-wife, and his hand might have wandered lower than it should, but Rebecca didn't react.

Judy Rae finished her latest song and stood quietly at the microphone. When she had the attention of the audience, she said, "Thank you so much everyone for coming tonight. I was particularly excited, as I'm sure you all were, to see some of my dearest Hollywood friends in the audience. It's been far too long. Elias Theropodous, Academy Award–winning director." She stepped back and clapped her hands. Elias stood up, grinning broadly. He bowed to Judy and then waved to the audience, accompanied by a round of thunderous applause. Next he bowed to Gloria, who limply lifted her arm and sort of wiggled her fingers. The diamonds on her bracelet flashed in the light of the chandelier above the center table.

Elias sat down, and Judy said, "For our next number, the band and I would love to give you . . ."

"You once told me you never dance, but dare I hope you'll make an exception tonight?" I turned to see Richard Kennelwood smiling at me. He carried a cocktail in one hand and a glass of whiskey in the other. "Or, if not, have a drink with me. I think this is what you were having earlier." He handed me the cocktail, and I accepted it.

"Thanks. I will have a drink, and I will dance. This seems like the night for it."

"Your mother's a marvel. She made Matthew look like he knew what he was doing out there. I don't think even he realized who was in control."

"That's what women do in life, isn't it? Make men look good."

He smiled at me. "Some women manage to make themselves look good."

"I hope you're not talking about me. Man or woman, the role of a hotelier is to make it all look perfectly effortless."

He laughed. "You got that right, Elizabeth. Although my father would disagree with you. As he so often did . . . does . . . with me."

Richard and I stood together and sipped our drinks and looked out over the ballroom. The big chandeliers threw light onto diamonds, rhinestones, and sequins; the air was full of perfume and tobacco smoke; laughter, the tinkle of glassware, and conversation mixed with the beautiful music.

The song ended, and before the next tune began, I saw Luke put his tray on a side table, check his tie was straight, and boldly cross the floor to stop next to Elias and Rebecca. I sucked in a breath. The staff are not supposed to interrupt dances in progress. Elias glared at the younger man, but Rebecca turned to the waiter with a smile and held out her arms. Elias stalked back to his table and dropped into the chair next to Gloria. She said something to him. He snapped at her and grabbed the fresh drink in front of him. Judy Rae was on her break and had taken the empty chair between Gloria and Olivia for a chat. The table was piled high with empty glasses and full ashtrays.

I took a couple of turns around the dance floor with Richard. I was, unlike my mother, no dancer, and Richard wasn't much better, but I enjoyed myself, and I believe he did too. Which is all that counts, really.

At ten thirty the dessert buffet was brought out and the guests surged forward to fill their plates with pineapple upside-down cake, banana cream pie, and angel food cake covered with a thick layer of pink icing dotted with maraschino cherries. Roger, Glenn, and Mary-Alice joined the line. While the dessert buffet was being served (and demolished) Olivia had slipped away. Gloria asked Mary-Alice to bring her a slice of cake, and she did so.

"I hope you're having a nice evening, Miss Grant." Velvet dropped into the vacant chair next to the older woman, and I stood behind them, leaving Richard to attack the buffet.

Todd and Rebecca had also taken their seats. Todd had a slice of everything on offer and Rebecca nothing.

"I am, dear," Gloria said. "Thank you. Reminds me of my long-ago youth, back in the glory days of the silver screen. Wouldn't you agree, Elias?"

"What?" the director snapped.

"I asked if this evening reminds you of your youth, so very long ago? The dinners we used to go to, the parties we had. Before the war changed everything."

"Unlike some, Gloria, my best days are not over yet," Elias said, unduly harshly, I thought. Gloria had simply been reminiscing, as one does at the end of a long, pleasant evening.

She dug her fork into her cake and put a small piece into her mouth. "Delicious. Well worth the calories. As for best days, Elias, that remains to be seen, depending on how this picture does. As you know, as we all know, the bigger the buzz around a picture, the further it has to fall."

Rebecca threw a frightened look at Todd, but he didn't notice. He'd caught sight of Velvet crossing the room after seeing one of her dance partners to the door. He leapt to his feet and hurried to intercept her.

"I'm not talking about fame or success," Gloria said. "But of youth. Yours is long past, Elias. Long past." She put down her fork, having eaten only one small bite, and gathered up her evening bag. "On that cheerful note, I'll bid you all a good night."

Everyone mumbled some sort of farewell.

"Be at the lakefront at eight o'clock sharp," Elias

growled. "I want that morning light for the farewell scene, and I want your lines perfect the first time. We don't have any more time for fooling around." He looked across the table at Rebecca. "As for you, wipe that stupid grin off your face. I need to go over your lines with you. I don't think you have the feel for the importance of the bungalow-colony scene yet. Meet me back at the hotel."

Rebecca's face, which had not been featuring a grin, stupid or otherwise, fell even further. Her lips formed a smile, although her eyes did not. "Whatever you say."

At last the evening drifted to an end. Judy Rae sang one final song and, to enthusiastic applause, promised to return the following night, and the orchestra began packing up their instruments.

Elias finished his drink in one long gulp. "Gary, it's on you to make sure we're set up and ready to go tomorrow at eight. I want that morning light, and it won't wait for us. Take Rebecca back to the hotel now. She's had enough to drink." He snapped his fingers. "Where's Mary-Alice got to?"

The secretary appeared as Gary and Rebecca left the table. "I'm here."

"Get the switchboard to give everyone a wake-up call at seven. If they don't answer, they're to keep calling until someone picks up the blasted phone."

"Okay," Mary-Alice said. She looked, I thought, very tired. It can't be easy running to Elias Theropodous's beck and call all day and still be at it past midnight.

"I'm thinking a turn at the tables at the Concord before going back to Kennelwood," Matthew said. "Anyone feel like trying their luck?"

"My luck?" Elias said. "I expect my luck to be in at Kennelwood. But first, my car had better be waiting outside if Freemont knows what's good for him. I'm not standing around all night waiting." He slammed his glass onto the table, got to his feet, and stalked away.

I grabbed a passing busboy and sent him to call for Elias's car.

"It'll be a few minutes," I said apologetically.

"In that case," Matthew said, "I'll offer him another drink. Elias! One moment."

"Good night, everyone," I said. "See you all tomorrow."

Gloria had made no further move to leave. She stood by her chair, staring after Elias. Her hands were clenched into fists at her sides, and her face was tight with anger as she glared at her ex-husband's back. She caught me looking at her and gave her head an almost invisible shake, and the anger disappeared.

"Men. What can you do other than feel sorry for them? Elias's days are numbered. He knows it, and he can't handle it." She waved her hand dismissively in the smoky air, and the light of the chandelier caught the diamonds on her bracelet. She brushed her lips across my cheek. "Good night, dear."

"Good night. Would you like me to call someone to escort you to the house?"

"No, thank you, dear. I'll go slowly and fully enjoy the evening air. The perfume from your gardens is marvelous at night."

She walked away. People stepped back to allow her to pass; several gentlemen dipped their heads to her, and women whispered excitedly to their friends.

I looked around the ballroom. Elias and Matthew had met with Glenn and Roger at the bar and were ordering a last round. Todd made no move to join them, preferring to chat to Velvet. He'd unbuttoned his jacket and loosened his tie and was boyish and charming, with the stubble on his jaw growing in and a dark curl flopping across his forehead.

"So," he was saying to Velvet as I joined them, "what do you do around here for excitement after work's done?"

"Sometimes there are parties in the staff cabins, and some nights the staff go into town to meet up with friends from the other resorts. As for me, I go to bed. I have to be on the dock at six thirty for prebreakfast calisthenics." She demonstrated by making an arc of her arms over her head and leaning to one side in a crackle of pink tulle.

"Can I join you?" he asked.

She laughed. "The class is for women over fifty."

"I meant in bed."

Velvet's face turned the color of her dress. While Gloria was staying in my room in the house I share with my mother, I was bunking in with Velvet. I was most certainly not going to have Velvet engaging in the staff custom of leaving a towel over the doorknob to warn the roommate not to come in because of company. I slipped my arm though hers. "Her boss runs a tight ship, and Velvet needs her beauty sleep."

Velvet gave me a look. I couldn't quite tell if it was of gratitude or disappointment.

Todd grinned. "Be warned, I never give up. Now, can I escort you two lovely ladies to your accommodation?"

"I've got this." Randy butted into our circle. "Your ride's about to leave, Todd." He nodded to Matthew and Elias, putting down their empty glasses as they headed for the door.

"I'll call a cab." Todd took one of Velvet's arms; Randy took the other.

What was I, chopped liver? I wondered if they were about to lower their heads and charge at each other with a clash of antlers. I was saved from embarrassment when Richard joined our cheerful little group.

"Thank you for a great evening, Elizabeth. I enjoyed it very much. Todd, it's late. I'll give you a lift back."

Randy couldn't hide his smug grin.

Todd hesitated, then he said, "I'll grab a cab later, thanks. Rebecca said you told her you used to be in movies, Randy. Anything I've ever heard of? The business got too much for you, did it? I suppose working here's a lot easier."

Randy growled, and I feared the antlers were about to come out again.

"Hey!" Todd said, "I've got an idea. As you know your way around the biz at the lower levels, I'll suggest you get a part as an extra. You're the lifeguard here, right? You can walk across the set once or twice. How about it? They'll give you union wages."

It was true Randy had tried to make it as an actor. He had the looks but little talent and, more important, no ambition. He gave up and left Hollywood after landing a couple of minor, very minor, roles and next tried his hand at Broadway. He didn't even get in the door, but somehow he fell into Olivia's circle and got himself a job here when she inherited Haggerman's. It was, however, not true that he needed the money. Randy, full name Randolph James Fontaine IV, was the scion of a blue-blood Boston family, and the despair of Mr. and Mrs. Randolph James Fontaine III. To the intense disappointment of his father, who hoped his only son would follow his family line into the law, Mrs. Randolph James Fontaine II indulged her beloved grandson to the extent that she financially supported his acting career, and when that failed, she continued providing him with a generous allowance even though he was now well into his thirties. In a couple more years, he'd be out of his thirties and probably still searching for a path in life.

Before the two men could come to blows, Richard interrupted. "You'll have a long wait for a taxi, Todd. Lots of folks from the other resorts came here tonight, and they'll be grabbing the cabs. They hoped to see Gloria and were not disappointed. You know full well Elias never offers anyone a lift. Except for beautiful women and moneymen. Tonight even Rebecca had to get a ride with Gary. Can you find your own way home, Elizabeth?"

He gave me a private smile, and I said, "Of course." A slow walk with Richard by the lake on a warm night would be lovely, but I needed Todd to be on his way.

Todd hesitated, and then he said, "Thanks. Morning comes early, doesn't it, and Elias'll fly into a rage if any of us is a minute late. I've never worked with the man before, but I'd been warned. If I want to be in an Academy Award–potential movie, I have to work with an Academy Award–winning temperament. You don't mind if I escort these ladies to their rooms first, do you?"

"Not at all," Richard said. "I'll come with you. It's a nice night for a stroll."

"Sounds like a good idea," Randy said. "As for union wages, buddy, you can—"

I quickly cut him off. "Are we getting any complaints about the beach and dock being closed during the filming? None have come my way."

Randy tore his eyes off Velvet, walking ahead of us between Richard and Todd. "Not that I've heard. People are more excited about watching the filming than swimming. The pool's open, so that's okay for those who want to swim."

My entourage and I descended the grand sweeping staircase. The lobby was crowded with people saying good night to their friends or debating having a nightcap on the veranda.

We stepped outside. The air was warm and still, full of the scent of the lake in front of us and the woods surrounding us. The lights above the veranda and lining the driveway broke the immediate darkness, but beyond that thin row the lake was a cloth of black velvet and the mountains nothing but an outline against the moonlit sky. The Skylark was pulled up to the bottom of the steps, blocking a line of taxis, and Freemont, immaculate in his cap and uniform, stood at attention next to the open door.

"Are you okay, Elias?" I heard Matthew say. "You don't look too good."

"Go on ahead," I said to Velvet. "I'll catch up." I hurried to join the men.

Elias stood at the top of the stairs, one hand on the railing and the other pressed to his chest. Beads of sweat had broken out on his forehead, and his face was very pale.

"I . . . ," he said.

I touched Matthew's arm. "Come with me. We'll find a chair in the lobby where Elias can rest until he's feeling better."

"Freemont, give me a hand here." Matthew took the director's arm while the chauffeur hurried up the stairs.

The row of taxis began beeping their horns and a man yelled, "I haven't got all night here."

"I'll help Mr. Theropodous," I said. "Please move the car, Mr. Freemont."

He glanced between his employer and me. Richard slipped through the crowd. "Do what Mrs. Grady says. We're okay here."

Freemont gave him a nod and ran down the steps.

"You," I called to a hovering bellhop. "Ask reception if we have a doctor in the hotel. Please, ladies and gentlemen, step aside. He needs to sit down."

Gradually the crowd parted. Richard and Matthew took Elias's arms. The director took his hands off the railing. He swayed, and then he leaned forward with a groan and discharged the contents of his stomach. Instinctively Richard and Matthew let go and leapt back. Elias Theropodous, three-time Academy Award–winning director, collapsed. No longer holding on to the railing, he lost his balance and tumbled the ten steps to the driveway.

There he lay, not moving.

Chapter 6

PEOPLE SCREAMED. SOME PRESSED FORWARD TO SEE what was going on, while others backed away. I ran down the steps, Richard and Matthew close behind me.

Freemont reached his employer before any of us and dropped to his knees. His big hands hovered above the unmoving form, unsure of what to do. Elias had landed face-down, one arm under him, the other thrown out at a bad angle.

"Call an ambulance," someone shouted.

"Roll him over." Richard crouched next to Freemont. "We have to make sure he can breathe. Careful of that arm though."

Elias lay very still, his eyes closed. He'd hit his nose when he fell, and blood streamed from it. His chest moved, slowly, but at least it was moving.

"An ambulance'll take too long," I said. "You can drive him to the hospital."

"I don't know where it is," Freemont said.

"I'll go with you," Richard said.

"No. I'll do that," I said. "Richard, can you take the others to Kennelwood? I'll call when I have news."

Richard nodded in acknowledgment.

"I'm a doctor. Let me through." A man in his early fifties, hair standing on end, pillow marks on his face, sweater hastily thrown over his paisley pajamas, arrived, shoelaces dragging behind him. "Did the gentleman have a fall?"

"He fell down the steps," I said. "But he threw up first, and he seemed to black out."

The doctor knelt next to Elias and lifted an eyelid. "Drunk?"

"He had a lot to drink," Matthew said, "but no more than I've seen him take before. It came over him very suddenly."

While the doctor asked about Elias's medical history, and Matthew said he didn't know, Freemont, Richard, and a couple of bellhops lifted Elias and gently laid him in the back seat of the car. He made no sound, and he did not wake up.

"Do you know where the Summervale hospital is?" I asked the doctor.

"I do not."

"Will you come with us?"

"I'd be happy to."

The doctor got into the back of the car and knelt on the floor next to the patient, and I climbed in the front, calling, "Richard, phone the hospital and tell them we're coming."

Freemont threw the car into gear, and we tore down the driveway. Freemont's hands were tight on the wheel and his eyes wide as he watched the narrow, curving, dark road. Traffic was heavy for the time of night, as people moved from one hotel to another after the evening's entertainment.

"Have you known this to happen before?" the doctor asked. "The blackouts, I mean?"

"Freemont?" I said.

He shook his head. "No. I'm his regular driver, sir, been with him for more than twenty years. Mr. Theropodous can put away the scotch or bourbon all the night long and be right and ready for work next morning. Never known him to pass out."

"Man's not as young as he used to be," the doctor said. "Some of these old guys, and I include myself, forget that. To our peril."

I thought about what Gloria had said earlier and how angry Elias had been when she reminded him he was no longer in the flush of youth.

A nurse and two orderlies waited for us at the emergency entrance to the hospital, and Elias was loaded onto a stretcher and rushed inside. The doctor followed them through the swinging doors at the end of a long corridor, but I was told to take a seat in the waiting room. Freemont remained outside with the car.

The waiting room of our small hospital is a cheerless place. Badly sprung, stained furniture, overflowing ashtrays and used coffee cups, scarred tables, decades-out-of-date magazines. I was the only person there, and I thought that was a good thing: they'd be able to see to Elias immediately.

I picked up a magazine at random. The picture on the cover showed a young, pale-faced, red-lipped woman with a wartime hairstyle, wearing wartime clothes. The headline proclaimed her to be the rising star of 1944. I'd never heard of her. Fame, indeed, is fleeting.

I looked up from the magazine as Matthew Oswald dropped into the chair next to me. He pointed to the picture. "Ruth Rosenweitz, also known as Ruthie Rose. She was a protégé of Elias's. Got herself pregnant, by her husband I might add, at the start of filming of what was to be her breakthrough picture. Elias fired her."

"They couldn't film around that?"

"They could, sure. But Elias wouldn't. I think he took it as a personal insult."

"That's sad."

"It has a happy enough ending. Her husband's now the junior senator from their state, and there's buzz about a presidential run in a few years. They say she's the power behind him." He nodded to the closed doors leading deeper into the hospital. "I'm guessing there's no word yet?"

"No," I said. "Have the others gone back to Kennelwood?"

"They have. I'll phone them with an update when I have one. You don't have to stay, Elizabeth."

"Perhaps for a while. I'd like to be able to tell Gloria how he's doing."

"Gloria. The best woman Elias ever had. In so many ways. I was sorry they divorced. She was a calming influence on him. I guess Elias didn't think he needed calming."

"You've known him for a long time?"

"Long enough," Matthew said.

We leapt to our feet when the door swung open. The doctor who was a guest at Haggerman's came through. He gave me a tight smile, and I began to introduce him to Matthew.

"Doctor . . . uh . . . ? I'm sorry."

"Fife. Ben Fife." The men shook hands.

"How's it look?" Matthew asked.

"Not good, I'm sorry to say. But I'm a pediatrician, not an emergency room physician. All I can say is they're working hard back there. A nurse called me a cab. I'm heading back to the hotel. Can I give you a lift, Mrs. Grady?"

"Thank you, but no. I'll stay awhile. Thank you so much for your help."

"Good night."

Ben Fife left. Matthew and I exchanged a look as we resumed our seats. I flipped idly through the magazine. He lit a cigarette.

"How much of this movie's finished?" I asked.

"You mean if Elias has to . . . uh . . . take some sick time?

Not much. The scenes in the Catskills are the first to be filmed with the principal actors. Bringing the entire crew and most of the stars on location for two weeks is an expensive endeavor. I don't want to see it go to waste. Outdoor filming is tricky, and I hate it. You're dependent on the weather, on keeping the sun in the same spot for the same scene, even if filming has to be over several days."

The doors to the rest of the hospital opened again and Dave Dawson, newly appointed chief of police of Summervale, came in. The redness in his eyes, the stubble on his chin, the rumpled untucked shirt, and the wrinkles on his pants told me he'd been roused from his bed.

"Mrs. Grady," he said.

"Deputy. I mean Chief. I haven't had the chance to congratulate you on your new position."

"Thanks," he said.

When I'd first met Dave Dawson I thought him slow, lazy, and largely uninterested in doing his job. I'd been wrong, and he'd proved himself. I was pleased his work had been rewarded. "What brings you here? I didn't hear anyone else being brought in tonight."

"Guy took ill at Haggerman's?"

"Yes, but he had a heart attack."

"Did the doctor tell you that?"

"No, but . . ."

"That's what we thought," Matthew said. "Are you saying he didn't?"

The double doors swung open, and a man in scrubs, a mask draped around his neck, came through. A nurse, her white uniform so highly starched it probably stood up in her closet all by itself, followed. Their faces were impassive, but something about the stiffness of those expressions told me the news was not good.

"I'm Dr. Higgins. Are you family of Mr. . . . ?"

"No," Matthew said. "I'm a longtime acquaintance and

business associate of Mr. Theropodous. We're here on business, and he has no family in New York State."

The doctor glanced at me.

"Manager of the hotel where he took ill."

"Doc?" Chief Dawson said.

"I'm sorry, but Mr. Theropodous died a few minutes ago."
Matthew shook his head.

I barely knew the man. What I did know I didn't like,
but still I felt a wave of sadness flow over me. I dropped into
a chair. It would be up to me to tell Gloria. Tonight, she'd
alternately chatted happily and fondly with him and been
furious at him. They had a complicated relationship, but I
suppose that was natural enough for a divorced couple who
worked together on occasion. It wouldn't be easy to break
the news.

"I called the police." Dr. Higgins nodded at Dave Dawson. "Because I believe the gentlemen died as a direct result
of something he consumed this afternoon or this evening."

"What does that mean?" I asked.

"You're the manager at the hotel where he's staying?"

"Not staying, no, but he had dinner with us."

The doctor turned to Chief Dawson. "I suggest you close
the kitchens at this lady's hotel and the one where he was
staying if he ate anything there today."

Chapter 7

PEOPLE COME TO THE CATSKILLS FOR THE FRESH MOUN-
tain air, to fish and to swim and to hike, to let their children
play in a way they never can in the streets of the city. They
come to snag a husband for themselves or for a daughter in
danger of being left on the shelf. They come looking for a
wife for life or a girlfriend for a weekend. They come to
reunite with distant relatives, childhood friends, or army
buddies. They come because their grandparents started
coming before the first war. They come to see comedy and
singing stars, and the next big thing.

A great many come for the food.

If Haggerman's kitchens were closed, no matter for how
long, we'd be finished.

It wasn't easy, but I managed to talk Dave Dawson out
of shutting us down. For now.

I pointed out that not one other person had come into this
hospital tonight with suspected food poisoning. I mentioned
that Haggerman's had a substantial number of elderly

guests. I told him Elias had eaten from the same food prepared for everyone and his drinks had come from the public bar. Yet no one else had taken ill.

"Might have gone to a different hospital," he said.

"Why on earth would anyone go farther away, when this hospital's perfectly good, and"—I waved my arms around—"nearly empty tonight? Call the ambulance services, call the other hospitals. Ask them."

"I will, Mrs. Grady. I will. But first, a moment, Doctor?"

The chief of police and the doctor went to a corner, where they talked in low voices. I considered edging closer to try to listen in, but one sharp stare from the steely eyes of the nurse had me reconsidering my plan. "I should call Richard Kennelwood," I said to Matthew. "He needs to know that his kitchens might be under suspicion also."

"Okay," Matthew said. "You do that. Then I'll call LA. The people financing this picture need to be told what's happening."

"Picture?" The nurse perked up. "You're in the movies?"

"Yeah. Believe me, sweetheart, sometimes I wish I wasn't. Most of the time I wish I wasn't."

"Where can I find a phone?" I asked her.

"A pay phone is by the emergency entrance. You passed it when you came in."

"I need to talk to the doctor about . . . arrangements," Matthew said. "Then we'll get Freemont to drive us back."

"Are you going to break the news to the others?" I asked.

"I'll have to. Mary-Alice will need to know tonight, but other than her, I want to do it once and once only. They all breakfast at different times, and some eat in their rooms. The crew and minor actors are staying at other hotels. I'll talk to them all at eight when they show up for tomorrow . . . today's filming."

"Gloria?"

"She's at your mother's house, right?"

"Yes."

"Would you be willing to tell Gloria? She should hear privately."

"Sure."

"Go and make your phone call."

I turned to leave. Then I turned back. I patted the tiny beaded evening bag looped over my arm. "Sorry, I don't have any money. I never carry money around the property."

He dug in his pocket and handed me a fistful of coins without counting them.

I found the phone and asked the operator to connect me to Kennelwood Hotel. She told me how much the call would cost, and I put coins into the slot. The coins dropped, lines clicked, and I was connected. I told the Kennelwood switchboard I needed to speak to Richard Kennelwood on a matter of urgency, and she said, "One moment, please. I'll try his home."

I waited. Static came down the line, but nothing else. "No one is answering," the voice said at last. "Shall I try Mr. Jerome Kennelwood?"

I hesitated. Richard's father was not a friend of ours. When Olivia and I first arrived to take over Haggerman's he'd bad-mouthed us throughout the entire Catskills hotel community as well as to the booking agencies. I'd recently had occasion to tell Jerome Kennelwood what I thought of him. In retrospect that might have been a mistake. I didn't think he'd handle it well if it was me who told him the police might order his kitchens closed.

"Is Mr. Kennelwood Jr. possibly in the bar?"

"I can try, but he might be anywhere. At this time of night, we can't summon him via the loudspeakers. He might not even be on the property. Perhaps you could leave a message and I'll find a page to attempt to deliver it?"

"Ask him to call Elizabeth Grady at Haggerman's, never mind the time. It's"—I checked my watch—"two fifteen now. I'll be home in about twenty minutes."

Back in the waiting room, the doctor had left, and Dave

Dawson was talking to Matthew. Matthew was telling him what Elias had been doing in the Catskills.

"Phone's free," I said to Matthew. I turned to Dave. "What makes the doctor think Elias was poisoned? He was in his sixties, and not exactly a calm, relaxed man. He had a heck of a lot to drink tonight, not to mention a large, rich dinner. He had a heart attack."

"They pumped his stomach, but they were too late. The doctor's going to send the stomach contents for analysis," Dave said.

My own stomach lurched. "They can do that?"

"Oh, yes. The doc's not swearing on the Bible the guy died of something he ate, but he said the signs are all there."

I didn't ask what those signs were.

"You yourself told him the guy threw up before he passed out."

"Yes, but . . . I thought he was drunk."

"They get a lot of food poisoning cases in this hospital. Kids, and adults, from the city who pick and eat berries and mushrooms without knowing what they are. Food left behind at the bungalow colonies, and the next lot happy to have the free grub without checking it out. Even some of the better hotels sometimes get in a bad lot of beef or the milk goes off."

"We didn't—"

Dave lifted his hand. "What you said made sense, Mrs. Grady. No one else has come in tonight with suspected food poisoning, and the doctor has his nurse calling the hospitals around here. In the morning if we start hearing about people having problems, I'll shut you down faster than you can blink. Some people react worse to that sort of thing than others, and a lot don't go to the hospital, thinking it'll pass, but you're right that plenty of elderly people and little kids are staying at your place. So, for now . . ."

"Thank you, Chief Dawson."

"If you're right, and no one else got sick tonight, and if

the doctor's right that Mr. . . . uh . . . the gentlemen was poisoned, then I have to ask how that happened."

"What do you mean?"

"He was unlikely to have gone for a walk in the woods and picked a mess of toadstools, right?"

"Right."

"He didn't dig around under the kitchen sink and find a bottle of rat poison and decide it looked tasty, and the doc says he didn't look like the sort of guy who cooks his own meals and tries to cut corners to save a few pennies."

"He definitely was not that. Are you saying you think he deliberately ate something bad for him? Why would he do that?"

"I have to consider that someone fed it to him."

"You mean . . . ?"

"He was murdered."

I dropped into a chair.

"I'm still looking to hire a deputy, and my officers are swamped with the season in full swing. I can't handle this by myself, so I'm going to have to call in the state police."

"Because they did such a fine job last time," I said.

He tried, and failed, to hide a grin. "We won't hold that against them. It's late and you must be tired, but before you go can you tell me what was going on tonight. That other guy, Mr. Oswald, explained about the movie crew and the private dinner. He said after dinner the group went to the ballroom. Is that correct?"

"Yes. I was a guest at the dinner myself, and I went to the ballroom with them."

"Was the food put on individual plates in the kitchen or brought out on serving platters for everyone to serve themselves?"

"It was dished up in the kitchen and the plates brought to the table by waiters. Two choices were offered for each course, no special orders. I can't see any of my cooks or waiters taking the opportunity to poison a guest."

"Never assume, Mrs. Grady."

"I'm no older than you, Chief Dawson. You can call me Elizabeth."

"Might as well. I'm still Dave."

"Dave. We had a bar set up next to the private dining room for the exclusive use of that group before and during their dinner. After dinner, Elias and his group joined the guests in the ballroom, where they were served from the main bar and helped themselves to the dessert buffet." I tried to remember who had been where when. "Before dinner we mingled in the reception room, and after dinner they were popping up and down all night, visiting tables, having visitors to their table. Some of them ordered drinks from a waiter, and some went to the bar themselves. About the only—" I sucked in a breath.

"The only?"

"Elias's secretary fetched his drinks for him. I can't say they were the only drinks he had, but she did spend a good part of the evening getting him drinks. As has been said, he drank a heck of a lot."

"What's this secretary's name?"

"Mary-Alice Renzetti."

Dave scribbled something in his notebook.

"You don't think . . . ?" I began.

"I don't think anything. Not yet."

"There's going to be a heck of a lot of unhappy people in LA tonight." Matthew came into the waiting room. "And one or two who are going to be absolutely delighted."

"What does that mean?" Dave asked.

"Elias had his enemies. Powerful men do."

"You think one of these enemies might have followed him here?"

Matthew shook his head. "I haven't seen anyone I recognized since we got here, other than Olivia Peters. Not anyone who isn't part of the shoot. Ready to go, Elizabeth? I'll drop you off on the way to Kennelwood."

I looked at the chief of police.

"You can go now," he said. "I have more questions for the doctor. I'll be at the hotel first thing tomorrow. You said this guy and his group are staying at Kennelwood?"

"Elias was, and some of the lead actors as well as me," Matthew said, "but not all the film crew. Everyone's been told to be at Haggerman's at eight to start the day's filming. I'm planning to break the news then."

"I'll be there," Dave said.

Matthew and I walked away. "Freemont," I said. "Has anyone told Mr. Freemont?"

"I didn't. I can't imagine a nurse went out to the car to tell him."

"He said he's been with Elias for twenty years."

"Yeah. Tough. Which makes me think. Can we go to Kennelwood first and then I'll have Freemont take you home? I'd like you to be with me when I break the news to Mary-Alice."

"Why? I don't know her."

"The woman's touch. It'll help, I think, if a woman's there."

I couldn't see why, and I was about to say so, but I changed my mind. Mary-Alice had been hovering around Elias most of the night. If anyone saw someone trying to poison Elias, it would have been her. If anyone had poisoned Elias, the most likely person was her.

▼

I STOOD SILENTLY IN THE DEEP SHADOWS OF THE WARM night as Matthew told Freemont that his employer had died. At first, I thought Freemont hadn't understood, but then I realized he was simply stunned. The parking lot of the hospital was mostly empty. A rapidly flickering light mounted high on a pole lit up the area around the Skylark. The chauffeur had been standing beside the car enjoying a smoke when we walked up, and Matthew spoke quietly to him.

"Dead," Freemont said at last. "I figured that man would live forever."

"No one lives forever," Matthew said.

"The police will want to talk to you," I said.

Freemont threw me a frightened look. "Why?"

"The police are . . . not entirely sure it was natural causes. They'll be wanting to know if Mr. Theropodous had any enemies."

"I don't know nothing 'bout anything like that."

"I'm sure you don't," Matthew said. "Come on, let's go. We're going to Kennelwood first, and then you can take Mrs. Grady to Haggerman's."

"I'll find my own way back," I said. "It's been a long day for everyone, and I don't want to bother Mr. Freemont any further."

"No bother, ma'am."

"Nevertheless, I'll find my own way home." I'd worry about how later. Freemont and his employer might not have been close, as in friends or even confidants, but they'd been together for many years. Freemont needed time to process the news.

He gave me a slight bow and held the door for me. I was about to get in when the screech of brakes had me turning around. A car, going far too fast, pulled up to the emergency entrance, and a short chubby man leapt out. For a moment I thought it was someone needing help, and I started to wish him well. He turned his head as he reached the doors, and the light above shone on his round face. Martin McEnery, a reporter with the *Summervale Gazette*.

My good wishes died. I had no doubt what had summoned him here in the middle of the night, and I feared it would do the reputation of Haggerman's no good.

"Ma'am?" Freemont said, and I slipped into the car with a mumbled apology.

Goodness but this car was comfortable, and immaculate. The Skylark was polished to a shine so bright it reflected the moonlight, and inside there was not a speck of dust on the seats or mud on the floor or streak on the windows. I settled myself into the luxurious seat and wiggled happily. Matthew got in beside me.

"What do you mean not natural causes?" he said. "What did that cop say to you?"

"I'm sure it's nothing, but he's wondering how whatever Elias consumed got into his food."

Matthew grunted. "Small-town cops. Nothing better to do, trying to make themselves seem important. No one murdered Elias, Elizabeth. If it had happened in Hollywood, the line of suspects would reach around the block. Isn't that right, Freemont?"

"Not everyone loved Mr. T.," the chauffeur agreed as the lights of the hospital faded behind us.

"But not here," Matthew said. "Everyone here might not have loved Elias either, but they needed him to finish this picture."

"What's going to happen now?" I asked.

"Tomorrow, we'll carry on unless I hear otherwise. Gary's more than capable of finishing a day's filming. The studio executives will meet in the morning, LA time."

I leaned forward. "Freemont, when you drove Mr. Theropodous to Haggerman's for the dinner this evening, did he have anything to eat in the car? Do you know if he had lunch earlier from the catering truck?"

Freemont chuckled. "Don't know 'bout lunch, but as for the car, I can swear to that, Mrs. Grady. No. Mr. T. didn't smoke, drink, or eat in the car, and he wouldn't let anyone else. If I wanted my lunch or supper while I was waiting, I had to stand outside, sometimes in the pouring rain or driving snow. Couldn't risk a crumb falling between the seats. Remember the time he threw John Ashcroft out of the car in the middle of Santa Monica Boulevard for lighting up a smoke, Mr. Oswald?"

"Yes, I remember. John was in a towering rage. Swore

he'd never work with Elias again. Next day the opening week's numbers came in for *Dying in the Moonlight*, and John never mentioned the incident again."

We turned into the private drive leading to Kennelwood Hotel and drove up the hill. The trees closed around us, and the powerful headlights lit up the narrow road as the leafy trees formed an arch overhead. We turned a bend, the trees fell away, and in front of us the bright lights of the hotel filled the night, as though beckoning us to approach. Kennelwood Hotel is older, bigger, grander than Haggerman's, but I like to think it's not any better. Because they have more guests and a larger entertainment budget, their show doesn't end at midnight but carries on into the wee hours. Dance music leaked out of the second-floor windows as Freemont pulled up to the lobby entrance. Matthew told him he could turn in for the night, and together the producer and I walked into the hotel. The chandelier hanging from the second-floor ceiling threw sparks into the water spraying from the fountain in the center of the lobby. The room was decorated entirely in gold and marble: gold curtains tied back by gold tassels, gold gilt on the ashtray stands, golden fabric covering the couches and chairs, imitation marble statues on either side of the grand marble staircase. Fans churned the warm, stuffy, smoke-filled air.

All the lights were on, the lobby bar was crowded with men, many of them wearing white trousers under dark blue jackets laden with gold braid and double rows of gold buttons. Elegantly dressed mixed groups clustered around lobby tables, and the sounds of music and laughter drifted down the stairs.

I assumed Mary-Alice would have been put up in staff quarters or one of the cheapest rooms Kennelwood has, but instead she was in the room next to Elias's.

"He likes her—liked her, I guess I should say," Matthew said when the night clerk had given us the room number, "to be at his beck and call, never mind the time. Elias always said he did most of his best thinking at night."

We got into the elevator. "Fourth floor," Matthew said to the uniformed operator, and we ascended.

Matthew knocked on the door of room 404. No answer. I put my ear against the door. All quiet. He knocked again, then he called, "Mary-Alice, it's Matthew Oswald here with Elizabeth Grady. I'm sorry about the time, but we have to speak to you."

Something inside the room shuffled, a floorboard creaked, and then the door opened a crack, and Mary-Alice peered out. Her hair was wound into a network of tight pins, a scarf tied around her head to keep the pins in place, and her face was white with night cream. She blinked rapidly. "What's going on? Is something the matter?" She peered into the hallway behind us. "Elias?"

"Can we come in?" I asked.

"I'm not dressed."

"I see that, and I'm sorry, but we would like to talk to you."

"I . . . I . . ."

The elevator bell pinged, and I turned to see Dave Dawson heading toward us. "I'm in time, I see," he said. "Good. Are you Mary-Alice Renzetti?"

"Yes, but—"

"I'm Chief Dawson, Summervale police. I have some questions for you."

Mary-Alice looked at me, her eyes wide and frightened.

"Please," I said. "We can't talk in the hallway."

She stepped back and slowly opened the door. Hers was a nice room, in the center of the hotel, facing the lake. Two single beds and a private bathroom. One of the beds was rumpled, the cover thrown off, the pillow depressed. The other was neatly made, the orange-and-brown blankets and pillows undisturbed. The drapes were closed, the wardrobe and dresser drawers shut, Mary-Alice's hairbrush, pocketbook, notepad, and pencil neatly laid out on top. One pair of shoes was tucked under the window. A glass of water, a book, and a portable alarm clock sat on the small table between the beds.

"What are you doing here?" I whispered to Dave. "I thought you were going to talk to the doctor some more."

"Changed my mind," he said. The room had one chair, and it faced toward the window. Dave picked up the chair, turned it around, and said, "Please, Miss Renzetti, have a seat."

Mary-Alice sat. She wore a pair of plain brown flannel pajamas, well worn and slightly tattered around the hems, which must be too warm for the humid night. She ignored the two men and spoke to me, "What's happened?"

Neither of the men said anything, so I answered. "I'm terribly sorry to have to tell you this, but Mr. Theropodous died this evening."

"Died?"

I took both her hands in mine. "Yes. I'm sorry."

She took a deep breath and stood up. "Goodness. That is a shock. That'll disrupt the production schedule. I assume, Mr. Oswald, you'll be in touch with the studio for their instructions?"

"I called them earlier."

"Good. Thank you for coming to tell me, Mrs. Grady. It was kind of you." She smiled at me.

She actually smiled.

"You did hear what I said?"

"Elias died. That's unfortunate, but I'm confident the studio'll see sense and continue with the filming."

"That's your only concern?"

"Are you expecting me to weep and wail and rend my garments, Mrs. Grady? Are you, Chief Dawson? If so, you're going to be disappointed. Elias was my employer, not my friend."

"You'll be out of a job."

"A minor concern. I've amassed a considerable amount of savings in the time I've worked for him. Now I'm free to do what I want with my life. I might even be able to offer some assistance to the new director. Why have you involved the police?"

"You haven't asked how he died," Dave said.

"His heart, wasn't it? I left Haggerman's before he did, got a ride with Gary and Rebecca. Rebecca went up to bed immediately, but Gary and I stopped for a quick drink in the bar. We were there when Richard Kennelwood came in and told us Elias had fallen ill and been taken to the hospital. Is that not what happened?"

"I've been told you fetched several drinks for Mr. . . . the deceased over the course of the evening," Dave said. "Is that true?"

Mary-Alice's eyes narrowed and she studied him. "I did everything for Elias other than cut his meat for him. I always do."

Dave Dawson straightened his shoulders and lifted his chin. "Mary-Alice Renzetti, I am—"

"One minute, please," I said. "Chief, might I have a word?"

"No, Mrs. Grady, you might not. This isn't a good time."

"Won't take a moment. Please? We can talk in the hallway."

"Mary-Alice and I'll stay here." Matthew gave me a quick nod that I took to be approval.

"Make it quick," Dave said. We stepped into the hallway and he shut the door.

"You can't arrest Mary-Alice," I said.

"I don't need your permission. But, because of the help you tried to be on the Westenham case, although I didn't need it, I'll do you the favor of asking why not."

"Because you don't know the poison, if it was poison, was in the drinks. It might have been in his food. It might have been administered some other way. We . . . you . . . don't know for sure, yet, but most of all because even if it was in his drink, almost everyone there had the opportunity to slip something into Elias's glass. I told you Mary-Alice had been fetching his drinks all night, but I had time to think it over in the car as we drove here, trying to remember what I observed earlier tonight. After the group went down to the ballroom, I wasn't paying a lot of attention, but I did keep my eye on them. Earlier, at the private dinner, I had no other duties, so I was paying attention. On both occasions, people were coming and going the entire time. Particularly before and after dinner, Elias left his drinks unattended. Before dinner, he went to the men's room at least once and left his glass on a side table when he did so. After the dinner, in the ballroom, he danced a couple of dances, and he joined the men around the bar."

"Meaning?"

"Meaning he wasn't watching his glass and neither was anyone else. Even Mary-Alice had to go to the ladies' room occasionally, and she wasn't seated at the main table in the ballroom. People came and went, some got up to dance and others sat down. Judy Rae, the singer, sat at their table for a while, and some of our guests were bold enough to come up and ask the ladies for a dance. People leaned over the table to be heard if the music was loud."

The elevator pinged, the doors slid open, and a couple, laughing uproariously, emerged. They were in evening clothes; she carried her shoes in her hands, and his tie was looped around his forehead. They spotted us—me in my frilly green dress, Dave in his rumpled uniform, and the laughter died. They edged warily to the far side of the hallway, pressing against the wall, and scurried on by.

"She's mighty cool about his death," Dave said when the couple had gone into their room and slammed the door behind them.

"She's not displaying the behavior you anticipated, you mean. Did you expect her to collapse in shock and grief? Please don't assume all women will always behave in certain predefined ways. We're not entirely predictable all the time, you know. Mary-Alice didn't like the man, and she isn't going to pretend to mourn him. I would have thought that sort of honesty would make your job as a policeman easier, not harder."

He studied my face for a long time. He said nothing, so I pressed my point. "How long does it take poison to take effect? Can you estimate when it was consumed? That would help narrow down the time frame. Maybe," I added hopefully, "it was something he had before coming to Haggerman's. He probably had breakfast here, and the catering truck provided drinks and lunch for the crew."

"Did you handle that? The catering?"

"No. They came from Kennelwood. From here."

"Depends on what was used and what the quantity was," Dave said at last. "We won't know that for a few days. Not until the results come back." He took a deep breath. "Okay, Elizabeth. You win. I won't arrest Miss Renzetti. At this time. June, my wife, is always telling me I leap to conclusions, particularly about what she's thinking, and I'm usually wrong."

He opened the door to Mary-Alice's room. The drapes had been pulled aside, and Matthew stood at the window, staring out into the night. Mary-Alice sat at the dressing table, writing in her notebook.

Dave cleared his throat. "Miss Renzetti, I need you to think over everything that happened tonight, and let me know if you saw anything suspicious, or can think of any reason anyone wanted your boss dead."

"I can think of plenty of reasons." She waved her pencil at him. "Mr. Oswald can give you more. But not on the part of anyone who's in the Catskills at the present. They all need this picture to be a success. Now, if you'll excuse me, I have a great deal to do to prepare for tomorrow."

"You're going to keep working?" I asked.

"I've asked Mary-Alice to give us a hand until we get things back on track," Matthew said.

Mary-Alice returned her attention to her notebook, and we left her to it.

"I'll be at Haggerman's in the morning," Dave said to Matthew. "I want to see everyone's reaction when you tell them the news."

We called the elevator and descended to the lobby. Dave put on his hat and headed out into the night. Matthew let out a long sigh. "What a mess." He walked away.

Three men staggered past him coming out of the bar, arms around one another, singing a sea shanty. They were young, their faces well tanned and their hair sun-streaked. They were dressed in double-breasted navy jackets, and one of them wore a captain's peaked hat. Participants in the regatta week.

I was about to leave, when I remembered I didn't have a ride. I groaned. My girdle was killing me, the bodice of my dress was too tight, I was desperate to get my shoes and stockings off, and I was absolutely starving.

"Elizabeth!" Richard Kennelwood crossed the lobby floor at a rapid pace. He'd taken off his jacket and tie. "I got word you needed to speak to me urgently. What are you doing here? Is everything okay? How's Elias?"

"I left that message ages ago, and you only got it now? Sorry, forget I asked. None of my business."

"Todd, Gary, Glenn, and Roger decided to have a hand of poker before turning in and talked me into joining them. One hand leads to another. One glass of scotch leads to another also. A bellhop finally found me, and I was on my way to a phone when I saw you."

"Just as well," I said. "When I left the message I forgot I'm not staying in my house tonight. Gloria's there, and I'm with Velvet, and her room doesn't have a telephone." I yawned. "Sorry."

"You're dead on your feet."

"Bad choice of words."

"Can I get you a drink? Bar's still open. Or maybe a coffee or hot chocolate?"

"Thank you, but no. I need a ride home. The reason I called you . . ." I glanced around. In the time I'd been upstairs, the evening had come to an end and most of the revelers had staggered off. The lights had been turned low, and the spacious lobby was almost empty. A handful of late drinkers had pulled chairs around tables. The sleepy night clerk leaned against the reception desk, and the glassy-eyed bellhop shook his head in an attempt to keep himself awake. Slow dance music, the type to see people off to their beds, drifted down from above.

Richard led me to a quiet corner. "You went to the hospital with Elias. What happened?"

"He died."

"Died? I'm sorry to hear that."

"Not just died, but the police and the doctor suspect he was murdered."

"Murdered? That can't be. I was there myself when it happened. So were you. He had a heart attack and fell down the stairs and hit his head."

"Not his heart, and the fall didn't kill him, according to the doctor at the hospital. He was poisoned. Dave Dawson has called in the state police."

Richard's handsome face was a picture of shock. "Surely the doctor made a mistake."

"I'd like to hope so, but . . . I called you because if he was poisoned, it was by something he ate or drank today. Yesterday, I mean. Did he have breakfast here? Do you know if he ate anything off the catering truck at lunch?"

All the blood drained from Richard's face, and he stepped back with a groan. "I don't know about lunch, but it's likely he had breakfast. Can poison take that long to take effect?"

"I've no idea. The police will be looking into that. And"— I lowered my voice although no one was near us—"word's going to spread. And fast. I saw Martin McEnery from the *Gazette* at the hospital. I suspect someone phoned him and told him what was going on."

"That's all we need."

"Haggerman's will be in the worse position," I said. "Elias had dinner at my place. Dinner, drinks, dessert, and he collapsed in full view of a substantial number of people." I yawned again, and Richard grabbed my arm.

"Come on. Nothing either of us can do until tomorrow. I'll talk to my kitchen staff, and I suggest you do as well. They need to be prepared for a lot of hard questions. I'll drive you home."

"You don't need to do that, you must be tired too."

"I'd like to take you. It's not far."

"Thank you," I said. "Who won?"

"Won?"

"At poker."

He grinned at me as he took my arm. "Elizabeth, I never lose in my own house."

Chapter 8

RICHARD PULLED UP TO THE MAIN ENTRANCE TO MY HO-
tel, and I waved off his offer to walk me to my temporary
accommodation. It would have been nice to have his company, to enjoy that walk I'd been thinking about earlier, but
there would be, I hoped, plenty of time for pleasant evening
strolls over the rest of the summer.

Lights shone from inside the hotel, along the veranda,
and above the paths, but no one was around. As I walked up
the hill to the staff cabins, the bright lights fell away and
only the occasional dim bulb illuminated the trail. The forest closed around me and I enjoyed the simple and all too
rare pleasure of being wrapped in silence. The worst of the
heat of the day had broken, and the night air was warm and
soft, full of the scent of the woods. On my right the creek
rushed over rocks toward the lake, and behind me, small
waves beat against the shoreline. Somewhere out on the lake
a loon called. A bat flew overhead, and small animals scurried into the undergrowth at the approach of my footsteps.

The porch steps of the female senior staff cabin creaked as I climbed them, and I had to give the door a hard shove to open it. A single light shone in the hallway, throwing the far reaches of the space into deep shadow. In the room to my right, someone was snoring as though to wake the dead. Bad choice of words, once again.

Velvet has a private double-size room on the second floor. As well as a single bed, she has enough space for a small couch—taken out of service in the guest rooms when a lit cigarette fell into the cushions—plus a table large enough to hold a toaster and a kettle and tea and coffee things. I hadn't carried my keys with me tonight, and I hoped she'd left the door unlocked. She had, and I edged it open, trying not to make a sound. I slipped in and closed the door behind me. A thin line of moonlight peeked through not-quite-closed curtains, giving barely enough light to maneuver by. Velvet's slow breathing came from the bed, but she didn't stir.

I slipped off my shoes and hiked up my dress prior to getting my stockings and girdle off, as I edged my way to the center of the floor and the mattress that would be my bed. My probing foot touched it, and I reached for the pillow under which I'd put my pajamas. I'd change in the bathroom down the hall.

My fingers touched something warm and moving. It growled.

I leapt back with a scream, lost my footing, and crashed into the table. The dishes rattled, and the kettle fell to the floor with a crash. The toaster followed it, and I, unable to keep myself upright, followed the toaster. A chorus of frantic barking began.

Velvet screamed. Someone down the hall shouted, "What? What?"

Velvet leapt out of bed, sweeping a candlestick off the side table as she moved. She loomed above me, brandishing the weapon, her pale face and night-tossed hair ferocious in the thin line of moonlight. "Elizabeth? What are you doing?"

A bulldog waddled over to me and licked my face. I shoved him aside and scrambled to my feet. "What's Winston doing here?"

Rapid hammering on the door. "Are you okay in there, Velvet?"

"Yes, we're fine. Mrs. Grady disturbed the dog." Velvet switched on the light. "Go back to bed, everyone."

"How can we be sure you're not being held prisoner and told to say that?" a woman called.

I opened the door and stuck my head out. Women clustered in the hallway, dressed in a wide variety of nightwear, cream on faces, curlers in hair. Curious faces stared at me. One woman brandished a baseball bat. "This isn't a movie," I said. "Go back to bed."

Grumbling to themselves, they did so. I slammed the door.

My aunt Tatiana's bulldog looked up at me, eyes shining, tongue hanging out, stubby tail wagging.

"What," I said, "is Winston doing in my bed?"

"I told you I was looking after him tonight," Velvet replied.

"You did not."

"I didn't? I intended to. Sorry." Velvet replaced the candlestick. "Tatiana's gone to have dinner with her friend who's the head housekeeper at Kennelwood. It's her friend's birthday, so she expected it would be a late night, and she doesn't want to pay for a taxi, so she's spending the night. She asked me to look after Winston. I thought I told you." She picked up the toaster, gave it a shake, and when nothing rattled too loudly or fell out, she put it back on the table. Then she did the same with the kettle. "Nothing broken."

"Except my pride in front of my employees. Which still doesn't answer the question as to why Winston is in my bed."

Velvet walked up to the dog, leaned over, and wagged her finger in his face. "I told you to stay in your own bed." She pointed, and the dog crossed the floor to settle himself in a plush beige dog bed, whereupon he promptly went back to sleep.

Velvet dropped onto her own bed. I pulled off my stockings and wiggled out of my girdle.

"As long as I'm awake . . . How'd it go at the hospital?" She took her watch off the night table and checked the time. "It's late. So late, it's early. Almost time to get up."

"Elias Theropodous died," I said.

"Oh no. I'm sorry to hear that. Have you been at the hospital all this time? You must be exhausted." She stood up again. "Do you want a cup of tea?"

"Yeah, that would be nice. I don't suppose you have anything to eat, do you?"

"Sorry, no. Randy, Todd, and I heard the commotion and went back to the hotel to see what was going on. Someone said Elias had fallen down the stairs and hit his head and he was being taken to the hospital. Is that what killed him?"

"Unzip me, will you?" I turned my back to her and she did so. I stepped out of my dress and scooped up my pajamas. Fortunately, they'd been under my pillow so they weren't covered in dog hair and slobber. "The doctor thinks he was poisoned."

"Poisoned!"

"By something he ate or drank at Haggerman's."

Velvet sucked in a breath. "That can't be good. Has anyone else been taken to the hospital tonight?"

"Not that I know of, and if no one else got sick . . . then Elias had to have been poisoned deliberately."

"You mean murdered? Surely not."

"I'm going to the bathroom. While I'm gone, think over this evening. Did you see anyone paying particularly close attention to what Elias was eating or drinking or possibly fiddling with his drink?"

Y

I DIDN'T GET TO BED THAT NIGHT. I CHANGED INTO MY PA-jamas, washed my face, brushed my teeth, and got ready to turn in. But when I got back to Velvet's room, she had a pot of tea on the table, and we sat together on her bed and talked. As the sun leaked through the curtains we went over and over details of the night before, while Winston moved from his bed to the floor at my feet. When we'd remembered all we could, for now, of the events of this evening, we naturally arrived at other topics of conversation.

"Todd's nice, don't you think?" Velvet said as she pretended to concentrate on stirring sugar into her third cup of tea.

"Nice enough, I guess. If you like the handsome, charming type. He seems to like you."

She looked up, eyes sparkling. "Do you think so, Elizabeth? I mean, he was paying attention to all the women last night, right? Even the older ones like Olivia and Gloria and some of the guests."

"That was part of the job. He had to be charming to Rebecca, and I got the feeling they aren't too fond of each other."

"I sensed that too. Do you suppose they're going to continue filming? Now that Elias is gone, I mean."

"Matthew Oswald said they'll carry on for now and wait to hear what the studio decides. Don't they say 'the show must go on'?"

Velvet's radiant smile competed with the morning sun streaming into the room. I reached out and put my hand on hers. "Take care. Move slowly."

"Have you ever known me to act rashly, Elizabeth?"

"Velvet, I have never known you not to."

♈

WE FINISHED OUR TEA AND GOT READY FOR THE DAY. Velvet tied her long blond hair into a bouncy ponytail and dressed for her morning exercise classes in white shorts and a short-sleeved, tight-fitting blue shirt nipped at the waist before taking Winston for a quick walk. I rummaged in her too-small closet for something suitable for me to wear. I hadn't brought much from my house, so I decided that yesterday's skirt with a fresh blouse would have to do.

"Are you coming for breakfast in the staff dining room?" Velvet asked when she was back from her dog-walking duties and Winston was slurping enough water out of his bowl to fill a small Catskills lake.

I secured my key chain to my belt. I'm always forgetting my purse, so I took a tip from an illustration of the chatelaine of a medieval castle, and I keep my keys (and I have a lot of them) clipped to my belt during the day. "No time for breakfast. I'm not looking forward to it, but I need to break the news to Gloria before they all assemble at the dock and Matthew speaks to them. I should have done it last night, but . . ."

"Can you take Winston to Tatiana? She's usually in the laundry room at this time of the morning."

"I'll look for her after I've spoken to Olivia and Gloria. If I go anywhere near the main building, I'll be sucked into one problem or another and I won't get to them in time."

🍸

I SHOULD HAVE KNOWN BETTER. NEWS TRAVELS MIGHTY fast in the Catskills.

As soon as Winston and I walked into our house I knew Gloria had already heard the news. She was in my bedroom, sitting in a chair in front of the dressing table, staring at herself in the mirror while a hotel hairdresser fussed over her. The actress wore a loose robe, and her eyes and nose were tinged red. She cradled a coffee cup in her hand. Olivia sat on my bed watching. She also showed signs of recent crying and twisted a lace handkerchief between her fingers. Another woman stood quietly in a corner, holding a small case.

"You heard," I said.

My mother nodded.

"I'm sorry. I should have told you last night, but I didn't want to disturb you."

"Wouldn't have mattered," Gloria said. "I still can't quite believe it."

"I didn't realize you and he were close. Close your eyes," the hairdresser said as she stepped back and sprayed hair spray over Gloria's head.

I not only closed my eyes but also held my breath.

"How's that?" she asked.

Gloria studied herself. "It will do." The hairdresser gathered up her things and left, mumbling sorry to me, and the makeup artist took her place behind Gloria's chair.

"I tried to call Matthew," Gloria said, "but he wasn't in his room and didn't answer the page. I'll assume today's filming will go as planned until I hear otherwise." The makeup artist opened her case and selected a small bottle. Gloria turned her chair so she was facing the woman, tilted her chin, and again closed her eyes. "Were you there, Elizabeth? Last night. With Elias."

"I went with him to the hospital. He fell down the steps and didn't recover consciousness. I'm sorry."

"Was it the fall that killed him?" Olivia asked. "Or did he have a heart attack and then fall?"

"Uh . . . ," I said.

My mother stood up, nodded to me, and left the room. Winston and I followed.

"Why do you have the dog with you?" she asked.

"Don't ask. How did you hear about Elias? I hoped to be the one to break the news."

"The hairdresser's brother-in-law's an orderly at the hospital. When he got home from work he told his wife that Elias Theropodous had been brought in and had died. That woman immediately called her sister, knowing she's been assigned to work on Gloria's hair. I can only assume the blasted woman has bragged nonstop to everyone in the entire mountains about that. She ran in here before we were barely awake, totally out of breath, and shouted out the news. You should consider firing her, Elizabeth. She said she didn't realize we didn't know, but she did."

My mother wasn't being overly harsh. Gossiping about

the guests was strictly prohibited. All that meant, of course, was that staff gossiped about them when I wasn't around. But to gossip about a guest to a guest? Yes, fireable.

"How did Gloria react when she was told?" I asked.

"With shock, I'd imagine. Why do you ask?"

"Weren't you there?"

"No. I let the hairdresser in and went into my room to start getting ready for the day."

"So you don't actually know that Gloria was shocked?"

My mother narrowed her eyes. "What does that matter to you? Gloria and Elias's relationship is their business."

"It's about to become ours, I'm afraid." I told my mother about the supposed cause of death and Dave Dawson's suspicions.

She fell into a chair with a moan. Winston sniffed at her legs. "The police. Here. Again."

"Matthew's planning to tell the entire crew when they gather at eight o'clock."

Winston leapt to his feet and let out a bark. Footsteps sounded on the porch steps followed by a knock at the door. I opened it to see a busboy bearing a tray laden with table settings for two and two covered dishes. "Good morning, Mrs. Grady. Miss Peters."

I held the door open, and he put the tray on the dining room table. Olivia and I always have our meals prepared by the hotel's kitchen. My mother doesn't cook. She'd never learned how, as from a very young age her life had been devoted to dance. Aunt Tatiana, who had learned to cook, taught me as a true daughter of New York Russian immigrants should. I generally enjoy it, but these days I don't have the time.

Olivia and her first husband had divorced almost as soon as I'd been born, and my mother had continued climbing ever higher through the ranks of Broadway dancers. She'd handed me to Aunt Tatiana and her late husband, Rudolph, to raise above their corner store in Brooklyn. Some years we

went months without seeing Olivia, particularly if she was
working on a movie in California, but she wrote to me when
she had the chance and phoned most Sundays. One of my
fondest childhood memories is of Uncle Rudolph clutching
the telephone and bellowing, "Long distance!" and me
scrambling across the floor to grab the receiver. My mother
had come for a visit on my tenth birthday, wrapped in a mi-
asma of French perfume, diamonds dripping from her ears,
silk dress rustling, bearing brightly wrapped gifts and casually tossing her fur coat over the kitchen chair. She told me
that, as I was now a big girl, I could call her Olivia, rather
than use the Russian accented *mama*, as Aunt Tatiana had
taught me.

My father, Paul Davis, who I've always been in regular
contact with, is a jazz musician, but I inherited not one whiff
of musical talent from either of my parents, and so I never
even considered following my mother into show business.
Instead, I went to business college and worked as a bookkeeper and later a personnel manager for a big department
store.

When Olivia unexpectedly inherited this Catskills resort, she asked me to manage it for her. "What do I know
about the hotel business? Or about any business? I trust
you, Elizabeth," she'd said over lunch at the Russian Tea
Room. "There are few people in the world about whom I
can say this."

Her caution was well earned: only a few months prior, her
third husband, the cursed Jack Montgomery, had fleeced her
out of her life's savings and disappeared.

I said yes without thinking about it. I didn't want to be
involved that closely in Olivia's life, but I was bored with
my job at the department store, tired of my small walk-up
apartment, and my romantic life (what there was of one)
was going nowhere.

How hard could it be, I'd thought, *managing an efficient, well-run, well-established hotel?*

Very hard, as it turned out.

I'd been stuck with the bill for lunch.

"I didn't order breakfast for you, dear," Olivia said. "Shall I?"

I checked my watch. "No time. I'll have them bring something to my office. It's seven now. I need to deliver Winston to Tatiana and check in at the office as to any crisis that's arisen overnight. Any more crises, I mean. I want to be at the dock when the movie people arrive. Come on, Winston, let's get you home. Winston? Winston? Where's the dog?"

Olivia shrugged. "He must have run outside when the waiter left. You know Winston. He'll find his own way home. Eventually."

Chapter 9

MATTHEW MIGHT HAVE INTENDED TO BREAK THE NEWS of Elias's death to the movie crew, but clearly that wasn't necessary. The news had traveled, and fast. When I made my way down to the dock, everyone—guests and staff as well as movie people—was talking about nothing else.

Promptly at eight o'clock, Matthew called for attention and led a short prayer for Elias. He then gave a small speech saying how much the man would be missed. He finished by telling us the filming would continue as planned until he heard otherwise. I peeked out from beneath my half-closed eyelids during the prayer and studied the people who'd gathered.

Rebecca wept openly. Gloria stood stoic and dry-eyed, next to Olivia, but I read nothing into that. She was enough of a professional to control herself so as to not to ruin her camera-ready makeup. The expression in her eyes told me she was very far away. Onlookers had gathered, both to watch the filming and to hear the news, and some of them cried or shook their heads in dismay. Otherwise, not many people, if any, appeared particularly upset. I'd heard far more people wondering if they were going to be out of a job than commiserating over the death of the director.

I suppose one doesn't get to be a three times Academy Award winner by being personally popular.

Dave Dawson stood at the fringes of the movie set, near the catering table. He was alone, and he spoke to no one, other than to exchange a few words with the Kennelwood staff laying out coffee and Danish.

Not many of the guests seemed to have noticed him. The chief was excessively thin with long arms and legs that swung in every which direction in a jangly gait. His cheeks were sunken and his nose too large, and he peered at the world through thick eyeglasses. Not exactly a movie image of a policeman, but I suspected the crowd assumed he was an actor, dressed in uniform for a scene.

"If there's one thing I know for sure about Elias T. Theropodous, he would want us to carry on working on his final picture," Matthew said. "Let's honor him, ladies and gentlemen, by doing the very best work today that we can. Gary Denham worked closely with Elias from the earliest days of this project and he's more than capable, and willing, to take over. Gary." With a great flourish Matthew indicated the chair stamped DIRECTOR.

Gary had been standing close to Mary-Alice, and they'd talked in low voices throughout the prayer and Matthew's speech. He gave Mary-Alice a nod and went to stand next to Matthew. "Thank you, Mr. Oswald, for the trust you've put in me. In all of us. Before we begin, I'd like to invite Miss Olivia Peters to do me the honor of sitting with me." He gestured to the chair next to the director's.

Olivia gave the clapping crowd a small wave and drifted across the lawn, her skirts swirling around her long legs. Behind me I heard a woman say, "Gloria Grant and Olivia Peters. The bridge club will be simply green with envy. Have your camera at the ready, Fred. I want to get a picture of me with them later."

Gary took Olivia's hand; they said a few quiet words and she settled herself into the camp chair. She looked lovely and dewy-fresh, as she always did in front of her adoring public. No doubt only I had noticed the slightest tilt to one side as she favored her good leg as she walked.

"Positions, everyone," Gary yelled. "I need absolute quiet, or I'll evict the onlookers." How he could evict several hundred of our staff and guests, I didn't know, but his threat did the trick and the murmurs of conversation died down. "Gloria, Todd, I know you're distraught, but I also know you'll do your absolute best today. As will we all."

The word I'd use for Todd wasn't *distraught*. He'd sauntered up to me the minute I'd stepped onto the lawn and asked, "Where's Velvet this morning?"

"She has callisthenics. The eight o'clock class normally uses the dock, but today they're by the swimming pool."

"Thanks," he'd said, and headed toward the pool.

He returned in time to hear the newly appointed assistant director calling his name. He and Gloria took their places at the end of the dock, and the camera, sound recorder, and lighting equipment were maneuvered into position. The morning sun was rising over the lake in a clear sky, and the forecast predicted another hot and humid day, perfect for ensuring that our guests would be glad they'd come to the mountains. Two bright orange paddleboats, containing movie extras, drifted past in the distance, and a pretty young woman in a flowered bathing suit and matching cap stood on the sidelines, ready to walk in front of the camera as the scene began. I was surprised to see Randy standing next to her, also dressed in his bathing suit. He rolled his shoulders and bounced on his toes, as though getting ready to bound onto the set. He must have been taken on as an extra after all.

The scene had been set up yesterday morning, when the camera took long panoramic shots of the actors in the distance. Today the camera prepared to move in close, and a sound boom hovered above.

This movie would be a wonderful advertisement for the Catskills in general and, I hoped, for Haggerman's in particular. A great many people, and not just in Hollywood, would be anxious for this film to be a success. First, of course, it had to be finished, and despite Matthew's assurances to the assembly, that was not yet a certainty in light of the director's death.

I studied the faces around me. The actors getting into position, the cameraman behind his camera, the men with the lighting and sound equipment, the catering crew, Gary in the director's chair next to my mother, the makeup artist standing at the ready, Randy and the bathing-suit-clad woman. Even Freemont was watching today, not needing to have the car ready at an instant's notice. Plus hotel people, off-duty staff, and staff who were supposed to be working but found watching a movie being made more interesting than their duties. All these people and many more stood to benefit if Elias had lived.

Who, then, wanted him dead?

"Action!" Gary yelled, and the person with the clapper board clapped it. Randy and the young woman walked between the dock and the camera. When they'd passed, the camera platform was pushed slowly forward, focusing on Gloria.

She stared out over the water at the rising sun. She wore a black-and-white-checked dress with a Peter Pan collar, black buttons running from neckline to hem, and a thin black belt. A black sun hat was carefully arranged to keep the shadows off her face. "Grandmama," Todd said, and Gloria turned. Todd walked onto the dock, followed by the camera and microphone. He was dressed in an army uniform that fit far better than anything I'd seen during the war. In the real army he'd be up on charges, with hair that long.

"So soon," Gloria said. Her voice was low, full of grief and of fear. Her eyes blinked rapidly as she tried to restrain the emotions threatening to overwhelm her.

"My ride's here," he said. "It's time for me to go."

She put her hand in the center of his chest. The light caught the size and power of the single diamond she wore. He covered her hand with his. "I consider our disagreement to be behind us," Gloria said. "Go with God, Reggie. Do what you have to do and make our country and our family proud."

"Grandmama," Todd said.

"Cut!" Gary shouted. Gloria and Todd moved apart. Todd stretched his neck and wiggled his shoulders to let out some of the tension. Gloria stretched her mouth and jaws.

One of my reservations clerks let out a long breath. "Oh my gosh. I have goose bumps. I cannot wait to find out what happens to him."

"He is soooo gorgeous in that uniform," said a file clerk.

I turned to them. "Work stopped for the day, has it? We have no one wanting to make a booking? No paperwork to be seen to? The business office opened at eight, did it not?"

"We're on our lunch break, Mrs. Grady," the reservations clerk said.

"It's eight thirty."

"An early lunch."

I glanced around the hillside. Most of my staff were out here. I hid a smile. It scarcely mattered. Most of the guests were out here too. For perhaps the first time in the entire history of the Catskills, people were voluntarily missing breakfast.

"Very well," I said. "You can have an early lunch."

"Thank you, Mrs. Grady."

"Thank you, Mrs. Grady."

"Roger. Todd. Gloria. Positions," Gary yelled.

Mary-Alice whispered in his ear, and he nodded.

Todd and Gloria moved toward each other. Gloria put her hand on his chest, and Todd placed his on top of hers. The camera hovering over them had pulled back as Roger got ready to join the scene.

"Action!" Gary called, and the clapper clapped.

Roger stepped onto the dock. His sliver hair was slicked back, and he wore a business suit. His face was tight with anger. "What's this? Your mother told me you're leaving today."

Gloria and Todd separated. "John, please," Gloria said. "Not now."

Roger ignored her. He faced Todd, bristling with anger and aggression. "You're planning to sneak away, like a thief in the night."

"I thought it best, Father," Todd said in a calm, reasonable voice, "that I do it this way. I've said my goodbyes to Mother and to Grandmama. You've made your position clear, and you and I have no more to say to each other."

"I'll decide when we have nothing more to say. I've invited a lot of important people to dinner tonight. People who want to wish you well, if you must go off to the army."

Todd sighed heavily. "Mother told me you invited Judith McNamara and her parents."

"Of course I invited them. McNamara is an important man around these parts."

"How much longer do you and Mr. McNamara intend to humiliate poor Judith? I am not going to marry her, no matter how much money she can bring to the marriage."

"Please. Don't argue," Gloria implored. "Not now. Not today of all days."

They ignored her. The two men faced each other. Everyone watching held their breath. Roger lifted his fist and swung at Todd's face. The onlookers gasped. Gary didn't yell cut and tell us to keep quiet, so I assumed they'd edit the sound out of the final version. From my vantage point, I could see that the blow missed Todd entirely, but he lifted his hand to his face and staggered backward. He stood at the edge of the dock, his eyes wide with shock. In the background, the two paddleboats reappeared, heading in the other direction. A flock of ducks few overhead. They hadn't been sent there by the director, but it would add a nice touch to the scene.

Gloria grabbed Roger's arm. He shook her off.

"I'm not going to fight you, Father," Todd said, his voice more full of sorrow than anger.

"You come to dinner tonight, you lavish attention on Judith, or I'm cutting you off. Completely and totally."

"I report for duty Monday morning. Esmerelda and I are leaving on the noon train. I'm sorry you'll not get the chance to meet her." Todd turned to Gloria. "You'll like her very much, Grandmama. When the war's over, I hope—"

Roger lunged forward and shoved Todd. Todd stepped back, his arms windmilling. Gloria raised her hands to her mouth, her eyes wide.

"Cut!" Gary yelled. "Good but not good enough. Fifteen-minute break and then let's try that again. Todd, your father has just attacked you. I need a lot more shock on your face."

And I had a hotel to run. I headed back, and spotted Velvet watching the excitement from the edges of the crowd. "What happened to your exercise group?" I asked her.

"No one showed up." She swept her arm in front of her, taking in the excited crowd on the hillside, the cluster of actors and assorted crew gathered around the dock. The makeup woman was patting Gloria's cheeks with an enormous powder puff. Todd had a cigarette in one hand and a coffee cup in the other. Roger was bent over Gary's chair, talking animatedly.

The paddleboats bobbed on the still water. For a moment, I wondered if the ducks were also waiting for their cue.

"All you can do," I said to Velvet, "is be available in case anyone does want to do activities today. What's Randy up to anyway?"

"He's been hired to be an extra. He told me about it over breakfast. Whoever they had pretending to be a lifeguard walking across the lawn got a better offer and took off. Todd told Gary that Randy has some movie experience, and he got the job. Wasn't that nice of Todd?"

I didn't say no, but I thought it. "Randy has a job. He works for me."

"It's a small part. He just walks in front of the camera. I guess they thought he looks good in his bathing suit." Velvet chuckled.

It might be a small part, but it seemed to take an awfully long time to film one scene. I left her and headed for Dave Dawson, still standing alone. He'd pulled his hat low over his face in an attempt to shield his eyes from the rising sun. "Where are your friends?" I asked.

"My friends?"

"The state police."

"Good question. I've no idea. Probably lost on the back roads, like last time. They were supposed to meet me here at seven thirty. I went to Kennelwood first thing and spoke to Mr. Oswald. He persuaded me to let the filming continue as planned. Something about having set the scene yesterday and the importance of catching the same light." Dave shook his head. He lowered his hand and blinked at me from beneath his glasses. "Probably not good policing, but Mr. Oswald was very convincing about the amount of money and publicity his movie's pouring into this area. He went to the trouble of finding out the name of our mayor and dropped it into our conversation. I was about to come looking for you. I want to talk to the people who knew Mr. Th—the dead man, and I need a place to do that."

"I'll have a meeting room put aside for you. I'll tell the front desk, and they'll direct you if you can't find me."

"Thanks. Do you have anything to add to what you said last night? Remember anything?"

"Sorry. No. Velvet and I talked it over, but she didn't notice anything significant either."

"She was there? At this dinner?"

"Oh, yes. You'll have no shortage of people to talk to. I saw you at the catering table. Did they serve Elias his lunch yesterday?"

"They say no. He's never come anywhere near them, although they think his secretary fetched the occasional coffee for him. And, before you ask, the coffee's served to everyone out of one big pot. They're from Kennelwood, so they don't know if missing lunch was his regular habit or not."

"Let me know if you need anything," I said. "Speaking of the catered lunch, it's unlikely you'll get anything to eat from them, that's only for the cast and crew. If you're here at lunchtime, it's on the house. Tell the maître d' I said so."

"Thanks, Elizabeth."

I next caught up with Matthew standing beside the flower beds surrounding the signpost pointing to the activity centers. Francis Monahan was pulling up weeds, and he gave me a shy smile of hello. I said, "Good morning."

I said the same to Matthew, followed by "Things seem to be going ahead as far as your movie's concerned."

"For now. Freemont's gone for the car. I'm heading to Kennelwood to make some calls to the studio people."

"Do you have an idea as to what they're going to decide?"

"To keep filming if they know what's good for them. And for their pocketbook. We've paid for the script, for the location shoot, paid the actors and the crew, brought everyone up here. We have good background footage and a couple of scenes in the can. Shots that can't be replicated if we wait more than a couple of days."

"Can I ask a question?" I said.

"Sure. What?"

"Why didn't they film Todd falling into the lake? He stood at the edge looking as though he was about to go in, and then Gary stopped filming. I would have thought that would make a great scene."

Matthew grinned at me. "Several reasons. Can't have Todd getting all wet and then the director needing to re-shoot the scene where he's dry. But more to the point, Todd can't swim. We don't want film of him floundering around. Wouldn't quite match the image he's trying to project. The character, Reginald, does go in the water, and when he gets out he leaves to meet his lady friend and catch their train soaking wet and in a rage. We'll film that scene in shallower water."

A taxi pulled into the curve at the entrance to the hotel, and two men got out. One of them looked around while the other handed money to the driver and waited for his change. They were both dressed in business suits and hats. One had a camera around his neck. They didn't go into the hotel but headed straight for the movie set.

Another taxi pulled up behind the first. This time the passengers were a man and a woman. Her mouth was a slash of red, her hair pulled back into a tight bun. She wore a brown tweed suit and flat shoes, completely out of place on a bright Catskills summer morning, and carried a heavy leather purse that showed signs of a lot of wear. The man was also in a suit and he carried a large black box.

"The ladies and gentlemen of the press," Matthew said to me.

"News travels. They would have gotten out of bed mighty early to get here so quickly. Those are New York City taxis. Must have cost them a fortune."

A private car was next to arrive. I recognized the driver as he got out and tossed the keys to a bellhop. Jim Westenham, crack crime reporter for the *New York Times*, touched the brim of his hat, and said, "Elizabeth. Good morning. You're looking as lovely as ever this fine morning." Jim and I had met earlier in the summer when his uncle died at the hotel under suspicious circumstances.

"Dare I ask what brings you here?" I asked.

"Big news, Elizabeth. Elias Theropodous died last night and it might not be from natural causes. A steady stream of cars and taxis pulled out of New York in the wee hours of this morning, and more will be arriving on the first train. We headed for Kennelwood, where we'd been told the man was staying. They told us the filming was happening here and . . . here we are. Do I get an inside scoop?"

"No."

102   VICKI DELANY

"You were at the hospital with Elias when he died."

"How do you know that?"

"I didn't. But you just confirmed it. All my sources said was that people from the hotel where he'd been having dinner brought him in. Not the hotel where he'd been staying, and you're the closest, and they're filming here this morning. A guess on my part. Hi." He thrust his hand toward Matthew, standing silently at my side. "Jim Westenham. *New York Times*."

Matthew accepted the shake. "Matthew Oswald. I know your name. You're a crime reporter."

"That I am, and proud of it."

"Was that Jane Donaldson arriving ahead of you? *New York Morning Standard*?"

"The Dame of Gossip herself, from a paper with no standards whatsoever. Oswald. Matthew Oswald." Jim grinned. "Do you, as a producer of this movie, have a statement for the press?"

"Not to a crime reporter, no."

"Jim," I said, "all I want is for Haggerman's name to be left out of it."

"Not going to happen, Elizabeth. This is a big story. Particularly if it turns out the man's death wasn't accidental. What do you know about that?"

I shook my head.

"Here's Freemont now," Matthew said. "Elizabeth. Mr. Westenham." Matthew headed for his car at a brisk pace.

"I hear Dave Dawson's now chief of police of your lovely little town," Jim said. "Good for him. Because I knew where it was, having been to Kennelwood before, I managed to grab a phone before the others could get to it and called the police for an update. Dawson's holding a press conference at three this afternoon." Jim pointed behind me. "Looks like they didn't get far." I turned to see the three newspapermen and the one newspaperwoman being marched off the film set by two rather burley gentlemen, the studio's security guards. My security staff are more used to chasing drunk teenagers away from the pool after hours or searching the woods for kids who got lost playing hide-and-seek than providing actual muscle.

"The people have a right to know," one newspaperman shouted.

"Run along now, and don't bother us again," said the larger and more formidable-looking of the security guards.

"Olivia Peters owns this joint," the oldest of the newspapermen said. "I bet she'll talk to the press." He ran past us, heading for the hotel. The man who'd come with him peered around and then wandered off.

"I'm gonna find some guests to talk to," the woman said to her companion. "Someone must have seen something. You keep that camera front and center. If they give us good copy, we'll imply their picture'll get in the paper."

She looked at Jim out of the corner of her eyes and gave him a tight-lipped nod of greeting as they passed us. Her photographer opened his box and began assembling his press camera as he walked. Jim smiled at them but said nothing. He did not, thank heavens, attempt to introduce us.

"If you'll excuse me," I said. "I have security of my own to call. I'm throwing those people off my property and posting a guard at the road. I'll evict you as well, if you start bothering my guests."

"You'd be better to face the story front and center," Jim said. "Get the facts out there. Better than rumor and innuendo."

"Better for who? Not me."

"Any chance of me getting that unused room again?"

"Not on your life." I stalked into the hotel. One of the bellhops was filling the newspaper box next to the reception desk with today's *Summervale Gazette*. I grabbed one out of his hands. The paper was so fresh, the ink almost rubbed off on my fingers. The last time I'd seen print so large, it had been to announce the end of the war.

FAMED MOVIE DIRECTOR DEAD!

DID ACADEMY AWARD WINNER ELIAS J. THEROPODOUS EAT SOMETHING AT CATSKILLS RESORT THAT DID HIM IN?

FILMING CONTINUES IN SUMMERVALE.

Elias's middle initial was T., but never mind that. I was grateful Haggerman's wasn't mentioned in the headline. I read quickly. Martin McEnery wasn't a very good reporter, which was the reason he was stuck here, in small-town Upstate New York working for a small-town newspaper, rather than living his dream with a byline at the *New York Times* or *Washington Post*. His article started with background, providing details of Elias's career, and then went on to talk about the movie he was filming here, including a list of the best-known actors. Only in the third paragraph did he mention Elias been staying at Kennelwood, and had been rushed to the hospital after dinner at Haggerman's. I considered having the paper removed from the box but decided to leave it. If anyone staying here didn't know what had happened last night, they would soon enough.

I asked the receptionist to reserve a meeting room for the use of the police and to call security to my office. I needed to get those reporters off hotel grounds and to post guards at the front gate to ensure they stayed out.

Jim Westenham and I had become friends, of a sort. I knew he wasn't a muckraking journalist. He could stay. For now. The moment I found him bothering my guests, he'd be out on his ear too.

Chapter 10

I WAS BENT OVER THE ACCOUNTS BOOK TRYING TO FIND a hundred unbalanced dollars, when Rosemary tapped at my door and came in.

"I thought you should know that guests are starting to talk, Elizabeth," she said.

"Guests are always talking," I replied. "There are two main activities in the Catskills: eating and gossiping, in that order. While the movie people are here, gossiping has temporarily taken first place."

"It's more than that. One of those newspaper reporters who was poking around earlier asked a guest if she had reason to be concerned about the safety of the food served here. Unfortunately, that lady was on her way to the beauty parlor, center of all gossip. Not to mention that the local paper did pointedly mention that the man died after eating here. Some people are wondering if Elias Theropodous was killed by something he ate, something prepared in our kitchen."

I put down my pencil with a sigh. It was coming up to lunchtime and I had a lot of paperwork to get through. "I was afraid of that. No one has taken sick today, have they?"

"Not that I've heard of."

"Elias ate what everyone else ate. If no one else got sick, then it can't have been the fault of our kitchen."

"I know that, Elizabeth, but people don't always see sense when it comes to these things."

The phone on my desk rang. I picked it up. "Mr. McIntosh from the booking agency's on the line," the switchboard operator announced.

"Then put him through to a reservations clerk."

"He insists he needs to speak to you, Mrs. Grady. Not a clerk."

I made a face at Rosemary as I said, "Put him through."

"Mrs. Grady!" the thick Lower East Side accent bellowed down the line. "I'm getting questions as to how safe it is at Haggerman's."

I moved the phone slightly away from my ear. "I trust your reply is that it's perfectly safe."

"So far, yeah, that's what I'm telling them. Folks drop dead at hotels and resorts all the time. Comes from catering to a bunch of old geezers."

"I hope you don't say that out loud."

"Give me a break here, Mrs. Grady. When the story gets in the papers and on the radio, people start calling me. So I'm calling you."

Once again, I explained that only Elias had taken ill, not even any "old geezers."

"Okay," he said. "Long as I don't hear any more 'bout it, that'll be the line I'll take." He hung up without wishing me a good day.

I put my head in my hands and groaned.

"Knock knock," came a voice from the door. "Anyone home?" Richard Kennelwood stood there, smiling bashfully, holding out a fistful of mismatched flowers.

I waved him in. "Richard, hi. Can you hold on a minute? I'll be right with you. Rosemary, anything else?"

"Deputy Dave . . . I mean Chief Dawson . . . is interviewing people in the writing room who were at the private dinner last night. He had a lot of questions for me about the drinks I made for Elias. I told him I made him a heck of a lot, but I didn't add a deadly poison to any of them."

"You didn't actually say that!"

"No. I'd never met the man before. I didn't even meet him yesterday, I just made him drinks. Dawson admitted I had no reason to kill him. He took away the bottle of bourbon though, for analysis, he said. Waste of time."

"Why?"

"I opened that bottle toward the end of the evening. I finished the one I'd been using and threw it in the trash. It would have been picked up this morning and dumped with all the other used bottles. Of which we get a heck of a lot in a day."

"Have the state police arrived yet?" I asked.

"They weren't there when Dave talked to me."

Rosemary left, and Richard handed me the flowers. A colorful mismatched mixture of geraniums, petunias, leaves of hosta, and other assorted garden plants. I smiled at him. "I hope you didn't pick these out of my flower beds. Francis Monahan will be in tears."

"I raided my own beds. My gardeners will have to deal with my disregard for their craft."

"Thank you." I put the flowers into the glass of water on my desk, admired them once more, and said, "What's up?"

The smile died, and he dropped into a chair. "What you and Rosemary were talking about. I'm hearing the same at my place. Elias had breakfast in the dining room yesterday, in full view of several hundred of my guests. Our kitchen catered the set. People are wondering out loud if he was killed by something in his breakfast or lunch. The chef told me a surprising amount of lox was left over this morning."

"They must be concerned. We never have lox left over."

"His point exactly."

I let out a long breath. "We had newspaper reporters here this morning. Including Jim Westenham."

"Oh, him." One corner of Richard's mouth twitched in disapproval. "A pack of them showed up at my place earlier and charged the phone room, trying to get updates. They soon left after being told the film crew was here. What did you do?"

"I told my security guards to order them off the property. Except for Jim. He can stay."

"Why?"

"Because I know him, and—"

"Don't say you trust him, Elizabeth. He's a newspaperman. Untrustworthy by definition. Remember what happened when you tried to lay a trap for his uncle's killer? He was supposed to help, but he had other ideas."

"That was a misunderstanding."

"If you say so."

"I do say so." Richard couldn't be . . . jealous of Jim, could he? Jim had taken me to dinner at Kennelwood (and the less said of that disastrous evening the better) when he was here before, but he went back to the city with no promises to meet again. "Last I saw of him today he was watching the filming. As for trust . . . Maybe I do trust him not to make up something about us, or to make it sound worse than it is. Elias's death is a big story, and I'm not sure it's a good idea to try to completely close us off from the press, they—"

"Mrs. Grady, you'd better come right quick." One of the office clerks stood in the doorway.

Richard and I both leapt to our feet. "What's happened?"

"Guest's taken ill. Jackson Brothers' Funeral Home's been called, and they're sending the ambulance."

"Why do they need me?" As had been said, we get a large number of elderly guests here. It's not uncommon for an ambulance to be called or a car grabbed for a rush to the hospital.

"It's a girl. A teenage girl. And it was something she ate."

Chapter 11

I BOLTED OUT OF MY OFFICE, RICHARD KENNELWOOD hot on my heels. We ran down the corridor and into the lobby. At that moment two ambulance workers came into the hotel, pushing their stretcher.

"Room 318," a receptionist called.

At this time of day, particularly with the movie crew here, the lobby was largely empty. But not empty enough. "What's happening?" people called to me. "Is it another poisoning?"

"Are we safe here?" a woman asked her husband.

I bit back a retort.

"You got here quickly," I said to the ambulance men, as we waited impatiently for the elevator.

"We were nearby. Heading to my place for our lunch break when we got the call on the radio."

"Good thing," Richard said.

A crowd had gathered around the door of room 318. A

bellhop was trying to get them to move, but he wasn't having a great deal of success.

"You'd think people would be outside enjoying the day," I muttered to Richard. "Not hanging around waiting for yet another disaster to fall."

He, wisely, didn't reply.

"What did she have for breakfast?" a woman called to me. "Can you find out? I'm not feeling too well."

I bit my tongue and followed the ambulance workers into the room, while Richard tried to help the bellhop assure people there was nothing to see.

A foul smell hit me, and my throat closed as I tried not to gag. A teenage girl lay on one of the twin beds moaning. The blanket had been tossed on the floor, and I could see that it was thick with a foul yellow substance. Lumps of the same substance were trapped in the girl's long hair. I turned my eyes away but not before my stomach rolled over.

A man and a woman who I assumed were the girl's parents hovered over her. The woman was weeping, and the man had his arm around her shoulders. A young girl watched from beside the window.

"Mommy!" the girl on the bed cried.

"She'll be okay," one of the ambulance workers said. "She's talking and she's brought most of it up. We'll take her in to be sure." He leaned over the moaning girl. "Can you move by yourself, darlin'?"

The girl rolled over. She groaned and then spewed up another stomachful. The ambulance man leapt out of the way.

"Is she dying?" someone called from the hallway.

"Drama queen," the girl by the window muttered.

I looked at her, and she rolled her eyes. She was about twelve, all knees and elbows, with straight dark hair, a scattering of freckles over her nose, and mischievous brown eyes. She had something clenched in her hand. She caught my eye and slowly opened her hand. A pill bottle. The girl winked at me.

"Maybe you should give that to the ambulance workers," I said. "They need to show it to the doctors at the hospital."

Her father heard us. He marched over and grabbed the bottle from her hand. "Get out of here, Lacy."

"Going, going!" she called in a singsong voice. She skipped merrily out of the room as the men helped her sister, still groaning, onto the stretcher. I followed the younger girl.

Most of the onlookers had been shamed into leaving, but a few lingered at the end of the corridor and heads stuck out of doors. Jim Westenham had followed the commotion and stood in the hallway, watching.

The stretcher came out of the room. "Mommy!" the girl on it cried again.

"I'll accompany your mother and sister to the ambulance," Lacy's father said. "You go for lunch, and I'll join you there."

"Yeah, lunch!" Lacy said.

"Do you know what happened?" I spoke to Lacy, and tried to keep my voice low.

"Was it something she ate?" Richard asked.

Jim Westenham edged closer.

"Oh, yes. It was something she ate." Lacy giggled.

My heart sank. It lifted again when Lacy said, "She ate all of Mommy's sleeping pills. Anything for attention."

I shouldn't have felt relieved, but I was. The girl hadn't been poisoned by her Haggerman's breakfast.

"None of my business," Jim said, and he headed for the stairs.

"Why would she do that?" I asked Lacy.

"At breakfast Daddy told Miss Fancy-pants she couldn't go into town tonight with that guy in charge of the paddle-boats she's been making gooey eyes at all week. She thinks she's soooooo grown up, but she's not; she's just a baby. I bet that paddleboat guy never even noticed her—she's so ugly—but she said he asked her. She got all mad at the table in the dining room, and Mommy told her not to make a spectacle of herself and sent her to our room. She didn't go to our room, she went to Mommy and Daddy's room and found the pills. There weren't enough pills in the bottle to kill her."

"How do you know that?" I asked.

Lacy grinned at me. "Because I check every day, of course. You're Mrs. Grady. Your mother's Olivia Peters. Carol wants to be a dancer like Miss Peters. As if. She's already waaay too big here." Lacy formed cups with her hands and held them up to her chest. Richard choked. I tried not to laugh.

"Maybe that's why that boat guy asked her out."

Richard choked again.

"I want to be an actress in Hollywood. I was in my class play last year, and Mrs. Johannsen said I'm really talented. I'd love to meet Todd Thompson. Can you introduce me?"

"If I get a chance," I said. "But they are very busy."

"Okay. I tried to say hi to Miss Grant and Miss Rae yesterday when they were talking with the gardener about the flowers by the pool, but Daddy dragged me away. He said I wasn't to bother them. I'm going to lunch now." She started to turn and then swung back. "Can you ask the cook to make hot dogs tomorrow? They had them on Sunday but not yesterday."

"I can do that."

Lacy skipped away and punched happily at the elevator buttons.

"What a horror of a child," Richard said.

"I liked her. I liked her a lot. Come on, let's go downstairs. I expect to have a lot of nerves to calm. It's far easier to start a rumor than to stop one."

The elevator doors swooshed open, and a hotel page emerged. He saw us, waved, and trotted down the hall. "Mr. Kennelwood. Switchboard's looking for you. You're needed at your place."

"Thanks," Richard said. "Did they say what it's about?"

"No, sir."

"If you're parked in the main lot, you'd be faster to take the staff stairs." I pointed to the end of the corridor and said to the page, "Will you show Mr. Kennelwood to the delivery doors, please?"

"I'll call you later, Elizabeth," Richard said before turning and following the page.

THE STOPPING OF RUMORS WASN'T HELPED WHEN WE found Martin McEnery from the *Summervale Gazette* enthusiastically fanning the flames. Unfortunately, he'd been in the lobby when the ambulance men wheeled their stretcher and their patient, moaning theatrically, out of the elevator, followed by the weeping mother and the concerned father.

I should have sicced Lacy on him, but she'd disappeared.

I marched up to McEnery. "Get out of here."

"Good afternoon, Mrs. Grady. Nice to see you again, looking as bright and cheerful as ever after the shocking events of last night."

"What do you want?" I growled.

"The truth. All any newspaperman wants. I saw none other than Jim Westenham a few minutes ago. If the *New York Times* has sent their top reporter after this story, it's a big one."

"I'll admit that Mr. Theropodous's death is of some interest to the entertainment and gossip columns," I said.

"Don't think Westenham works gossip. He's a crime reporter, right?"

"The police are dealing with it," I said. "You should interview them."

"I tried to. Dave Dawson's new to the post. He's stepping warily."

"Meaning he's not rushing to any conclusions," I said.

"What happened just now? A young girl suddenly over-come with illness? Being rushed to the hospital? Was she poisoned by something she ate in the same manner as Elias Theropodous?" He held his pencil over his notebook and gave me a mean smile.

My mouth flapped open. I shut it. I could hardly tell this odious man that one of our young guests had made a show of trying to kill herself because her parents wouldn't let her date a Haggerman's employee.

"I trust," I said, "you'll respect the family's privacy."

His eyes gleamed. "I need something for my paper, Mrs. Grady. Are you going to give it to me or . . ."

The word hung in the air.

I was saved by the timely arrival of Jim Westenham. He slapped McEnery on the back so hard the other man pitched forward. "I thought I'd head into town, grab some lunch. Check things out before the press conference at three. I might pop into your paper's office, Martin. Ask the owners if they know their reporter's trying to dig up dirt on one of the town's largest employers."

"I'm in pursuit of a story, Westenham, same as you."

"If, and it's still an if, Elias Theropodous was deliberately poisoned, that's a story. Regardless of what happened to him, the medical problems of a young guest and the distress of her family is not, and never will be, any story I'll report on."

McEnery attempted to puff himself up. He looked at me. I clamped my lips shut.

"I'm going back to town," he said. "I'll drop into the police station, check with Chief Dawson as to the status of the investigation."

"You do that," Jim said.

McEnery clamped his hat on his head and stormed off. I held my breath when he passed Lacy's father coming in after seeing the ambulance off, but McEnery didn't pause. Several people rushed Lacy's father, asking what was go-ing on.

"Quite all right. Quite all right," he said. "My daughter seems to have come down with a bad case of the flu. Her mother's with her, and they're going to the hospital to have her checked out. Just a precaution." Head down, he slipped past me going in the direction of the dining room.

"Girls these days." A stiff-backed, silver-haired matriarch sniffed as she tapped her way across the lobby with the aid of a gold-topped cane. "Haven't got a lick of common sense. If you want my opinion, her foolish parents allowed her a glass of wine at dinner. Wouldn't have been permitted in my day."

No one asked the lady how a single glass of wine the night before could send a girl to hospital the following day.

Some of our male staff did try to ply the young female guests with liquor or offer to get them into the bars in town. The girls, like Lacy's sister, were young, on vacation, surrounded by college boys, stretching their wings. It didn't always end happily.

"Thanks for getting rid of McEnery," I said to Jim. "I really, really do not like him."

"If he's headed to the police station, he's going to be sadly disappointed," Jim said. "Deputy Dave's still here. Unlike his predecessor, who made sure everyone knew he was around by leaving the car out front, Dave parked in the staff lot. He's still interviewing people about last night."

"Is that why you're hanging around? Hoping for a chance to talk to him?"

Jim grinned and spread his arms out. "As I seem to be the only newspaperman in the place . . . yup."

I shook my head. "Not here. Not in my hotel. If you want to interview the chief, I've heard he likes the Red Spot Diner on Main Street."

"I'll keep that in mind. Thanks. Speaking of lunch . . ."

"Were we?"

"We are now. Do you have time to join me? I hear the food's good here."

"No, I don't, sorry. If you're hoping to stay in the area tonight, you should get on the phone and try to find yourself a room. Things fill up fast around here in the summertime." I walked away, conscious of Jim's eyes following me.

When he'd been here last, he'd taken me out to dinner and had been very pleasant company. Jim was good-looking and full of charm. But he was a newspaperman, first and always, and I didn't entirely trust him. I'd learned, the hard way, about men and their self-serving charm.

Instead, I found myself thinking about Richard Kennelwood and his small but totally delightful bunch of hand-picked flowers. I mentally shook my head. *Not a good idea.* I had no time for romance. This summer had to be all about getting the hotel established under my management and ensuring it remained profitable.

🍸

RICHARD HAD, IN TURN, BEEN THINKING ABOUT ME, although not in a way I might have wanted. I'd barely dropped into my office chair, picked up my pencil, and tried to remember what I'd been doing, when the phone rang. I sighed and picked it up.

"Elizabeth," Richard said when he'd been put through. "Everything okay there?"

"Far as I know. Martin McEnery tried to say if I didn't talk to him, he'd bother the parents of that girl who was taken to the hospital, but Jim Westenham had him scurrying out of here like a frightened rat."

Richard's voice turned sharp. "What's Westenham got to do with it?"

"Nothing. He happened to come in when we were talking."

"He just happened to be passing, did he?"

"Yes, he did. Why are you calling, Richard?"

"Maybe only to check in." His voice softened. "My

father . . . I'm sorry to have to say this, Elizabeth, but he told a group of our guests that Haggerman's had been ordered closed because unsanitary conditions in the kitchen killed a diner."

Richard probably didn't even need the phone to hear my shriek. "*What?*"

"That's why I was asked to get back here in a hurry. He was chatting to guests down by the pool. One of the pages overheard, and he had enough sense to report it to his supervisor. Who had enough sense to know we don't need a lawsuit and called me."

"Lawsuit's the least of it," I muttered.

"I had a talk with my father and explained that that's not true. He said, 'So what? It's a good story.'"

I growled.

"I then pointed out that accusations such as that can bounce back and bite us. Elias had breakfast in our dining room that day, and everyone saw him devouring enough lox to feed a whale. I think I got through to him, Elizabeth, on that score if not the danger of libel one."

"Thank you. And thank you for telling me."

"Forewarned is forearmed. I told you when we met that I don't do business the way my father did. Business is business and competition is good, but I firmly believe we're all invested in ensuring that every one of us in the Catskills—hotels, boardinghouses, bungalow colonies—do well for the success of us all. Have you heard anything more from Dave?"

"He's still conducting his interviews. I've been told he's having a press conference at the station at three, but I've no idea if he has anything to say we don't already know."

"Take care, Elizabeth."

"I will. You too." I hung up. I chewed on the end of my pencil for a long time and stared out the window into the overgrown shrubbery crowding my office window. The phone rang a few times, but I didn't pick it up. One of the clerks slipped in with a stack of pink message slips, and I indicated to her to leave them on my desk.

This was not good. Not good at all.

I couldn't sit here in my office wondering what disaster was about to fall next.

Time for me to do something.

Chapter 12

CHIEF DAWSON, THE RECEPTIONIST INFORMED ME, HAD left. "Without arresting anyone," she added with a touch of disappointment. The state police had never arrived.

I'd decided to "do something" but I couldn't actually think of anything I should be "doing." I could ask questions. Maybe people would talk more freely to me, the friendly hotelier, than to the police.

I went outside. Filming had returned to cabin one. I held my hand above my eyes to shade them from the sun and peered into the distance. The pillars of the cabin porch blocked my view of the on-camera action, but I had a clear view of the onlookers. My mother was seated next to the director's chair. Gary was on his feet, waving his arms around. Mary-Alice hovered next to him. Gary pointed left. Mary-Alice pointed right. Gary then pointed right. Matthew Oswald stood to one side, arms crossed over his chest, watching.

Instead of heading toward the filming, I went the other way. I trotted down the driveway and rounded the main building. I found Freemont and his Skylark in the guest parking lot. The chauffeur was leaning against the hood of the car, reading a newspaper. As I got close I was sorry to see the paper was the *Summervale Gazette*.

He heard my approach, quickly folded the paper, and straightened. "Afternoon, Mrs. Grady."

"Mr. Freemont."

"Just Freemont, please. Mr. Freemont's my daddy. Still going strong at ninety, I must add."

"I'm pleased to hear that. Freemont."

"Is Mr. Oswald ready to leave?"

"No. That's not why I'm here. Have you had lunch? You're welcome to take your meals in our staff dining room while you're here."

"That's kind of you, Mrs. Grady. I brought sandwiches from my lodgings today, but tomorrow, if we're still here, I might do that. Mr. Oswald isn't quite the stickler for instant obedience, the way Mr. T. was." I tried to read his face when he mentioned his late employer but it remained impassive. Like all well-trained servants (and hotel managers) he'd learned to control his expression. "Can I help you with something, ma'am?"

"Not really. I'm just . . . well, to be honest, I'm curious. About Mr. Theropodous, I mean. Have the police spoken to you?"

"Yes, that Chief Dawson, he did. I had nothing to tell him. Mr. T. had his breakfast at his hotel, ate nothing for lunch, which was normal in a working day—and every day was a working day for Mr. T.—and came here for dinner with the rest of them."

"You said you've worked for him for a long time."

"Twenty-one years." The lines on his face folded. "I'm going to miss him, Mrs. Grady. I'm going to miss him a lot."

"Are you going to be out of a job?"

He shook his head. "Don't you worry 'bout me. I'll be fine. Mr. Theropodous paid well, and I've got my savings. I've been thinking of retiring soon anyway."

"That's good to know." The sun was directly overhead, beating down on my hatless head. Heat rose from the pavement and radiated in almost visible waves off the metal of the car. I felt a trickle of sweat slithering down my back. In the far distance, a grounds worker pushed a wheelbarrow, and a woman came out of the laundry shed, her arms laden with towels.

"I've been driving movie people around for more than forty years," Freemont said. "I've learned to keep my ears shut, but I've also learned to read what people aren't saying. You want to know who might have killed Mr. T. I didn't."

"I didn't mean—"

He lifted one hand. "That's all right. The policeman asked me that too. I'll tell you what I told him. Mr. Theropodous was a hard boss, in that he expected the best, and he expected it every time. Not everyone can give their best every time. Like Mr. Oswald and I were saying last night, Mr. T. had his enemies. I won't say he was a good man, 'cause he wasn't to a lot of folks, but he was good to me. He stood up for me plenty of times, like when restaurants or hotels told me I had to leave, or young punks thought they could get a few laughs by bullying an old Black man." The edges of his mouth turned up and something in his dark eyes lifted as he remembered. "Yeah, I'm gonna miss the old coot." He studied my face. "I like you, Mrs. Grady."

"You can call me Elizabeth."

"Probably best not to. I realize Mr. Theropodous's death isn't likely to do the reputation of your hotel any good, particularly if the police never find out who killed him. He and I got on well 'cause we understood each other. He was the boss, and he told me what to do. I was the chauffeur, and I did it. He turned mean when he didn't get his own way, and that was happening more than it used to. This picture was Mr. Theropodous's last chance. His last two movies didn't do as well as the backers expected, and plenty of younger men out there anxious to show what they can do. He'd been told to keep this one strictly on budget, but he wasn't one to cut corners. Whole reason Mr. Oswald's even here's to keep an eye on Mr. T.'s spending."

"You aren't saying the movie studio ordered Elias to be killed to stop his movie?"

"Oh, no. Nothing like that. Money that's been spent can't be gotten back. I'm only trying to tell you the way things stood."

"Younger men. Like Gary Denham?"

Freemont shrugged. "I'm not pointing no fingers, Mrs. Grady."

"Did you work for Elias when he was married to Gloria Grant?"

"That marriage was ending when I was hired. She had a temper on her, that one, and didn't care who was listening. So many of them think the servants are part of the furniture and never bother to watch what they're saying."

I laughed. "Same for anyone who works at a hotel."

"I learned some new words when I started driving Miss Grant. She found out he was foolin' around with a young actress name of . . . I don't remember. So many of 'em over the years. Miss Grant divorced him. The actress soon disappeared, and not long after, he married Annie Fitzpatrick. Annie was nice, a lady, I liked her. But she didn't last long, either as Mrs. Theropodous or in the movies. Mr. T. told me he was done with marrying them. More bother than it was worth." He chuckled.

"What about you, Freemont? Are you married?"

"Forty-five years next summer. Four kids, eleven grandkids. I'll be glad to get home to California to see them all."

"Thank you for talking to me. If you need anything—coffee, a glass of water, or a soft drink—tell the kitchen I said you're welcome to it."

"I'll do that. Thank you kindly." He touched the brim of his hat.

* * *

I HADN'T LEARNED ANYTHING I DIDN'T ALREADY KNOW: Elias Theropodous was difficult to live and work with.

"Mrs. Grady to the office. Mrs. Grady to the office." All over the property loudspeakers boomed and the tinny voice echoed off the mountains and across the lake. They must be having a break from filming, if the loudspeakers were back on. I ran down the hill, tripped on a patch of gravel, and barely saved my knees and my stockings, not to mention my dignity, by a bit of fast footwork that would do my mother herself proud.

I CHEWED ON THE END OF MY PENCIL. IT WAS AFTER FIVE o'clock, and the business office had closed for the day. I was trying to plow my way through the endless stack of paper on my desk, but I was finding it extremely hard to concentrate. After the switchboard operator put two calls through to me from newspaper reporters, I told her to screen my calls and tell anyone from the press I wasn't available. Those calls reminded me of what had happened, and my thoughts kept returning to that desperate drive to the hospital. I went over yesterday evening, again and again, trying to place the movements and actions of the movie people.

Who, I thought, would have not only wanted Elias dead but had the wherewithal to bring a pill or a vial of some sort of poison with them to a formal dinner, and then grab the opportunity to use it when it presented itself.

My head snapped up.

Had someone wanted Elias dead?

Was it possible they'd misjudged the dose? Had Elias suffered from underlying health conditions that made a small amount of . . . whatever it was . . . deadlier than it might otherwise have been?

If so, that could change the picture considerably.

Earlier, I'd decided that no one who'd been at the dinner last night would have had a reason to kill Elias. Every one of them was invested in seeing the movie finished.

The bosses in California had decided to continue filming without Elias, but that wouldn't have been a guarantee. I don't know much about movies, but I know a great deal about business. There comes a point when you have to know when to cut your losses. It's possible the movie studio would have decided either to drop the movie, despite the money they'd already spent, or to bring everyone back to Hollywood to complete the filming on a soundstage.

Even Matthew hadn't known what the final decision would be.

Had the killer's intent not been to kill the temperamental director, but to make him sick? Put him in the hospital for a while? Long enough for filming to continue without Elias?

Long enough for Gary Denham, the assistant director, to take the reins and show what he could do? Long enough for Matthew to get some control over Elias's spending?

Had it been a practical joke taken to extremes? An actor or crew member angry at one insult too many, worried about being taken off the project, or wanting to get back at the boss for some slight?

If that was the case, then the possibilities were endless. Anyone at that dinner could have been responsible.

Excepting me, Velvet, Randy, and Olivia of course.

I groaned. I'd hoped with a few casual questions, and some hard thinking, I'd be able to determine who'd done it. I'd then take my case to Dave Dawson, and he'd make the arrest.

And life at Haggerman's Catskills Resort would get back to what passes as normal.

Once again, my phone rang. It was the front desk.

"Sorry to bother you, Mrs. Grady, but Mr. and Mrs. Smith from room 219 say their toilet isn't flushing."

"What?"

"Their toilet isn't—"

"I heard you. Why on earth are you bothering me with this? Don't we have a maintenance department? Don't I have plumbers on my payroll? Can't George fix everything God ever made, and a heck of a lot he didn't? Isn't—"

"Sorry, Mrs. Grady. Sorry. I . . . I . . . One minute, please, I'll get it sorted out immediately." Her voice shook and she whispered into the phone. "They're standing right here, watching me. I tried calling the maintenance building, but no one's answering."

I debated who to fire first. The receptionist or the maintenance workers. Instead, I threw down my pencil. "I'll come out and mollify the Smiths. Send a bellhop to the maintenance shed and get someone."

"The bellhops are all busy."

"Then do it yourself!"

"I . . . I . . . Yes, Mrs. Grady." She sniffled.

"Page maintenance and ask them to call you. Then tell them what you need. Can you do that?"

"Yes, Mrs. Grady."

"Tell the Smiths I'll be right there."

Grumbling about wasting my time, I marched through the empty business office, past the silent phones, the dim lights, the covered typewriters, and into the corridor. From the depths of the kitchen came the sound of someone yelling at someone. I employ good department managers, and I pay them well. Better than the previous owners did, because as far as I'm concerned, the main job of department managers is to handle problems in their department before they get to me.

I plastered on my biggest smile, opened the door to the lobby, and stepped out. A man and a woman in their sixties stood in front of the reception desk, scowls on pudgy faces and arms crossed over more-than-adequate chests. The young woman behind the desk blew her nose and wiped away tears.

The man snapped at me as I approached. "Are you the so-called manager?"

"Yes, I am. I'm Elizabeth Grady. I—"

"Isn't there a man in charge?"

My smile faded fractionally. "A man? No, there's me."

"Isn't that nice, dear," Mrs. Smith said. "So modern. A girl boss."

"I don't want a girl boss," he said. "I want a man who can fix my problem. And I want him now."

Considering I had no intention, even if I had been a man, of picking up a plunger and personally seeing to his toilet, I said. "About your problem. I'll have someone fix that immediately."

Mrs. Smith smiled at me. Mr. Smith looked dubious.

"Are you planning to attend tonight's entertainment in the ballroom?" I asked. "If so, I'll mention to the bartenders that your first drinks will be on my account."

Mr. Smith appeared to accept that I did have the authority to make that order, and some of the hostility faded from his face. All he wanted was a freebie, in any event. The receptionist put down the phone and told them a plumber was on his way to their room.

"Don't let the guests intimidate you," I said to her once the Smiths had gone away happy. She was a pretty girl, young enough to be in her first year with us. "Problems happen and we're equipped to handle them when they do. Some guests will try to get something out of it, and some of them think bullying will help."

She sniffed and dared to crack a small smile. "It worked."

I laughed. "So it did. All you can do is be pleasant in return." Then I took a more serious tone. "Never, ever, let them make you cry. Walk away if you have to, after excusing yourself, take a few breaths and then come back."

"I'll remember that. Thank you, Mrs. Grady."

I didn't say, *One more incident like that and you'll be moved to the housekeeping department.* But I thought it.

A man leaned across me and barked at the clerk. "Where can I find a telephone?"

"There's a telephone for the use of guests in the writing room, sir. Give the switchboard operator the number you want and she'll place your call. The charge will be put on your bill." She gave him directions, and he marched off without bothering to thank her.

Telephone calls. The switchboard.

I crossed the lobby at a rapid pace and slipped into the small, dark, enclosed room across the hall from the main business office. As usual the telephone room was full of wires and smoke.

"Connecting you now. Go ahead, sir." The operator plugged in the connection and breathed out cigarette smoke. The ashtray next to her was overflowing with ash and butts, and her coffee cup was full. She was an older woman, thin on top but heavy-bottomed and thick-legged, with a deeply lined face, hair dyed a solid dark black, and eyes that had seen (or heard) it all. She'd been working this switchboard for many long years. "Hi. Can I help you?"

A light on her panel lit up, and she said, "Haggerman's Catskills Resort."

Her hands flew, smoke blew, she drank coffee, and she said, "One moment, please. What's up, Mrs. G.?"

For a moment I didn't realize she was talking to me. "Oh. Were you working on Sunday?"

"Yup."

"Do you remember getting a call from Los Angeles for Mr. Theropodous?"

"I get a lot of calls, but not often from Hollywood for a big-time director, so I remember that one, yeah. Good afternoon, Haggerman's Catskills Resort. One moment, please. I put the call through to the writing room. I'm sorry, sir, no one's answering. Can I take a message?" She scribbled on a pink message pad. Somehow she was able to smoke, drink her coffee, write down the message, answer another call, and converse with me all at the same time. "Connecting you now. What about it?"

"Are you talking to me? I was wondering if by any chance you . . . accidentally, of course, overheard any of the contents of that call."

She grinned and swung in her chair to face me. "Are you asking if I listened in on a guest's private conversation?"

"Just this once."

"That's the guy who died after dinner yesterday, right? I heard about that. Yeah, maybe I didn't disconnect my line fast enough when he took his call. I heard a heck of a lot of yelling, coming from both directions. The caller was a man. New York City accent, for all he was phoning from California. He told Mr. Theropodous something was unacceptable. Mr. Theropodous replied that he did things his way and he wanted no interference. The caller said he was going to get interference whether he wanted it or not. Good afternoon, Haggerman's Catskills Resort. Hey, Johnny, how's the family? Glad to hear it, I'm putting you through now. A bunch more yelling, and the caller told him he could be replaced and Mr. Theropodous said, 'That'll happen over my dead body,' then—"

She stopped talking. Her fingers stopped moving, the cigarette froze halfway to her mouth, lights flashed on the panel, and she didn't answer them. "Oh my gosh, Mrs. Grady. You don't think—"

"You're sure the incoming call was from Los Angeles?"

"Positive. So the guy on the other end of the phone couldn't have killed him, right?"

"Right. Are you going to answer that?"

"Answer what? Oh. Good morning. I mean good afternoon, Haggerman's Catskills Resort. They might have sent someone though, right?"

"Anything's possible. Did you hear any more?"

"Nah. Calls were coming in." She pulled at plugs. "I don't make a habit of listening to guests' calls. You know that, right? I mean, just this once 'cause it was a Hollywood big shot on the line."

I nodded, even though I didn't believe her. "I'm going to tell the police about this. They might want to talk to you. If so, tell them what you told me."

"Okay. Good afternoon. Haggerman's Catskills Resort. Mr. Reynolds no longer works here."

I slipped out of the telephone room.

Had the Hollywood people decided to take Elias at his word and terminate him? Permanently? The person who called might have been in California, but was it possible they had people in New York they could send on such an errand? If they wanted to?

Did Hollywood movie moguls bump off errant directors?

I didn't know how things worked in Hollywood, but I knew someone who did. I went to my office for my purse, and then I headed home. I'd check in with Olivia and get dressed for this evening's cocktail hour. I don't usually attend the hotel social events, and I was not in the mood to make polite conversation tonight, but if rumors were circulating about Haggerman's being unsafe, I needed to present my smiling face and assure everyone that all was well.

FILMING AT CABIN ONE HAD FINISHED FOR THE DAY, AND the crew were rolling up their equipment and loading it into the truck while Gary issued instructions.

"How'd it go?" I asked him.

"Good. Great, truth be told." He beamed at me. "I probably shouldn't say this, but everyone seemed a heck of a lot more relaxed than when Elias was around. He put the fear of God into his cast and crew. Sometimes that can be a good thing, but not when it makes them overly nervous about making a misstep. Me, I prefer to put my trust in my actors. They know their characters better than I do. Of course," he added quickly, "in the bigger scheme of things,

Elias'll be sorely missed. His name'll still be at the top of the credits. The inspiration and vision behind this picture was strictly his. Anyway, we're done here, Mrs. Grady, and I thank you for your hospitality."

"Done? I thought you were filming here tomorrow."

"As I said, everything went well. I have to go over the last couple of day's footage, and if I see any problems we'll be back. Otherwise tomorrow and the next day we're at some bungalow colony down the road. Thanks again."

"I'm looking forward to seeing the final product," I said.

"I think you'll like it. Your place looks great on film, and we got some good background shots of the hotel and the grounds."

Feeling pleased, I set off down the lakeside path, heading for home. My evening dresses, other than the one I'd worn last night and sent to the laundry this morning, were in my closet at the house, and I hoped Gloria wasn't napping in my room.

Instead, I spotted her relaxing next to the pool, the picture of movie star glamour in a flower-patterned bathing suit, huge sunglasses, and an even bigger sun hat. A bright pink cocktail was in her right hand and *Photoplay* magazine was on the table next to her. Mary-Alice, looking not at all Hollywood glamour in her dark blue skirt, thick stockings, flat shoes, and plain spectacles, balanced awkwardly on the edge of a lounge chair next to her.

"An encounter with the woman would have a dramatic impact that's otherwise missing," Gloria was saying as I walked up to them. "Elias refused to understand that women— Elizabeth, darling, how nice to see you. Why don't you sit down and have a drink? Or better yet, run and get your suit on. You work far too hard, your mother says."

"Thank you, but no. I'm glad you're having a chance to relax. Gary told me today went well."

"It did."

I studied Gloria's face. Even without makeup and despite her age, her skin was almost flawless. The delicate lines at the corners of her eyes and mouth gave the porcelain complexion an air of vulnerability that only added to her stunning looks. Her cheekbones were high and sharp, her eyes enormous blue pools under the thin line of sculpted brows, and her jawline as sharp as if it had been cut with a knife. If she'd had work done, it had been by a skilled surgeon.

What I didn't see in her face was any sort of sorrow. I glanced at Mary-Alice, sitting primly on the lounge chair, her ankles crossed, her hands folded in her lap. No grief there either.

As if she read my mind, Gloria said, "Your mother suggested we go to the cocktail hour this evening, but I think not. The hotel doesn't need to pretend to be mourning Elias—he wasn't staying here, after all—but I can't be seen enjoying myself too much." She peered at me over the top of her sunglasses. "I've shocked you, haven't I?"

"No," I said. *Shocked* might not be the right word, but I would have expected Gloria to show some grief. She and Elias had been married at one time, after all.

"No one here's mourning the man, Elizabeth. We all, even me, worked for or with him. We didn't love him. I don't suppose many people loved him. If any. You didn't, did you Mary-Alice?"

Mary-Alice started. "Me? I . . . of course I am. Mourning him, I mean. He was a . . . brilliant director. A genius. All of Hollywood should be in mourning."

"He was a brilliant director . . . once. But his time had passed, and you of all people know that, Mary-Alice, so please don't pretend you don't."

The lifeguard's whistle blew, and Randy stood up from his high chair to shout at two children running on the side of the pool. The kids slowed down and walked very fast. A mother called to her children to get out of the pool, and they pretended not to hear. The sun was dipping in the west, and although it would be daylight for a long time yet, all around us families were packing up their books, towels, sun hats, drinks, snacks, and toys. Time to go to their rooms and rest or to get ready for the evening.

"The show must go on," Gloria said. "I'm glad Matthew decided to continue with the filming. We've done such good work so far."

"Matthew decided?" I said. "I thought the producers in Los Angeles made the final decision."

Gloria laughed lightly. "They might think they decided, but there was never any doubt they'd do whatever Matthew told them."

"The police seem to think that . . . uh . . . Elias might have been poisoned deliberately."

"I'm aware of that. The young policeman spoke to us earlier, and he had a great many questions as to who handled Elias's food and drink yesterday."

Mary-Alice shifted uncomfortably.

"Can either of you think of who might have wanted to kill him?" I asked.

"Easier to think of who didn't want to see him dead, isn't that right, Mary-Alice?"

Mary-Alice was already sitting stiffly on her chair, but her back and neck straightened even more. "I don't know what you're implying, Gloria."

"I'm implying nothing. I'm simply stating what we all know. A man like Elias doesn't inspire loyalty. People work for Elias because being associated with him does their professional reputation good. When that is no longer the case . . . then it's time to terminate the relationship. One way or the other." Those amazing blue eyes stared into mine. "Not that I'm suggesting anyone in our little film family had anything to do with his death. But Elias did tell me, in the strictest of confidence of course, that he was not happy with Todd's performance."

"That's not true," Mary-Alice said. "Todd—"

"Perhaps he didn't confide in you about that, dear," Gloria said sharply. "Elias told me he needed me to draw more from Todd. As if it's my responsibility to make spoiled pretty boys look better than they are." She settled her sunglasses back on her face and picked up her magazine. "It's starting to get a mite chilly now that we're in the shade. I think I'll go up to the house."

"I'm going to grab a dress out of my closet, and I'll leave you alone," I said.

As I walked away, I heard Gloria say to Mary-Alice, "You will consider my idea, dear." It was not a question.

I ran into Todd and Velvet coming my way. They were walking close together, and although they were not touching, her cheeks were a bright pink, and he was grinning broadly. They looked so perfect together they might have been in an advertisement for soap or toothpaste. Both of them young, tall, slim, attractive, lightly tanned. Todd was still in the white blazer that was his costume for the cabin scene, and Velvet wore her short white tennis dress and swung a racket in her hand.

Velvet's face turned even pinker when she saw me. "Todd's been watching me give my tennis class. He suggested we have a game tomorrow."

"Not that I'm up to the level of a professional like Velvet," he said.

Her blush deepened and she giggled. "Hardly a professional. I give instruction to people who've never seen a racket before, much less played the game."

"Still sounds like a professional to me." Todd winked at me.

I glanced at my friend, all blushes and giggles. *This*, I thought with a sinking heart, *is not going to end well*.

"I'd like to come back tonight," Todd said, "to catch the show, maybe have a couple of dances with Velvet. And you, of course, Elizabeth. But Matthew's put his foot down. To look like we're going out and having a good time so soon after Elias's death would not be good for our image. He canceled the Concord outing tonight and ordered us all to stay at our hotel."

"There are worse places to be confined to barracks than Kennelwood," I said.

"You can say that again. I invited Velvet to have dinner with me, but she says she has to work. You're the boss, Elizabeth, give her the night off, why don't you?"

Velvet swatted at him with her racket. "Oh, you."

Todd and Velvet were facing toward the lake, their backs to the hotel buildings and the pool; behind them I could see Mary-Alice and Gloria leaving the pool area. Gloria had pulled a floor-length blue-and-white-striped wrap over her bathing suit and slipped her feet into high-heeled sandals. The sun was behind her, and her hat and sunglasses shielded most of her face, but I could see the tightness of her mouth and the angry set of her shoulders. Mary-Alice said something to her, and Todd turned at the sound of her voice.

Gloria's face changed as though a spotlight had come on, and she gave the actor a beaming smile. "There you are, you darling boy. Mary-Alice and I were talking about you. I've had some ideas as to how to improve on our farewell scene, and Mary-Alice wants to talk it over with you. Why don't the two of you share a cab back to the hotel? You know Matthew's on the warpath about expenses, so no need to get two cabs when one will do, now is there?" She slipped her arm through Velvet's. "Have you been playing tennis, dear? I used to be quite the player in my day, but I haven't been on a court for simply years."

"I'm the tennis instructor here," Velvet said. "If you'd like a game, I can sign you up for one."

"If only I had time. If only I had time. What are you standing around for, Mary-Alice? Aren't you planning to speak to Gary about what we discussed?"

Todd bowed slightly. "I know when I'm dismissed. Ladies. I'll see you tomorrow." He started to walk away with Mary-Alice.

Out of the corner of my eye I noticed a bathing-suit-clad Lacy, sister of the girl who'd been taken to the hospital earlier, peeking out from behind a bush with eyes as round and wide as a beach ball.

"Todd!" I called. "One minute, please."

He turned back to me, and I said, "Here's someone I'd like you to meet." I gestured to Lacy. She blinked at me, and I waved her forward. She stepped out from behind her tree. Her mouth opened. It closed again.

"Hi," Todd said.

"This is Lacy," I said. "She's a big fan of yours, Todd."

"That's nice to hear," he said, huge toothy smile in place. "I hope you're having a good vacation, Lacy."

"It's—it's. . . . the best vacation ever!"

"This is a nice place, all right," he said. "I'm heading back to the hotel now. Would you like to walk with us, Lacy?"

She gasped and tripped over her own feet in the rush to fall into step beside him.

I turned back to Velvet with a smile, but my smile died. I didn't care for the way she was watching them go. Velvet had been my best friend since we were very young. I loved her dearly. I wanted her to be happy, and I genuinely wanted her to fall head over heels in love, if that was what would make her happy.

But I didn't trust Todd Thompson. I didn't trust his all-American good looks, his ah-shucks charm. More than that, I worried that Velvet was falling in love as much with the idea of Hollywood than with Todd himself. And Hollywood was nothing but a fantasy. Still, she was an adult woman, and she'd make her mistakes without my interference.

As I had made my own. Maybe I was concerned over nothing. My marriage had been such a disastrous mistake,

I had to consider that I was overly worried about Velvet doing the same.

I gave my head a shake and noticed Randy watching us—watching Velvet rather—from high in his lifeguard chair. His face, I thought, mirrored my own.

"I'm going to the cocktail party tonight," I said to my friend. "I need to present the calm face of the hotel to anyone who might be worried about sampling the canapés. You planning anything until the dancing starts?"

Todd, Mary-Alice, and Lacy disappeared around a bend in the path, and Velvet remembered my existence. "Anything planned? No. I'm way behind on writing to my grandmother, and I'd better get a letter off to her before she sends the police to see if I've been kidnapped."

We walked along the lakefront path together. Paddleboats were coming in, and rowboats heading out for an evening fishing. From one of the cabins a woman called to her children that it was bath time, and in another someone was playing a radio far too loudly. A screen door slammed, and a girl screamed in mock terror.

I hoped it was mock. But then another girl laughed, and the first one joined in.

We reached the bend in the public footpath, where it divides in two. One direction heads away from the lake, going uphill and skirting the woods toward the last of the guest cabins and beyond that to my house and the staff quarters. Continuing straight, the path passes a sign marked STAFF ONLY, through a line of trees and across a small, fast-moving rocky creek, to the service dock, boathouses, and equipment sheds.

Something rustled in the undergrowth, and Winston burst through the trees, stubby tail wagging, ears standing up, a cluster of dead leaves and twigs caught in the fur under his belly.

"Silly dog." Velvet bent over and plucked the foliage off

him. "Always into something. Do you think I could be an actress?" She spoke quickly and didn't look at me.

I hesitated and chose my words carefully. "I think you can be whatever you want to be, Velvet. Except maybe a professional football player, although even that wouldn't surprise me if you put your mind to it. Are you, uh, thinking about it?"

"I wanted to dance. You know that. But it didn't work out. I . . ." She plucked the last twig off Winston, gave him a slap on his rear end, and straightened up. "Todd says I have the looks the camera loves."

"Has Todd asked you to come to Hollywood? With him, I mean?"

"No, and he'll only be here for a few more days. He . . . I think he likes me, Elizabeth. I like him."

"What does your heart say?"

"My heart reminds me that California's a long way away. That my parents and my grandmother are in New York. That you're here, Elizabeth. You need me."

Did I need Velvet? The hotel didn't need her. We could always get another outdoor activities director. Did I need her?

Absolutely.

"Promise me you won't rush into anything," I said. "Sometimes, when we act too hastily, we can make mistakes. Serious mistakes. Mistakes that cannot be undone."

She heard something in my voice and studied my face. "Are you trying to tell me something, Elizabeth?"

I'd never told Velvet how unhappy I'd been in my short marriage, what a disaster it had been to fall in love with Ron Grady and get talked into a quick wedding. Perhaps I should. Perhaps my experience could be a warning to her about rushing into things. I took a deep breath, but the words died in my throat. "No. Just saying think it over carefully, and you'll do the right thing."

Chapter 13

I CREPT THROUGH THE DARK, EMPTY BUSINESS OFFICE into my own small office, switched on the overhead light, and shut the door. I peeked out the back window to ensure no one was lurking about, and then I called the switchboard and asked her to place a call for me. "This is private," I said. "Do not listen in." It was time, I'd decided, to find out what I could about the Hollywood people. One Hollywood person in particular.

"Mrs. G.," the operator sniffed, "I'm insulted you need to say that."

"Nevertheless, I'm saying it."

Plugs were attached, buttons pressed, the line hummed and cracked, and then a voice said, "*New York Times.*"

"I'd like to leave a message for one of your reporters, please. Mr. Jim Westenham."

"Go ahead."

"Can you ask him to contact Elizabeth Grady at Haggerman's. He should have my number, but in case he doesn't . . ." I rattled it off.

She repeated it, assured me the message would be passed on, and we hung up.

🍸

I WENT TO THE COCKTAIL PARTY.

It had been less than twenty-four hours since Elias's death, but most of the talk had died down, and I was pleased to see it. The death of a major Hollywood director was mighty big news, but nothing could compete with the news that Douglas Reightenham III, now Dr. Doug Reightenham, had invited the McPhersons' youngest daughter, the one everyone said was pretty enough but would never get a husband with her attitude, for a turn around the lake in a paddleboat, whereupon he'd produced a ring with a giant diamond and asked for the honor of her hand, and the girl, rather than being suitably grateful, had leapt overboard—despite being fully dressed—and swum to shore. She'd shortly thereafter been seen surrounded by her suitcases, hailing a taxi to take her to the train station while her parents had alternately wept and railed at her and her elder sisters looked mighty pleased.

Judy Rae, the singer, was ordering herself a sidecar at the bar.

"That looks nice," I said. "I'll have one of those too."

When I had my drink in hand I joined Judy in a quiet corner. "I didn't get a chance to tell you how much I enjoyed your show last night."

She put her drink on a side table, took a cigarette out of her small evening bag, and lit it with a silver lighter. "Thank you. I heard Elias died not long after." She picked up her glass and blew out a long plume of smoke. "That was very sudden."

She didn't sound particularly broken up about it. I must have looked surprised because she grinned at me. "What, you expected me to say how sad I am?" She lifted her glass. "To Elias Theropodous. Too bad he didn't shuffle off his mortal coil years ago."

My drink went down the wrong way. When I finished coughing, Judy said, "We had a history, Elias and I, and it wasn't a good one. Not for me anyway, although I suspect he never gave me another thought. I'm not going to pretend I care one way or another if he lived or died. Although I'd prefer you don't mention that. I'm aware the police have been poking around here today."

"Did Chief Dawson speak to you?"

"No. Being the entertainment at a place like this is existing in a netherworld. I'm neither a guest nor an employee. Meaning neither and thus both, so I get all sides of everything. The staff are saying the police are concentrating their attention on the movie cast and crew. The guests are saying it was a mob hit. They seem to think Hollywood's made up of nothing but the mob." As she spoke, Judy's hands moved constantly, lifting her cigarette to her scarlet lips, or taking a sip of her drink. Was she nervous? Hard to tell, as I'd never spoken to her before other than to welcome her when she arrived. "If not the mob, then communists. One thing I can say for Elias, he was most definitely not a communist."

I didn't like the sound of that. We'd had a red scare at Haggerman's recently, and guests had threatened to check out. I didn't need anyone bringing those rumors up again.

"What happened?" I asked. "Between you and Elias, I mean?"

She turned her head to one side to blow smoke away from me, but she kept her dark eyes fixed on mine. "I was young. I was talented. I was ambitious." She struck a pose. Her deeply cut, formfitting dress showed off her wide hips and large bosom. "I was also substantially thinner than I am today. What I had, and still do, which you can't say for a lot of them, was some degree of self-respect. My acting

career ended before it had barely begun when I was fired
from the first movie I'd been cast in. It was a mid-budget
musical and Elias was the director. He fired me because I
wouldn't sleep with him." She sipped her drink. "His loss.
The movie didn't exactly bomb, but it wasn't the success it
could have been. Hollywood's loss, as I decided I was better off in New York pursuing a singing career. My gain. I
get to sing in nice places like this."

"When was that?" I asked.

"So long ago, I hardly remember. Fifteen years maybe.
I won't say it didn't sting at the time. I genuinely thought all
a woman needed in Hollywood was talent. That and looks
maybe. I was wrong, and I was angry. But I got over it."

Had she? She'd been friendly enough to Elias last night,
but she was—they all were—show business people. Running a big hotel is a lot like being in show business. I also
have to keep up a cheerful appearance at all times. Nothing
is ever wrong. The guests are never wrong. Nothing breaks
that can't be fixed instantly, and that includes peoples'
feelings.

Judy, I remembered, had stopped at Elias's table to chat
between her sets. Meaning, she'd been near his drinks. It
was no secret the movie people were coming to the show.
She would have been able to be prepared.

"Miss Rae, I'm such a big fan. Would you be so kind as
to sign my napkin? I can't wait to tell all the ladies at bridge
that you sang for us." A guest, thinning gray hair sprayed
into a stiff helmet, diamonds around her throat and on her
fingers, fringed dress twenty years out of date, thrust a hotel napkin and a pen toward the singer.

"It would be my pleasure," Judy said. "What's your
name, honey?"

I left them to it and went to check out the buffet table.
The wolves had descended the minute the offerings were
brought out, but a few scraps remained. I scooped up a
couple of celery sticks filled with bright orange Cheez

Whiz. I was licking the gooey cheese off my fingers and wondering when, and if, I'd have a chance to get a proper dinner, when Jim Westenham came into the room.

He looked around, spotted me above the heads of the people between us, and came my way. "Good evening, Elizabeth. May I say you look quite lovely tonight?"

I was in my second-best evening attire, a sleeveless black dress with a full skirt, thin belt, and V-neckline. I smiled at him. "Thank you. What brings you here?"

"You do."

"Me?"

"You left a message at the paper?"

"That was quick. I didn't expect you to get back to me until tomorrow."

"You called moments before I checked in for the night. I knew you'd be busy, so I decided to come over rather than trying to track you down to come to the phone. You'll be pleased to hear I was stopped at the gate and asked my business. They're keeping reporters out, but I dropped your name liberally so the guard let me through. Helped that he remembered seeing me last time I was here. What's up? Do you have news on Elias?"

"No. It's about something else. Can I buy you a drink?"

"Never say no to that."

We went to the bar, and Jim ordered a scotch on the rocks. When he had his drink in hand we left the crowded, noisy room to talk in private. I leaned my back against the railing at the top of the grand staircase. Laugher and conversation swirled around us.

"First," he said, "I'll fill you in on the press conference if you haven't heard."

"I haven't. Dare I hope Dave announced he's arrested the killer and it had nothing to do with Haggerman's?"

"Nope. Sorry. It wasn't particularly newsworthy. Not much we didn't know. Some of the gentlemen and a lady of the press tried to get him speculating, but he stuck to the facts as he knows them. Suspected poisoning. No other reports of illness at the time concerned. Unlikely to have been deliberately consumed on the part of the deceased. Therefore . . ."

"Therefore?"

"What Dave called suspicious circumstances and the papers are calling murder. What I'm calling murder, Elizabeth. I filed my story, and that's what I reported."

"Fair enough," I said.

"I can tell you something that wasn't part of the press conference. Dave Dawson spent most of the day, along with hunting down suspects in the murder, trying to find out where the staties were."

"The state police? You mean they didn't arrive? Where were they?"

"No one knows. They say two detectives were dispatched, but they never showed up. Dave thinks they might have gone to the wrong town."

"Has the autopsy been done?"

"Not yet. It's scheduled for tomorrow. It'll be a few days after that before Dave gets the analysis of the contents of the man's stomach."

My Cheez Whiz rolled over.

"The gentlemen and ladies of the press are still hanging around, hoping for further developments. There was a kerfuffle at Kennelwood this afternoon when Richard had to almost physically haul his father away to stop him from giving an ill-advised statement."

My face twisted. "Jerome didn't try to blame Haggerman's, did he?"

"He was heading that way, but Richard intervened in time. Or so I've been told. I wasn't there. As the representative of the *New York Times*, I'm not after the gossip. Just the facts."

I refrained from offering my opinion on that. I turned and leaned over the railing, looking at the lobby below us.

Bellhops carried suitcases to the elevators as a handful of guests checked in. Other guests were gathering for a drink with friends before going in for dinner, the men in suits and ties, ladies in evening dresses. One of the outdoor-activities staff, flashlight in hand, whistle around neck, waited by the doors with a clipboard as children gathered around her for the guided nature walk in the evening woods.

"Other than that," Jim said, "I've nothing to report. If Dave has any leads he hasn't told me about them. Why did you call me?"

"Do you have contacts in Hollywood?"

"One or two. Why do you ask?"

"I feel almost embarrassed asking this, but . . . I mean, it's none of my business, but . . . that is, I . . ."

"You want to find out more about Todd Thompson."

I turned. "How did you know that?"

"I'm a newspaperman. It's my job to figure out what people aren't saying. Todd Thompson has focused his substantial charm on Velvet. You don't trust him."

"How do you know that?"

"Because I know you, Elizabeth. You don't take anyone or anything on face value. Velvet's your friend, and you're concerned about her. Fair enough. I've done some reading on this bunch as part of putting together a story. Todd's a rising star. Big things ahead of him, they say. As part of being a rising star, he gets his picture in the gossip magazines with one pretty starlet on his arm after another. His name's never been linked with any one of them in particular. I can ask around. Find out if all that's true. It often isn't. The big studios own their actors, and that means they own the actor's image. Todd plays roles as the all-American hero and general good guy. His image has to be kept squeaky clean. I won't make any promises, but I'll see what I can find out."

"Thank you," I said. "I do appreciate it."

"Can I take you to dinner?"

"Thank you," I said again. "But as I told you, I never eat

in the dining room. I'm only here now in case any of the guests are feeling nervous about what happened last night, and my smiling face will reassure them all is well." I bared my teeth and stretched my lips into a huge smile.

Jim laughed. "I feel so reassured."

"I'll come back later for the entertainment and do the same, so I need to have my dinner in some degree of peace and quiet. I . . . I hope you understand."

"I understand perfectly, Elizabeth." He checked his watch. "It's still early on the West Coast. Early enough to make some calls." He swallowed the last of his drink and gave me a salute with the empty glass. "Thanks for this."

"You're welcome."

I watched him walk down the stairs. He nodded politely to people as they passed and stepped aside to let two elderly ladies by. I hoped he did understand. Jim was nice, and I liked him. But *like* was as far as it went. His invitation to dinner had been casual, seemingly offhanded, but I thought he meant more to it than the words implied, and so I declined. As I said, I never eat in the dining room—too many people want to stop by my table and complain—but I could have invited him to my house or Velvet's room and ordered something for us.

I don't know why Jim Westenham inviting me to dinner put me in mind of Richard Kennelwood, but it did.

I grinned to myself. Maybe I was becoming a Catskills girl already. Catskills people—Mountain Rats, they like to call themselves—are an insular bunch.

A Catskills girl.

A Mountain Rat.

Gloria had told us Elias Theropodous had grown up in the Catskills. I'd forgotten that. We assumed he'd been killed because of something to do with his Hollywood world, but maybe that wasn't it at all. Could it be possible a hometown secret had caught up with him all these years later?

Chapter 14

"SHE HAD ME AT EGG CREAM," VELVET SAID.

"Same for me," I said. "And a grilled cheese sandwich to go with it, please."

"Make that three egg creams," Lucinda McGreevy told the waitress.

It was ten o'clock in the morning on Wednesday. I'd left a stack of unanswered pink message slips on my desk, an accounts book that refused to balance, a pile of unopened envelopes, and come into town for a late breakfast. Knowing Velvet had a gap in today's schedule between eight o'clock calisthenics for teenage girls on the dock and a round of the ever-popular Simon Says to lead at noon on the beach, I'd invited her to come with me.

I'd said no more than "for an egg cream at the diner," and she was sprinting in the direction of my car.

The Red Spot Diner, located in the center of Summervale's main street, is famous for its version of the frothy soda drink. "Best in the Catskills," they claimed, and I agreed.

"As seems to be becoming a habit," Lucinda said once we'd placed our orders, "Haggerman's is the talk of the town."

"Talk we don't need," I said. "I hate to say it, but that's why we're here."

"I figured as much," Lucinda said. "That's okay, Elizabeth. You're busy. I'm busy. We're all too busy in the summer to simply spend time being friends."

As if to prove her point, Lucinda's mother walked past our booth and gave her daughter a disapproving glare.

"It's okay, Mom. I'm having a quick break before the next rush." Lucinda smoothed her skirt. Her dark hair was tied back, and she wore the diner's waitress uniform of a red dress under a white apron liberally sprinkled with giant red polka dots.

"You can have a break," Mrs. McGreevy said, her accent tinged with memories of the back alleys of Naples, where she'd spent her early childhood, "in October."

"If I live that long," Lucinda said.

I laughed, and Mrs. McGreevy turned her Italian-mother scowl on me. I ducked my head. We'd been seated directly beneath a slowly turning fan mounted on a high shelf, and the moving air felt delicious on my overheated neck and arms. The temperatures were supposed to be in the low nineties for the next couple of days, and the humidity would rise along with it.

The waitress put three egg creams on the table and slid a plate of grilled cheese and french fries in front of me.

I'd timed our visit carefully, hoping my friend could take a moment to catch her breath (and enjoy an egg cream) between the breakfast rush and the busy lunch hour.

Lucinda's family's restaurant is the most popular casual place in Summervale. It's centrally located, making it popular with townspeople on their lunch break as well as tourists and summer visitors looking for a quick, plain but delicious, reasonably priced meal.

Meaning, it was gossip central. Lucinda, who'd grown up helping out in the diner, knew just about every one of the longtime residents and many of the newer ones, like me. We'd met over the winter and became instant friends. As she said, it's hard to find time for socializing over a Catskills summer. Everyone has just a few short weeks to make most of what money they'll need to get by the remainder of the year.

I took that first marvelous sip of egg cream, feeling the sparkling soda water and thick chocolate syrup dancing on my tongue. Velvet, who'd said she didn't want anything to eat, plucked a french fry off my plate.

"People have been talking about Elias Theropodous's death?" I asked Lucinda when I could speak again.

"There's been a lot of talk, yes. Word's getting around that he died not long after eating at Haggerman's, but I think you're in the clear. It's obvious no one else got sick at the same time. I heard something about some teenage girl being taken away in an ambulance, but the consensus seems to be that she got into her parents' private liquor supply."

"Things happen at a busy hotel," I said.

"And in a busy diner," Lucinda said. "Even before the man died, everyone in town was in a tizz about having the movie people here. Rebecca Marsden went shopping in the dress store, and there's now a picture of her hanging in their window. Todd Thompson and a couple of guys dropped into Mike's bar one night, and I don't think the bar girls have washed their hands since. I've heard people who aren't guests are being thrown out of Kennelwood for trying to find the actors' rooms and that you've got a guard at the road turning away newspaper people."

"Have you heard anything from the police?" I squirted a mountain of ketchup onto my plate next to the fries.

"Dave came in for breakfast this morning soon as we opened. He looked like he hadn't slept. One of the patrol officers was with him, and they were talking, heads down, whispering. I might have overheard a word or two when I brought them their scrambled eggs and hash browns. And coffee, lots and lots of coffee. Seems Dave got a call from the mayor last night, suggesting it wouldn't look good for the reputation of the town if anyone associated with the movie is found to have killed the man. It seems the mayor's hoping we'll get more movies being filmed here. His Honor sort of suggested it would be better if the killer was found to be an itinerant drifter."

"An itinerant drifter," Velvet said around her straw, "who moved comfortably around a private dining room and the ballroom of one of Summervale's finest hotels. The mayor hasn't thought that through."

"He tends not to do that," Lucinda said. "The movie shoot's bringing money and publicity to town. That's all he cares about."

"Martin McEnery isn't trying to keep the murder under wraps or downplay it's significance," I said. "What's the mayor's relationship with the owners of the *Gazette*?"

"Good to excellent. But the editor has a dilemma. They're a respectable paper, and they can't be seen playing favorites—or downplaying a murder—to make the town look good. That might be called covering up a crime."

I pondered that for a minute, while I ate my sandwich and finished the egg cream. "I specifically came in to ask you about something other than town gossip around the movie. Did you know Elias was originally from Summervale?"

"Yeah, I did. Local boy makes good. You'd have to be a long-time resident to know about that though. I know because Mom told me about him the other day. He might have grown up in Summervale, but he left as soon as he finished school and never bothered to show his face here again. Not

even to visit his family. On this trip, he's made no attempt
to visit people his family had known or who he'd been
friends with when they were kids. I'm surprised you even
know about it. Did he tell you?"

"Someone told me he was from here. Maybe I'm wondering if the reasons for his death lie in his past."

Lucinda lifted her right arm. "Mom!"

Mrs. McGreevy was taking advantage of the temporary
lull in business to relax on the stool at the cash register and
flip through *Life* magazine. She looked up when her daughter called.

"Mom, can you come and sit with us for a minute?"

The older woman climbed off her stool and crossed the
red-checked floor. "I do not sit at a table in the middle of
the day," Mrs. McGreevy said. "Nor should you, Lucinda.
What will people think? You don't have lunch to prepare?
You don't have dishes to wash?"

"Elizabeth's asking about Elias Theropodous." Lucinda
slid out of the booth and stood up. "You knew him, right?
Sit down and tell us about it. Can you bring Mom a coffee
and maybe a piece of pie," she called to the waitress. "What
would you like, Mom? Lemon meringue or blueberry?"

"I have no time for pie," the older woman said as she
dropped onto the bench seat. "Blueberry. With ice cream."

Lucinda gave me a wink. "I'll get the door if anyone
comes in. You knew the Theropodous family, right, Mom?"

"I haven't thought of Elias in years," Mrs. McGreevy
said. "Until this movie silliness started. Elias was a good
bit older than me, so I didn't know him well, but he was in
school with my brothers. My oldest brother, Carlo, was
friends with him, as I remember."

The waitress put the pie on the table. It was a huge slice,
oozing blue juice, the flaky pastry perfectly browned, accompanied by a scoop of vanilla ice cream.

"Oh," Velvet said.

"Can I get you a piece?" the waitress asked.

"After that egg cream?" Velvet pushed her empty glass across the table. "Why ever not?"

Behind me, the bells over the door tinkled, and Lucinda slipped away.

"Elias said something about him and Jerome Kennelwood knowing each other a long time ago," I said. "That must be what he meant."

"Jerome. Like boy like man. He was never very nice." Mrs. McGreevy lifted a fork laden with pie and ice cream to her mouth. "Elias left the Catskills as soon as he graduated high school. His parents and his brother stayed in Summervale, but he never came back."

"I was told he left when his parents died," I said. "You mean that's not true?"

"No. No one wants it to be known he abandoned his family first chance he got. Over the years, there was talk of Elias, now and again, and people made a point of going to see his movies and being proud of a boy from Summervale doing so well. The pride soon turned to resentment. The Theropodous family were never well-off. Not dirt-poor, but no better than anyone else around these parts. The father worked at the hardware store, as I remember, and Elias's mother cleaned at the hotels. We expected she'd be able to stop cleaning when her son became a big Hollywood director, but that never happened. They didn't seem to have any more money than they ever had. They died, must be twenty or more years ago, before the war anyway, and talk began to die down. Things around here changed—the war came, and then new people moved to the Catskills. People forgot he was a local boy."

She chewed and shook her head. "He didn't come to his mother's funeral. I remember that. People said that wasn't right, even though he sent the biggest bunch of flowers many of us had ever seen. Better he'd bought her a new pair of boots when she was alive, they said. Some of the people, my age, his age, remembered his name when we heard about him making his new movie here." She shrugged and continued to eat. "But we no longer care about local boy doing good. He left and he didn't give us another thought. Even Carlo never heard from Elias again."

Velvet's pie arrived, and she happily dug in. My back was to the restaurant, and across from me Mrs. McGreevy's eyes flicked around the room while she ate and talked. The chimes over the door rang again, and Lucinda's soft voice welcomed the new customers. The early lunch crowd was beginning to arrive.

"That's all I can tell you, Elizabeth." Mrs. McGreevy scraped her plate clean. "I have not seen Elias since I was young, and until this week I have not thought of him or his family for many long years."

"Thanks anyway," I said. I was disappointed, but I'd known it would be a long shot. What sort of a secret would be so bad it would fester for forty years and end in murder?

Mrs. McGreevy started to stand. "I don't think even Nikos has had any contact with Elias, but you could ask him. They might have gotten together this week, for old time's sake or to drink a toast to the memory of their parents."

"Nikos? Who's Nikos?"

"Elias's brother. He works for you."

"He does?" I quickly ran down a mental list of my employees, those whose names I know anyway. Haggerman's employs hundreds of people, and I don't have much contact with most of them. I couldn't think of anyone named Nikos. I threw a question to Velvet, and she shrugged in response.

Lucinda had noticed her mother getting ready to stand up, so she came back to join us and caught the tail end of the conversation. "Does this Nikos go by another name, Mom? Nick, maybe?"

"So many young people want to have an American name these days," Mrs. McGreevy said. "What's wrong with the good family names? All my children have proper Italian names."

"Yes, yes," said Lucinda with the proper Italian name. "I think I know who you're talking about, Mom. Is it Nick Timmins? His name's Nikos, but I don't know if Timmins is his true family name."

"Nick Timmins?" I said. "My saladman?"

"Yes, that's him." Mrs. McGreevy said. "Used to be Nikos Theropodous. Enough talking. Back to work, Lucinda."

"In a minute, Mom."

"My saladman is Elias Theropodous's brother?" I said as Mrs. McGreevy returned to her post.

"Sounds like it," Lucinda said. "Nick was in here on Saturday for breakfast. He was with a man about the same age as him, who I didn't know. What did this Elias guy look like?"

I described the director as best I could, while Velvet ate pie and ice cream and nodded.

"That sounds like him," Lucinda said. "I remember it was Saturday morning because Mom was at the dentist. She broke a tooth the night before and had an emergency appointment, so she missed breakfast shift. It was Saturday and we were so rushed, and the new assistant line cook was off sick, so I was helping in the kitchen. I heard a lot of yelling and came out to see what was going on. Nick Timmins and this other guy were shouting at each other. Like they were really mad, Elizabeth. I was afraid they were about to come to blows, and the cook threw them into the street. They didn't even finish their breakfast. The other guy stormed out. Nick threw some money on the table and then he left too. I didn't hear what they were arguing about, and I didn't see what happened after that. I forgot all about it until now, because I didn't realize it might matter. The guy Nick was fighting with sure sounds like Elias Theropodous."

🍸

"WHERE TO NOW?" VELVET ASKED WHEN WE WERE STANDING on the sidewalk outside the Red Spot Diner.

"I need to talk to Nick Timmins. Interesting that he had a big fight with his long-estranged brother two days before the man died, don't you think?"

"You don't know they were estranged, Elizabeth. Plenty of families don't talk to one another much, if at all, but that doesn't mean they actively disliked each other. Families, siblings in particular, drift apart. Not that you'd know, being an only child, you lucky thing."

"Only one way to find out," I said. "As for what to do now . . . I wonder if Dave Dawson knows about this."

"Only one way to find out," Velvet said.

The diner's conveniently located between the police station and the newspaper office. We walked the ten steps down the sidewalk. The heat was intense, the belt of my dress was too tight, and my girdle and stockings were attempting to cut off circulation. I surreptitiously adjusted the waistband of my girdle to get some air flowing.

"I can see you're wearing stockings under that dress, but please tell me you don't have a girdle on," Velvet said.

"Guilty as charged." I eyed her flowing trousers and loose comfortable blouse enviously.

She chuckled. "Lucky me, who doesn't have to sit in a stuffy office all summer long and look smart and professional."

I growled at her, but her eyes sparkled with laughter, and she continued chatting happily. "I, on the other hand, am required to look outdoorsy and sporty. I'm thinking shorts this afternoon and a light cotton top."

I marched ahead of her into the police station.

An officer sat at the front desk, his chubby index fingers poking hesitantly at a typewriter. The office was small, dark, cramped, and far too hot. A small fan sat on a table in the corner, accomplishing nothing much at all. From the back, I could hear the sound of someone singing an Irish ballad, very poorly indeed.

The cop looked up when we came in. "Mornin'. Help you, ladies?"

"I'm Elizabeth Grady from Haggerman's, and I was hoping to have a word with Deputy— I mean Chief Dawson. Is he in?"

"Nope." He dragged a handkerchief out of his pocket and wiped sweat off his forehead.

"Do you know when he'll be back?"

"Nope."

"Do you know where he's gone?"

He narrowed his eyes. "What's that got to do with you, honey?"

"Nothing," Velvet said. "Other than that we have information pertinent to an important criminal matter, and we believe the chief of police might find it interesting. Even if you, sir, do not."

He gaped at her.

"My friend means that if Chief Dawson isn't far away we can find him and save you the trouble of delivering a message," I said.

"I do not," Velvet said.

"Yes," I said, "you do."

The singing continued coming from the back. I smiled at the officer. Finally he shrugged and said, "Guess I can tell you. Seeing as to how you're from Haggerman's. Chief's gone to Kennelwood to talk to the movie people about that killing you had."

"We didn't have a killing," I said. "Mr. Theropodous died at the hospital."

Another shrug.

"Have the state police detectives arrived?"

"Nope."

"Any word on when they will arrive?"

He wiped more sweat away. "When they find the town, I reckon. Can you type?"

"What?"

"The clerk's off sick, and I need to get this report finished before the chief gets back and . . ."

"Better learn to type, then." Velvet grabbed my arm and dragged me out the door. "Thanks for all your help."

"What got into you?" I asked her when we were back on the sidewalk. "It's never a good idea to offend the local police."

"Can you type indeed? It's after eleven. I need to get to work."

"As do I."

We passed the newspaper office, heading for my car, and I slowed to peek in the front window. June, the receptionist, was Chief Dawson's wife, and I considered going in to ask if he'd said anything to her about the case. Then I saw the other people in the lobby, and I increased my pace.

Too late. They'd spotted me. The door flew open and Jane Donaldson, the female reporter who'd been at Haggerman's yesterday morning, ran out. "Mrs. Grady! A moment of your time."

"Run!" I said to Velvet.

"Okay. I can do that. I need to work off that egg cream and that pie anyway. But it was worth it. Both of them were. Why must we run?"

"Newspaper reporter. Not a friendly one."

Velvet slowed and turned to look.

"You are not running," I pointed out.

"Mrs. Grady." Jane sprinted after us. She was dressed in the same severe brown suit she'd had on yesterday, but today she wore a pink blouse with a floppy bow tied around the neck. Her shoes were thick-soled and practical with a solid low heel. Better for running than the strapless sandals I had on.

"I'm sorry," I called over my shoulder as I kept walking at a brisk pace. "I do not have a statement for the press, and I have an emergency to deal with at the hotel. A plumbing emergency, I mean. Nothing for you to concern yourself about."

"Has anyone else died after eating at your hotel?" she called to us.

A passing man whipped his head around.

"I wouldn't repeat that if I were you," Velvet said.

I grabbed my friend's arm. "Don't get into it with her."

"Repeat what?" the woman said. "It happened, didn't it? I'm only wanting to hear your side."

"I have no side," I said. "It was unfortunate, yes. But Mr. Theropodous's death had nothing to do with my hotel."

"Are you referring to Haggerman's Catskills Resort?" she said in a too-loud voice. "That remains to be seen, doesn't it?"

A woman in a baggy, ill-hemmed housedress dragged her two children across the road to get out of our way. I kept walking.

"Mrs. Grady, I suggest you talk to me. I am going to write this story, with or without your statement. You want to present your side, do you not?"

I whirled around. "I have no side. What happened, happened." Now who was getting into it with her? I took a breath. "I'm sorry, I have to go." I walked away.

I'll say one thing for Jane Donaldson, the Dame of Gossip. She was persistent. Her voice followed us down the street. "My newspaper is widely read in New York City. You get a great deal of your guests coming from the city, do you not? People who read newspapers."

I stopped walking and turned again. "Are you threatening me?"

"Perish the thought. I'm asking for an interview. My readers are interested in what Elias Theropodous's last words were." Her eyes narrowed and the edges of her thin lips turned up. "In what he ate for his last meal. And where that was."

"I . . . I . . ."

"What paper are you with?" Velvet asked.

"The *New York Morning Standard.*"

"Hey!" Velvet said. "What d'ya know! That's my uncle Brian's paper. You remember Uncle Bry, Elizabeth. He came to my birthday party last year. Great guy. I love him to bits. Sorry, I didn't get your name."

"Jane Donaldson," the reporter said.

"Jane Donaldson. I'll mention to Uncle Bry that you chased us down the road and frightened innocent women and small children out of your way. When I call him, I'll ask if he needs a statement from Elizabeth. She can give it to him directly. Bypass the middleman, or middlewoman, I should say. Bye!" Velvet marched down the street, her hand firm on my arm. The reporter made no attempt to follow us.

When we were safely in my car, I said, "I've never met your uncle Brian. I didn't know he owned a newspaper."

Velvet laughed. "Mighty quick thinking on my part, if I do say so myself. I went out with a guy once who was an advertising editor at that miserable rag. He told me the owner, Brian someone, is a mean son-of-a-you-know-what, but he's a solid family guy and he dotes on his sister's kids. They all call him Uncle Bry. Jane'll realize I was bluffing pretty soon—she probably already has—but it set her back for a moment and got us away without more of a scene." Velvet settled back in her seat and laughed heartedly.

Chapter 15

I BYPASSED CHECKING IN AT THE OFFICE AND HEADED straight for the main kitchen. It was coming up to lunchtime, and I found the place in its usual state of chaos. Chef Leonardo was brandishing a knife at a cowering busboy.

"Do put that down, Chef," I said. "We don't want any accidents around here." I turned to the busboy. "Do you not have any work to do?"

"No, ma'am. I mean, yes, ma'am, Mrs. Grady ma'am. I was just going to wash that knife."

"You touch my knife, boy, and I'll have your fingers," Chef Leonardo growled.

The busboy fled. He was new. I could tell because he didn't yet realize that despite numerous threats the chef hadn't removed anyone's appendages. Not yet.

"I'm looking for Mr. Timmins. Do you know where he is?"

"Dead, I dare hope." My chef brought the knife down on a piece of beef, no doubt imagining it was the saladman's head. They did not get on, to put it mildly.

In a kitchen operation the size of ours—350 guests, more than a hundred employees, nine meals a day (guests, children, staff), plus room service, late-night dessert buffet, cocktail party, afternoon tea on the veranda, not to mention numerous other special occasions—the chef and the saladman are on the same seniority level and each has his own department and staff. The chef cooks the hot meals, the saladman is responsible for cold foods such as salads and desserts and sandwiches.

"I saw Mr. Timmins going to the cold room a few minutes ago, Mrs. Grady," a cook's assistant said.

"Thank you," I said.

I found the saladman rummaging through a basket of blueberries and berating a tearful young kitchen helper for throwing out too many.

"But . . . but . . ." she wailed. "I thought they didn't look fresh enough."

"Are they rotting?" he shouted. "Are the worms eating them? Are they— What do you want?" he snapped at me, his employer.

What was there, I thought, not for the first time, *about these men who cooked professionally that made them so ridiculously temperamental?*

"I don't want our guests served berries at the point of being bad," I said.

"You have money to waste throwing out good food? You're lucky you didn't grow up the way I did. We ate what we were given, and we were thankful for it."

Now that I knew about this man's relationship to Elias Theropodous, the resemblance was obvious. Nick was a good bit thinner than his brother, but he had the same height, the same prominent nose, except that Nick's didn't show the obvious evidence of drink, the same thinning brown hair, although Elias's had been professionally styled in an attempt to hide the bald spots.

"Can you give us a moment, please?" I said to the kitchen helper.

She was only too glad to flee.

It was delightfully cool in the cold room, surrounded by pitchers of juice, boxes overflowing with fresh fruit and vegetables, eggs, and a double row of chocolate puddings in small glass bowls. I briefly considered making some extra money renting the place out by the minute to heat-struck guests.

"It's your money to waste." Nick gestured to the berries. "But you'll be angry at me if my department goes over budget. Not like the butcher's bill that fraud in the kitchen—"

"I'm not here to talk about food or even money. Although that berry there, the one on the top, has mold on it."

He shrugged. "I'll serve it to the staff. They'll never notice."

"I'd rather you didn't serve it to anyone." I plucked it off the top and tossed it in the trash. I then rummaged through the basket with my hands. "The rest of them look okay. Please don't cut corners. We don't need anyone else falling ill here."

"If anyone falls ill, it'll be because the meat isn't cooked property. I've told you—"

I lifted my right hand. "We're getting way off topic here, and neither you nor I have time to spare. Tell me about your brother."

Something flared behind Nick's eyes before the shutters slammed down. He picked up an apple and studied it with far more intensity than it deserved. "What brother?"

"Elias Theropodous. I've been told he was your brother."

"What of it?"

"Why didn't you say something? You know the police have been looking into his death. The staff is talking about little else."

"I don't listen to staff gossip."

"You met him in town on Saturday morning. You were overheard arguing."

He put down the apple. "If you want to talk to me about the berry supply, Mrs. Grady, we will. But my private life is none of your business. Now, like you said yourself, I have work to do. Lunch service is about to begin."

"Your brother died after eating here, at Haggerman's. The police have been asking questions of our staff and guests. Newspaper reporters have been poking around. People in town have been talking about us, and not favorably. All that makes it the business of this hotel and thus of me."

He hesitated. "I hadn't seen my brother in more than forty years. He never even came to my parents' funerals, although he sent flowers. Flowers to show us how rich he was, not out of respect. He went away. He became rich and famous. He married beautiful women and bought them beautiful expensive things. I didn't expect anything from him—we'd never gotten on, even as children—but he could have offered our parents a helping hand as they got old and unable to work so hard." Nick snorted. "He didn't. We didn't have a happy childhood, Mrs. Grady. Our father was a hard man, quick with his fists, and our mother was a weak woman. But they were our parents. After our father died, I wrote to Elias. I told him Mother needed help, that she couldn't put in the hours cleaning the hotels the way she used to. I did what I could, but I had a family of my own to care for. Do you know how he responded to my plea?"

I shook my head.

"He sent me a check for ten dollars."

"That's . . . not much."

"Ten dollars over forty years? Barely enough for a meal for two in a fine restaurant in New York City. It was humiliating having to ask for money, even if it was to help our mother in her old age. The amount he sent was intended to be even more humiliating. I had no more contact with him until last week. I heard he and his film people were in Summervale, and he was staying at Kennelwood. As you said, the staff are talking about little else. Elias made no attempt to contact me, which didn't surprise me. I surprised myself, sending him a note asking him to have breakfast with me on Saturday. He came. He was by himself. I recognized him the minute he walked into the diner. He wore a good suit, a suit that probably cost more than you pay me in a year, and a fancy watch. But it was the same old Elias. Same resentments, as though forty years hadn't passed and our parents hadn't died long ago." He dropped onto a stool.

"You argued."

"Yes. It was a mistake, seeing him. I shouldn't have—"

The door creaked open, and the kitchen helper's head popped in, her eyes wide with trepidation. "Sorry, but I need—"

"Get out!" Nick roared.

Her eyes opened wider, she gasped, and the door slammed shut.

"I'm the older brother," Nick said. "I should have protected Elias when we were children. But I didn't. I ran with a hard crowd, and I left him alone to deal with our father and try to look after our mother. He couldn't do it. So he left them, left us, permanently."

I said nothing. Nick twisted his hands together. He'd been a cook in the army in the first war, and his hands were crisscrossed with old scars. A fresh bandage was wrapped around his right thumb. Finally he gave his head a shake and stood up. "I'm sorry our last words were hard ones. I'm sorry we both forgot we'd been brothers once." He walked past me, opened the door, and disappeared into the hallway.

I let out a long breath. I hadn't asked him if he'd killed his brother, or if he'd wanted Elias dead. If Nick had been responsible, he wouldn't have told me, but that didn't matter. It wouldn't have been possible for Nick Timmins, aka Nikos Theropodous, to have poisoned his brother. He hadn't come into the private dining room or the ballroom on Monday night. He didn't belong there, and he had no reason to ever go there. If he had come in, I would have seen him. He could have poisoned the food before it was brought out, but he wouldn't have known which plate was Elias's at dinner or what he'd choose from the dessert buffet.

I'd tell Dave Dawson about their relationship, but I was confident Elias's death had nothing to do with his angry, still bitter brother.

🍸

I NEEDED TO GET SOME WORK DONE, BUT WHEN I WALKED into the business office, one of the clerks said, "Mr. Westenham was here to see you."

"When was that?"

"Ten, fifteen minutes ago? I told him you'd gone into town. Sorry, I didn't know you were back. He said he'd pop around to your house and pay a call on Miss Peters and then check back for you."

"Thanks. I'll see if I can find him. If he comes in while I'm gone, ask him to wait, please."

Her phone rang, and she swung back to her desk to answer it.

I found Olivia and Jim relaxing in the shade of our porch with glasses of iced tea in front of them. Winston let out a bark at my approach but didn't expend the energy required to lumber to his feet. My mother lifted her fan in greeting and gave me a welcoming smile. "Nice to see you in the middle of the day, dear."

"I heard you wanted to talk to me," I said to Jim. I eyed the ice-filled pitcher on the table. "That looks good."

Olivia put her fan down and stood up. "I'll get you a glass."

My mother always manages to look cool and dewy-fresh despite the heat. Her lipstick was perfectly applied, her lashes thick with mascara, and not a hair escaped her chignon. Her blue cotton dress didn't contain the slightest hint of a wrinkle, and sweat didn't stain the arms or neckline.

I tried not to adjust my girdle, which was sticking un-

comfortably to my hips after the short walk from the hotel.
I sat down and leaned back in my chair with a sigh.

"Having a hard day?" Jim asked.

"Not particularly. But the heat gets to me sometimes."

"Gets to us all," he said. "Which is why half the popula-
tion of New York is in the Catskills."

"And the other half is planning to come. Thanks." I accepted a glass from Olivia and poured myself a drink. I
took a long grateful sip as she tucked her skirts beneath her
and settled back down. She resumed fanning her face.

"I'm thinking of doing a story about the generational
appeal of the Catskills to New York families," Jim said.
"So I thought I'd interview your mother."

"In my role as a hotelier," she said.

"You're not working on Elias's murder?" I asked.

"I can do two things at once," he said with a grin. "Truth
be told, I can do three things. I made a few phone calls, like
you asked me to."

"Phone calls? What about?" Olivia asked.

"Would you mind," I said, "if I ask you to excuse yourself. It is kinda private."

A spark leapt into my mother's eye. "Private?"

"Not what you're thinking. Whatever that might be."

The spark faded. "Very well. I'll be in my room. I have
some letters to write."

"Before you go, where's Gloria today?" I asked. "I don't
see any signs of the movie people. Gary told me if he was
happy with what they'd done, they'd be finished here. Are
they?"

"For now, at any rate. The director and some others view
the raw footage, what they call rushes, to decide if it's ac-
ceptable, and then adjust the filming schedule accordingly.
Gloria wasn't sure if that has been completed yet, or if Gary
would be satisfied with what was filmed under Elias's direction, but they've reserved time at some bungalow colony
for a few days. One or two small but important scenes with

Todd and Rebecca will be shot there. Gloria has no part in those, but she tagged along to watch them setting up today, getting background scenes and shots of extras wandering around. They plan to start filming with the principal actors tomorrow. She's enjoyed her time here, but she's looking forward to getting home. I've enjoyed having her. It's great fun to chat about the old days sometimes."

"I placed a few calls to friends of mine working the Hollywood beat," Jim said. "I learned one thing of interest. Elias wasn't the original choice for director. Gary Denham was."

"Gary?" Olivia's fan moved languidly. "The assistant director? You mean he was demoted? He can't have liked that."

"They went with a director with the bigger name and more solid reputation when Elias unexpectedly had a gap in his schedule. The picture he was supposed to be working on folded. The public reason the other picture stopped was artistic differences in the writing team. The real reason was that Elias had far grander plans than the producers were prepared to pay for. They got cold feet and pulled it. WolfeBright Pictures then got Elias on the cheap, and they demoted Gary to assistant director. People in the know say *Catskill Dreams* was Elias's last chance to stay relevant, and he was in danger of blowing it. The studio was getting increasingly concerned he was going way over budget."

"That sounds like the way Elizabeth runs my hotel," Olivia said. "She expects the very best from everyone, but then tells her department heads to cut back their expenditure."

"Business is a balance," I said, stung at what I considered unfair criticism. "Doesn't mean I have to serve rotten blueberries though."

"What do blueberries have to do with anything?"

"Never mind."

"Gary would have been furious when the role of director

was taken from him," Olivia said. "How fortunate for him that he was reinstated. If the picture does well he'll tell everyone it's because he took it on and managed to save it. If it's a bomb, obviously that's because Elias made such a mess of it to begin with."

"Very fortunate," Jim said.

Olivia got to her feet in a smooth cool blue river. "I'm going to order lunch. Do you want anything, dear?"

"I ate already."

"Jim?"

"Thanks, but no. I need to be on my way."

"Todd Thompson?" I said once Olivia had gone inside, and Winston had wandered off in search of squirrels to play with.

"Married," Jim said.

I wasn't expecting that. "Whoa! Really?"

"Really. He married his high school sweetheart when they were eighteen. They moved to LA shortly after that, and both of them tried their hands at acting. She got nowhere while he almost immediately started getting solid roles, and he hasn't looked back. She didn't like living in California and returned to Fort Wayne, Indiana, to live near her parents."

"They're still married? Todd and this woman?"

"Oh, yes. It's common knowledge in Fort Wayne as well as the back offices of the movie studio. He visits her a couple of times a year. Her and their children. A set of twin boys and a baby girl."

I stared at him.

"Yup. Close your mouth, Elizabeth. You'll catch flies."

I did as instructed.

Jim chuckled. "I'd say Todd does more than just visit when he goes home."

"You say it's common knowledge. Why don't the gossip magazines report on it?"

"Because it's in the interest of WolfeBright Pictures,

who have him under contract, to keep Todd's marital and parental situation on the q.t., and it's in the interest of the magazines to keep up the pretext he's a playboy-about-town. No one wants to see pictures of him reading a bed-time story to a two-year-old, or helping his wife wash the dishes after supper."

"What am I going to tell Velvet?"

"Up to you to do what you want with what I've told you, Elizabeth. I can't say if Todd's trying to charm Velvet be-cause he's hoping to bed her, or if he's simply playing the role he's been assigned to the hilt. Todd might not even know. I don't much care about his marital situation and romantic affairs, or about the reputation of his movie stu-dio, but a double life is hard to keep up. It messes with people's minds."

"How do you know that?"

He grinned at me and stood up. "I'll tell you about it someday."

I put down my glass and also stood. "I'll walk back with you. I don't suppose you know what Dave Dawson's been up to today?"

"He went to Kennelwood first thing this morning with more questions for the movie people. No sign of the state police yet. The autopsy's scheduled for this afternoon, and Dave said he'll speak to the press after that. Which is why I need to get into town."

"Will you let me know what he has to say?"

"It'll be on the radio and in tomorrow's papers, but sure."

I hoped to get into my office without any guests stopping me to chat, or to complain, so I walked with Jim on the staff path that cuts around the rear of the main hotel build-ing to the car park. Winston burst out of the trees and fell into step beside us. It was quiet at this time of day, not many staff around, as they were mostly at work. My aunt Tatiana came out of the laundry building reading from the papers on her clipboard, and the bulldog ran ahead to greet her.

"I might do a story one day," Jim said, "about the behind-the-scenes workings of a big Catskills hotel."

"I thought you were interested in the people who come here as guests," I said.

"I'm interested in lots of things. People mostly. Average, ordinary men and women trying to make a living, raise their families, and find some fun in their lives. I'm increasingly uninterested in the crime beat. Same old same old. Mob Guy One offends Mob Guy Two. Mob Guy Two offs Mob Guy One, and Mob Guy Three is out for revenge. And so it goes. Which is why, when a character like Elias Theropodous is murdered, it makes a big story. Gives reporters like me something new to talk about."

The path ends at the back of the hotel, next to the parking lot. A small overgrown trail breaks off here and goes around the side of the hotel to the back door of my office. Very convenient when I need to sneak out without the staff seeing me go.

"I'll call you after the press conference." Jim trotted away.

I started to turn for the office when the roar of a powerful car engine caught my attention. Two girls who worked as nannies for the hotel ran past me squealing with excitement, and I heard whistles and a boy exclaim, "Wow!"

Wow indeed. A 1951 Chevrolet Styleline convertible, pale yellow with a cream interior, screeched into the small staff section of the parking lot. More girls gathered around to admire it, and several of the male staff began kicking at the tires or rubbing their hands over the body work. Even Jim stopped in his tracks to have a look.

To my considerable surprise, none other than Luke Robinson was behind the wheel. He opened the driver's door and leapt out, grinning from ear to ear.

"Take me for a ride!" a girl squealed.

"Yes, yes. Take us for a ride." Her friend jumped up and down, clapping her hands.

"Plenty of time, ladies, plenty of time," Luke drawled. "This baby and I aren't going anywhere."

"How many horses it got?" a boy asked.

"More than you can handle, pal," Luke replied.

Two guests walked up, men in their forties. One let out a low whistle. "Nice wheels."

"Thank you, sir."

"Is this your car, son?" the other man asked.

"Yes, sir. Like it?"

"Sure do. Wouldn't mind one like that myself, but the wife wouldn't be too keen."

"Nice to be young and rich, eh?" the first man said. "How's it handle?"

"It's a beauty of a ride, sir. Handles like a"—Luke threw one of the wide-eyed nannies a smirk—"wild woman."

The girls screamed with laughter.

Luke saw me watching. He put his hands on his hips, cocked his head to one side, and gave me what he probably considered to be a seductive grin. "Hey there, Mrs. Grady, want to go for a spin?"

I walked toward them, making a big show out of checking my watch. "I believe they're still serving lunch. Shouldn't you be in the dining room, Luke?"

"It's okay, Mrs. Grady. I arranged with Miss Sullivan to skip a shift. I'll make it up." He kept his eyes on my face and ran his hand lightly over the hood of the car. "I can make it up to you, if you'd like?"

One of the boys choked. A girl giggled. The two guests had dropped to their knees in the dust and were peeking under the car.

"None of the rest of you have any work to do?" I said to the onlookers.

"Yes, Mrs. Grady. Sorry, Mrs. Grady." They began to slip away.

I followed them. I don't know much about the price of cars, but I know something. When Olivia inherited the hotel and she and I made plans to leave Manhattan for remote Summervale, I insisted that she buy a car for our use. I wasn't going to be trapped in the mountains, particularly in the winter, without a way of getting out. I spent a lot of time looking into the price and value of cars. The vehicle we eventually bought had had a previous owner and had been comfortably within our budget. The car Luke was so ostentatiously showing off must have originally cost in excess of two thousand dollars. If he bought it used, it would still have been far more than a summer waiter should be able to afford.

Luke had never before shown any signs of having money. He was a college student, first-year law at Columbia, working here for the summer to earn next year's tuition. He didn't dress any better than the other waitstaff; he lived in staff accommodation, and until now he'd taken the bus into town with his friends on their nights off.

Where had Luke suddenly come into enough money to afford that car?

I took a guess, and I didn't like what I came up with.

Luke had been the waiter at Elias's private dinner on Monday night. He'd been working in the ballroom after dinner, chatting to guests, dancing with the ladies. Until now, it hadn't so much as crossed my mind to consider that Luke had been the best positioned of anyone to slip something into Elias's food or drink. I thought back to that night. We had cocktails before dinner. Some people went to the bar for their drinks, some asked the waiters, including Luke, to get them. Mary-Alice had fetched Elias's drinks, but I didn't know whether she'd ordered directly from Rosemary at the bar or asked a waiter to do that. At seven o'clock, everyone took their seats around the table, me included. We carried our unfinished drinks with us. Wine was served with dinner, but I didn't remember seeing Elias having wine. He stuck to his bourbon. The food was plated in the kitchen, and brought out by waiters. Ladies were served first and then the gentlemen. If he wanted to, Luke would have been able to place a particular plate in front of a particular person. I hadn't considered him as a suspect because he had no motive.

Only a short while ago, I'd dismissed Elias's brother as a suspect because although he had a motive—years of pent-up anger and humiliation—he'd had no opportunity.

Put the two together—Nick's motive and Luke's opportunity—and I had two very strong suspects.

Had Nick Timmins, my saladman, paid Luke the waiter to kill Elias Theropodous?

Chapter 16

I SLAMMED THE OFFICE DOOR BEHIND ME, PICKED UP MY phone, and asked the switchboard to place a call to the Summervale police station without even bothering to switch on the fan. The surly officer who answered told me the chief was in but not taking any calls. I told him it was important, and he said he'd check.

I waited a very long time indeed, anxiously chewing at the end of my pencil, suspecting the officer was playing games with me, but eventually the line clicked and Dave Dawson said, "Elizabeth. This isn't a good time. The mayor's having a press conference in a few minutes, and I'll have questions to answer. I can see town hall from my window, and I can tell you it's a mob scene out there. Reporters have come from a long way away."

"I appreciate that, and thank you for taking my call. I'll try to be quick. I discovered something that might be of importance. Did you know that Elias's brother lives in

Summervale and they got into a heated argument at the Red Spot Diner on Saturday morning?"

"No. I did not know that. How do you?"

"They were overheard by everyone in the diner, and Lucinda McGreevy told me about it. At the time, it was nothing but two old men arguing and getting themselves thrown out, and no one knew who Elias was. Lucinda didn't tell you because she didn't know either, until she was talking to me and put two and two together. Elias's brother changed his name and is now called Nick Timmins, and he works here. At Haggerman's. He's the saladman."

"You think this Timmins . . . ?"

"I think nothing. I'm telling you what I know, that's all. I should also tell you that the waiter who served at dinner that night has just bought himself a fancy new car. An expensive car. A far more expensive car than a young man should be able to afford on a summer waiter's salary."

"I remember the waiter. Luke Robinson. I spoke to him. He claims not to have noticed anything untoward all evening. I'll need to talk to him again." He paused. "It's entirely possible he got the funds for this car by legitimate means. If not, it would be a heck of a risk on his part to rush out and spend the money so soon. Attract attention to himself."

"Luke's an arrogant college kid, and not all that bright for all he's intending to become a lawyer. I doubt he stops to worry about consequences. If you like, I can speak to him about it. Save you a trip out here if it turns out to be not necessary."

"That would be a help, thanks. Try not to put words in his mouth."

"Meaning?"

"Don't come right out and ask him if he was paid for poisoning a guest."

I was rather insulted. "I can be more subtle than that."

He chuckled. "I'm sure you can. In return, I'll tell you what I'm about to announce to the press. Mr. Theropodous consumed a poisonous substance shortly before he died."

"That's what the doctor suspected, but I suppose it's good to have it confirmed. Can you be sure it was given to him deliberately? Deliberately administered to him by someone else?"

"People have been known to kill themselves by taking poison," Dave said. "But I have to say in light of what we know of Mr. Theropodous and his state of mind that evening, I consider it to be highly unlikely that's what happened."

As, I had to admit, did I.

"What sort of poison was it?" I asked.

"That's still to be determined, but there's no shortage of dangerous substances lying around out in the open at the ordinary home. Or hotel. The sort of thing you can buy at any store: rodent killer and pesticides in particular. Easy to find, but putting it into someone's food or drink makes it murder, Elizabeth. The pathologist estimates the man consumed the poison within two hours before feeling ill, and it was in his drinks."

"Meaning it definitely was taken at my hotel."

"Yes, but rest assured it couldn't have been an accident or as a result of food incorrectly prepared. You're in the clear there."

"That's good to know. I wasn't aware we were still under suspicion."

"The state police wanted to have your kitchen shut down."

I choked. Beads of sweat dripped down my forehead. If Haggerman's failed, I could go back to the city and find a job as a bookkeeper easily enough, but this hotel was all Olivia had in the world.

"I managed to convince them that would be premature," Dave continued. "The mayor helped with that. Something about a large donation to the state police benevolent fund on the part of the town. You might also consider making a contribution."

"I'll do that. I'm assuming the state police finally arrived?"

"They showed up a short while ago. They claim they were sent to the wrong town. As though I don't know the name of the town I live in." With that Chief Dawson hung up.

I got up to switch on the fan and stood in front of it for a few minutes, my arms held up and my legs apart, letting the lukewarm air swirl around my body. It didn't help much. I dropped back into my chair, and once again picked up the phone. "I need to talk to Luke Robinson," I said to the switchboard operator. "He's a waiter, but he's been given time off at today's lunch shift. When last seen he was in the staff parking lot. Can you send a page for him, please, and have him come to my office. If not in the parking lot, check his room. If not there, he'll have to be summoned by the loudspeakers."

"Got it," she said.

I opened my office door to admit the clatter of typewriter keys and the sound of women yelling into telephones and then resumed my position behind my desk to await my caller.

Richard's flowers were already beginning to droop in the heat. I reached out and touched the soft variegated leaf of a hosta, and I felt myself smiling.

I took my fingers back, and opened the reservations book for next week, but I scarcely read a word. I chewed on the end of my pencil and thought about the best way to ask Luke about his car.

Could I come right out and accuse him of taking bribes?

I didn't have long to think it over. Obviously the page had found him in the parking lot, holding court over his new car. He knocked on my office door less than five minutes after I'd placed the call.

I looked up to see Luke standing in the doorway, smirking. He was a thin, gangly boy, with good skin, prominent cheekbones, and deep-set dark eyes. He might have been good-looking except for the weak chin and the perpetual smirk and cock-of-the-walk attitude that was, as far as I knew, totally unwarranted.

"You wanted to see me, Mrs. Grady?" He stepped into the office and half turned to shut the door behind him.

"Leave the door open, please," I said in my best stern, no-nonsense boss voice. I didn't want any misunderstandings here.

One eyebrow rose, he shrugged, and stepped farther into the room. He shoved his hands into his pockets and leaned against a wall. "Okay."

"Take a seat," I said.

"Okay." He sat.

I studied his face. I saw arrogance, rudeness, not a lot of intelligence. I didn't see fear or guilt.

Underneath the cover of my desk I wiped my hands on my skirt. Maybe this wasn't such a good idea.

Oh, well. He was here now.

"Gloria Grant claims to have—shall we say—lost . . . a bracelet. A diamond bracelet."

Luke's eyes narrowed. "So?"

"She wore it to the private dinner on Monday evening and hasn't seen it since. You remember the dinner, Luke. You were the waiter."

Something jumped behind his eyes. "I don't know about any bracelet."

"She remembers having it on when she left the dining room and went to the ballroom. It was, as I'm sure you'll remember, a very social evening. Lots of people coming and going, well-wishers dropping by her chair for a chat, couples dancing."

"I didn't see anyone take her bracelet, if that's what you're asking."

"She says the last time she definitely remembers having the bracelet was moments before you, Luke, escorted Miss Marsden back to their table after you and she had a dance."

Luke might not be too bright, but he had good instinct for self-preservation. He understood what I was saying and leapt to his feet. "I never took any bracelet. The ditzy old broad lost it, and you're accusing me 'cause I'm the best scapegoat."

"Please don't talk about our guests that way," I said sternly. "Miss Grant clearly remembers that you brushed against her arm. She also remembers looking up at you and giving you a smile because, let's be honest here, Luke, she thinks you're most charming."

That was a lie and a half. I hoped to knock Luke off guard, and it worked. He preened, one eye lowered in a half wink, and he gave me what he probably thought was a charming grin. "What about you, Mrs. G.? Do you think that too?"

"What I think doesn't matter. Miss Grant wants her bracelet back. She won't report its disappearance to the police, as long as it's returned. No questions asked."

"I don't know anything about any bracelet. Like I said, she's a spoiled old b—woman. The clasp was probably wonky and it fell off and she was too drunk to notice. She had a heck of a lot that night; they all did. Heck, that old guy died. I spoke to the cops about it: told them I couldn't help them. One of the busboys must have found the bracelet, snatched it up, and stuck it into his pocket. It's long gone by now." He shrugged and started to stand. "Sorry I can't help with that, Mrs. Grady. If you need anything else . . ."

"Sit down," I said.

Such was my tone, he dropped back down.

"I don't intend to forget about it, or to ask no further questions. I've reported the theft to the police and they're taking it seriously. The reputation of this hotel, of all the hotels in Summervale, is of utmost importance to the local authorities. As was mentioned, a large number of people were in that room the night in question, but not many people were physically close enough to Miss Grant to loosen her bracelet, remove it from her wrist, and drop it into a purse or pocket unnoticed." I looked at Luke.

Beads of sweat were dripping down his forehead. All the arrogance had fled, leaving a frightened boy behind. I almost felt sorry for him. Luke feared he was about to be accused of something he didn't do, something that hadn't even happened.

Would he try to get out of the theft charge by admitting to having slipped something into Elias's drinks? Easy enough to claim he hadn't known what was in the . . . whatever it was. That someone had asked him to play a trick on the director.

"I'm talking to you, Luke, because you've obviously sold the bracelet and used the proceeds to buy that car. I asked Miss Grant the value of the bracelet and the sum she mentioned was about what a car like that one of yours would cost. If you confess, I'll ask the police to go easy on you."

Luke was attending Columbia Law School. His future in the law, I decided, was dim. He had the most readable face I'd ever encountered. At my words, every line of tension simply melted away. A spark came back into his eyes and his shoulders relaxed. The edges of his mouth lifted in a sneer. "Sorry to disappoint you, Mrs. Grady. I didn't buy that car. It isn't mine."

"You didn't? It isn't?"

"Nope. Buddy of mine who works at Kutsher's had to leave the area suddenly. He said I could look after his car for him while he's away."

"Oh," I said. "That's good to hear." Reading between the lines, I suspected Luke's buddy was spending some time in jail and needed someone to keep the car running in his absence. Unlikely he wanted Luke to offer rides to every influential man or pretty woman at our hotel, but that was none of my concern. Where the friend got the car was none of my concern either, nor was the possibility that it would soon be repossessed.

"If you don't believe me," Luke said, "I can show you the registration papers."

"That won't be necessary. Thank you for coming in and talking to me. I'm glad we cleared this up." I picked up my pencil.

Luke stood. "I'll keep an eye out for that bracelet, okay?"

"Bracelet? Oh, the bracelet, right."

He almost sprinted out of my office. So shaken was he, he didn't even offer to take me for a ride in the car.

I felt rather pleased with myself as I firmly shut the office door behind him. The possibility that Luke had put the poison into Elias's drink was still there, but I had to consider it unlikely. I might be wrong, but I didn't think the waiter had that much guile in him to be able to bluff me so effectively. He was vain, and strutting and arrogant. If that car did belong to him, he'd never be able to bring himself to say it didn't, no matter the consequences.

I had the fan on high and the window open, but the heat was steadily building. Feeling as though I'd roast if I didn't do something about it, I loosened my belt, pulled off my stockings and girdle, and stuffed the offending garments in my drawer under a pile of hotel brochures. I then went back to work.

I hadn't spent long checking over the kitchen expenses (exorbitant) when my phone rang. I picked it up. "Mrs. Grady."

"Frank Steinberg, *Los Angeles Times.* Does Haggerman's Catskills Resort have a comment about the autopsy report on Mr. Elias Theropodous?"

"What? I mean . . . we're sorry about the man's death, but he wasn't a guest of Haggerman's."

"I've been told he died after a party at your place."

"Lots of people were at that party, and none of them took ill. I was at that party, and I am in perfect health. Good day." I hung up. The phone rang again.

"Mrs. Grady."

"This is Jane Donaldson, *New York Morning Standard.* I'm hoping I can come around and have an interview with you, Elizabeth. Earlier today, Chief Dawson said—"

Click.

I called the switchboard. "I thought I left instructions not to put through any calls from newspaper reporters."

"Sorry, Mrs. Grady. Those last callers didn't identify themselves."

"If it is reporters, tell them I am not available. If they ask to speak to anyone else, you are to tell them we are all unavailable."

"How'm I gonna know if they're newspaper people?"

"Ask them! Ask everyone!" I slammed the phone into the cradle and took a deep breath. I picked up the phone again, and said, "Mr. Jim Westenham is an exception. I'll speak to him if he calls."

I got up and marched to the office door. "Darlene!"

The clerk's head popped up. She blinked at me from inside a cloud of smoke. Everyone else stopped what they were doing to watch.

"I want a memo prepared for the attention of all staff. See that it's posted everywhere, absolutely everywhere staff will see it but guests will not. Anyone found to have given a statement to a newspaper reporter without my personal approval will be fired on the spot."

"Yes, Mrs. Grady."

I looked around the room. "Did you all get that?"

"Yes, Mrs. Grady."

IT WAS ONLY WHEN I STRETCHED AND STOOD UP, READY to switch out the lights, get properly dressed once again, and head home, that I realized I'd forgotten to tell Dave what I'd heard about Gary and the job of director.

I hadn't forgotten what I'd learned about the marital situation of Todd Thompson, but I had absolutely no idea what to do with that information. Velvet would not thank me for interfering.

Chapter 17

"WHAT WOULD YOU DO," I SAID TO MY MOTHER AS I helped myself to mashed potatoes, "if you knew a friend of yours was considering making a big mistake, and you knew it was a big mistake but the reason you know is that you went behind her back to find out what was going on."

"Oh, *lastachka*," Aunt Tatiana said. "Like when you married Ron Grady."

"Why was that a mistake?" Olivia asked. "I thought Ron was lovely. Such a charmer." She turned to Gloria. "Elizabeth's husband died in the war. He was a true American hero. Such a tragedy, they'd only married a few weeks before he left for Europe."

"My condolences," Gloria said. "So many women lost so much."

I concentrated on cutting my pork chop and avoided Tatiana's eyes. I'd always suspected Aunt Tatiana knew more than she'd ever let on about my whirlwind wartime romance and quickie marriage.

"What would being honest accomplish?" my aunt said in answer to my question. "A woman will do what she believes she must when she is in love, and she will forget all bonds of friendship and of family if it is necessary to do so to maintain her illusions."

"And such," Gloria said, lifting her wineglass in a toast, "is the stuff of great movies. You should come to Hollywood with me, Tatiana. I can find you work as a script-writer."

"Pshaw," said my aunt. Winston had settled himself at her feet, apparently snoozing but on the alert in case anything fell off the table.

We four women were having dinner at our house. The heat of the day had scarcely dispersed when the sun went down, and the air was so sticky it was almost physical. The windows were thrown open to let in the soft breeze off the lake, and two fans had been set up at opposite sides of the room. I'd gratefully torn off my dress and undergarments and dressed for a casual dinner in shorts and an open-necked, short-sleeved cotton blouse.

Gloria had declared that she was not in the mood to go up to the hotel and be charming to everyone who interrupted her meal wanting an autograph, and so Olivia suggested dinner in, and invited Tatiana, Velvet, and me to join them.

Velvet, Olivia told me, had declined because she'd taken the night off and was dining at Kennelwood. I didn't care for the sound of that, but I said nothing.

"I'll talk to Velvet if you want me to," Gloria said.

"What do you mean?" I asked.

She pushed her unfinished plate of food aside, leaned back in her chair, and reached for the pack of cigarettes at her elbow. "I assume that's who you're talking about. It's obvious Velvet is falling under Todd's spell. I am aware that Todd is not, shall we say, quite what he appears, although I'm contractually forbidden from saying more than that."

"Elizabeth knows," Olivia said.

"Knows what?" Tatiana asked.

"How do you know I know?" I said to Olivia. "Were you listening at the window earlier?"

"Of course I was listening at the window earlier. Don't pretend to be so shocked, Elizabeth. You can hear a squirrel rolling over in its sleep through the walls of this house. If you wanted privacy you and Jim should have gone for a walk. Come to think of it, you and Jim should take a walk more often. A nice, quiet, private walk. If you know what I mean."

"I do not," I said. "This chop is tough. I'm going to suggest Chef Leonardo find a new pork supplier."

"It's not the meat, it's the cook," Aunt Tatiana said. "When we first arrived, I offered to teach him to prepare good, solid Russian food, and I thought he was going to explode with rage. Man's a fool." She scooped up a forkful of potatoes.

"If by Jim, you're talking about that newspaperman," Gloria said around a plume of smoke, "he's quite handsome. Is he courting you, dear?"

"No," I said.

"Not because of any lack of interest on his part," Olivia said.

"Potatoes have too much butter," Aunt Tatiana said.

"No such thing as too much butter," I said. "Jim and I are friends. That's all."

"Do you want me to talk to Velvet?" Gloria asked again. "Over the years, I've met more than a few beautiful women who arrive in Hollywood full of dreams and end up brokenhearted and on the street."

"As have I," Olivia said. "Plenty of men out there ready to take advantage of girls and their dreams. Velvet has a good head on her shoulders. She's no fool."

"Any woman is a fool if she thinks a bad man loves her," Gloria said. "How old is she?"

"Same as me," I said. "Twenty-seven."

"Too old to get her start in Hollywood," Gloria said. "I'll tell her not to waste her time."

My mother pushed her meat around on her plate. "It's a hard business, acting. The only one harder is dancing."

"It's harder working in a hotel laundry, O," Aunt Tatiana said. Olivia refuses to answer to her birth name of Olga, considering it too common, not to mention too Russian. Tatiana refuses to call her sister Olivia, considering the change of name to be an insult to their parents and their proud Russian heritage. So they compromised, and Aunt Tatiana always simply calls my mother O.

"You know what I mean," Olivia said.

"Maybe don't mention anything to Velvet," I said. "Not yet. We'll see what happens. Filming's wrapping up soon, isn't it?"

"We have two days at the bungalow colony and then, provided the rushes are satisfactory, it's back to the city and into the studio. As the plan is now, I have only one more scene myself, when Todd returns from the war and visits his grandmother, but scripts change all the time. I hope this awful heat breaks soon. If it's this hot in the mountains, it must be positively unbearable in the city." She crushed her cigarette out in the plate in front of her, next to the abandoned pork chop and mashed potatoes.

"Anyone for dessert?" Olivia said. "I specially requested the angel food cake tonight. More wine, Gloria?"

Over dinner, I debated whether to tell the women what I'd learned from Dave Dawson, but as the contents of the wine bottle went down, and we chatted and laughed, I decided not to. The autopsy results would be in the papers tomorrow, and we were having a nice evening tonight. No one, least of all me, wanted to think about poison being slipped into someone's drink.

I got to my feet and began gathering up the dishes. The

phone rang as I passed it heading for the kitchen, and I dropped my load on the counter and answered.

"Elizabeth. I'm glad I caught you," Richard Kennelwood said.

"I'm having a relaxing night in. What's up?"

"We had a fire in the kitchen."

"A fire! Is everyone okay? Do you need anything from us?"

Olivia, Tatiana, and Gloria caught the word *fire* and stopped talking to listen.

"We're all fine, thanks. No one was hurt, and not too much damage," Richard said. I gave the watching women a thumbs-up, and their faces crumpled in relief.

"As for needing anything, that's why I'm calling. The fire was in the baking kitchen. We lost all our bread and most of the baked goods intended for tomorrow, and the oven has been damaged. My chefs'll be cooking all night. We're supposed to be catering lunch for the film crew tomorrow at Sparkling Waters, and we can't manage that as well as catch up on what's needed here. I was wondering if you could do it?"

I thought quickly. "I can't see it, Richard. Dinner's over at the hotel and the chef might have left for the day. The saladman will be preparing the evening's dessert buffet, but if I consult him and not the chef, I'll have a war on my hands. I can't commit to using their supplies and their workers without talking it over with the both of them. I have an idea. How much does it pay?"

He named a handsome sum, and I said, "Can I call you back?"

"I'll be here."

I pressed the button on the phone's cradle to disconnect the call, released my finger, and called the switchboard. "Can you put me through to the Red Spot Diner in Summervale, please?"

"Connecting you now, Mrs. Grady."

"Hello?" Lucinda said.

"How would you like to earn some extra money?"

*   *   *

I SET MY ALARM CLOCK FOR THE UNIMAGINABLE HOUR of 6:00 A.M. When it sounded, I switched it off quickly, conscious of Velvet's light breathing coming from the bed. I'd made arrangements with Lucinda and Aunt Tatiana for catering the movie crew, and it had been late when I finally said my good nights to Gloria and Olivia and made my way to Velvet's room in the staff quarters.

I'd been lying in bed, awake and staring at the thin beam of moonlight slipping through the cheap curtains when Velvet came in. She tripped, giggled, said, "Sorry," and giggled again.

"I have to get up early tomorrow," I said.

"Sorry."

She undressed without switching on the light, went down the hall to the bathroom, and climbed into bed when she returned. The springs squeaked, the mattress shifted, and my friend sighed heavily. The windows were open to the night air, and the fan on the dresser moved slowly, but the room was still stiflingly hot. I didn't ask Velvet how her evening had gone. I was afraid that if I did, and she told me it had been wonderful, I'd end up telling her what I knew about Todd. I hadn't yet decided if I was going to do that.

"'Night," she said.

"Harrumph," I replied.

The fan whirled softly in the corner.

WHEN I GOT UP, I DRESSED QUICKLY IN THE DARK AND DID the best I could with my hair and makeup in the bathroom and slipped downstairs. Velvet had rolled over, murmuring softly in her sleep, but she didn't wake.

Muffled snores came from behind some of the closed doors, and from others I could hear women getting ready to start their day.

A band of pale gray was rising over the lake when I headed for the hotel, and birds were calling to one another from high in the trees. A wind had come up, blowing straight off the water toward me, and that boded well for the prospect of a slightly cooler day. Not many lights were on in the guest rooms or cabins, but the kitchens and the laundry rooms and garden and maintenance sheds were ablaze. Work in a hotel starts early.

I found the head breakfast cook at work in the kitchen, checking a batch of coffee cakes in the oven, and I told him what I needed. He hailed a yawning dishwasher and ordered him to give me a hand. I sent the boy to the storage shed to get trestle tables while I searched for George, head of maintenance, and organized the use of a truck for the day.

That done, I went to my office to try to get a few hours of work done. I was falling so far behind, I worried I'd never catch up.

By nine o'clock, I'd made such good progress on the accounts I was able to start plowing through the pile of pink message slips to return calls when I thought people would be in their offices. I'd left my door open, and I'd heard the clerks arriving to start work at eight. Women chatted, chairs were pulled out, covers thrown off typewriters, desk drawers opened, cigarettes lit, coffee made, and phones began to ring.

"Sorry to bother you, Mrs. Grady," a head popped around the corner, "but we thought you'd want to know. The police are here. They're in the kitchen."

I threw down my pencil.

Fortunately this time the police had arrived at mealtime, and the security guard had the sense to direct them to park around the back, so not many guests knew they were here. Also fortunately Chef Leonardo hadn't arrived yet, so he wasn't going to throw a tantrum and get himself arrested for threating bodily harm to officers of the law.

I'd met Detectives Stanford and Flynn of the state police

before, and I hadn't been particularly impressed with their efficiency or professionalism. This morning, they'd been served coffee and were munching on a plate of scrambled eggs and toast when I came in. "Good morning, Detectives," I said in my cheeriest tone. "What can we do for you today?"

"We're here about the guy who died on Monday. Poisoned, the autopsy says."

"Yes."

Staff dodged around us. Assistant cooks flipped eggs or laid slices of lox on plates or supervised the industrial-size toasters; bakers took breads and cakes out of the oven; waiters called for more juice or demanded to know where their order was; busboys carried in towers of dirty dishes; and dishwashers banged away at pots and pans.

"We want to talk to the cooks and waiters and other folks who were working that night." Flynn stuffed eggs into his mouth.

"Most of them aren't here yet," I said. "Our kitchen operates more than eighteen hours a day, so people work in shifts."

"Yeah, that's what he"—a stab of a fork in the direction of the breakfast chef—"said. We'll come back later, then. Say, around lunchtime. Any more toast there, sweetie?" Flynn called to a passing cook's helper.

🍸

AT ELEVEN O'CLOCK I SENT A TRUCKLOAD OF ASSORTED Haggerman's employees who Aunt Tatiana had rounded up into town to help Lucinda pack up her night's cooking and baking and take it out to the film shoot, and I drove myself to Sparkling Waters Bungalow Colony.

My supervision probably wasn't necessary, but I wanted to check the activity for myself. Over the phone last night, we'd arranged that Lucinda and her mother would prepare the food and Haggerman's would provide soda and juice and what was needed in the way of trestle tables to lay it all out on, as well as dishes, cutlery, and glassware. Lucinda couldn't spare workers from her small restaurant, so I sent some Haggerman's staff to the diner this morning to help her get it all out to the film shoot, and then serve and clean up.

When I got to the Haggerman's staff parking lot, I found Velvet and Olivia waiting impatiently for me by my car.

"Are you two coming?" I said.

"I thought I'd enjoy the outing," Olivia said. She'd wrapped a yellow-and-blue scarf around her hair and tied it under her chin, and put on enormous sunglasses.

"I saw Olivia heading this way, and asked her where she was going," Velvet said. "And I decided to come too."

"Don't you have work to do?" I asked, maybe a fraction more harshly than I should have.

"I got one of the girls whose day off it is to take my morning classes," she said. "I should be back in time for tennis this afternoon."

She looked lovely this morning. Positivity glowing with health and happiness. I didn't ask how her dinner date had gone—I didn't want to know. I growled at them to get into the car.

"That's quite the car over there," Velvet said, pointing to Luke's friend's Styleline. "That's the staff area. The car must be in the wrong place."

"And therein lies a story," I said.

❦

LUCINDA DIDN'T LOOK AS THOUGH SHE'D BEEN UP ALL night, although she had. By the time we arrived at the filming location, she had everything well in hand. Most of the food would be served cold—sandwiches and various salads—with pies, cakes, and cookies for dessert, along with juices and soda, tea and coffee.

I'd lent her what staff Aunt Tatiana and I could grab with little notice and temporarily spare, from Francis, the gardener's assistant, to a dishwasher I found having a smoke behind the kitchen door after breakfast service was finished, to a dance instructor who'd sprained her ankle. Long tables had been laid across a section of the lawn, and they groaned under the weight of the offerings. Lucinda stood behind them, smiling broadly, her polka-dot apron on and her long dark hair tied behind her head. She gave me a big thumbs-up.

A couple of cars were pulled to the side of the highway near the entrance to the bungalow colony, and reporters stood together in small groups, watched over by a security guard. The guard recognized me and waved me through.

Equipment trucks and trailers lined the bumpy road into the bungalow colony, and the movie crew had taken over a section near one of the cabins, positioned so the brown waters of the small lake provided the background. The camp was ill-named: nothing at all sparkled in the waters of that lake. It was more like a pond—shallow and muddy, thick with weeds and rushes.

Wide-eyed guests hung around the perimeter of the filming area while bathing suit–clad children ran back and forth. Thick cables crisscrossed the weed- and crabgrass-choked lawn, the cameras were set up and ready. Gary sat in pride of place in the director's chair while Mary-Alice hovered over him, and the makeup artist dabbed at Rebecca's face with her brushes. Gloria sat next to Gary, her eyes hidden behind huge sunglasses and an enormous straw hat over her hair. Judy Rae was seated beside Gloria.

Todd, dressed in his perfectly tailored army uniform, stood in the shade of the cabin that would be the center of the scene, smoking. He spotted us picking our way around the network of equipment, threw his cigarette to one side, and bounded toward us.

Or, I should say, he bounded toward Velvet.

"You came! Great." He smiled at her. She smiled back.

My fingers itched to smack that grin off his face. He tore his attention away from Velvet and bowed to the women with her. "Miss Peters, how nice to see you." He extended his arm. "May I?"

Olivia glanced at me and wiggled her eyebrows as she took his arm. "You may."

They walked away, making me feel, once again, like chopped liver. He helped Olivia settle into the chair next to Judy, also resplendent in sunglasses and an umbrella-size hat, where she could have an uninterrupted view of the action. Gloria and the singer greeted my mother with cries of welcome.

More than a few of the watching women, I noticed, were more excited at seeing Olivia, Gloria, and Judy than the younger actors. A large man in a suit stood next to the row of chairs, feet apart, hands behind his back, staring across the lawn rather than toward the film set. Security, keeping pesky fans at bay.

Velvet and I found places to stand behind the three women.

"Places, everyone," Gary yelled. "Quiet on set."

Behind us, parents shifted their feet and shushed children.

Makeup done, Rebecca took her position on the cabin's front porch. This place hadn't been chosen to show the Catskills to its best advantage. The cabin that would be in the movie, like the others packed close together and stretching in a long double line toward the lake, was noticeably in need of some sprucing up. Flecks of paint peeled off the door and window frames, the gutters drooped, the porch railing tilted ominously to one side, and what plants remained in what had once been flower beds were being slowly choked to death by weeds.

This place had been chosen, I assumed, as an illustration of the class and income differences between Todd's character, the scion of a family getting rich(er) off the war, and Rebecca's Lower East Side factory worker.

It's customary for guests in the bungalow colonies to share common areas as well as cooking facilities. The scent of boiled cabbage and burnt meat was so strong, it was too bad the camera wouldn't be able to capture it.

"Aaaaand action!" Gary shouted. The clapper board clapped and the camera and sound boom moved slowly in on Rebecca. Todd stood just out of range. He gave Velvet a huge grin and a wave and then returned his attention to his job.

Rebecca was sitting on a porch chair, pretending to read a book. She looked up as though she heard a sound. Her eyes widened and her mouth fell open. She jumped to her feet, gasping and clutching her hands to her chest. The book fell to the ground. The camera moved back, and Rebecca took a step forward. Her eyelashes fluttered, she gasped again, and said, her voice breaking with emotion, "You've come."

Todd stepped into camera range. "I've come," he announced in that deep, rolling voice, the patrician accent the pride of many a voice coach.

"Cut!" Gary shouted. He stood up and hurried across the lawn toward the actors. He leaned into Rebecca's face and screamed, "That has got to be the worst piece of amateur dramatics I've seen since my son's first grade Christmas pageant."

All the color drained out of the actress's lovely face. "I . . . I . . ."

"No," Gary screamed, "I'm wrong. It's the worst piece of acting I've ever seen."

Todd slipped out of range.

"I did it like I rehearsed for Mr. Theropodous," Rebecca said.

"Oh dear," Gloria said softly.

"She is rather . . . stiff," Olivia said.

"Yelling at her like that," I said, "is not going to help."

"I'm sure the camera loves her," Judy said.

Rebecca was beautiful, but she looked nothing at all—to me anyway—like a factory worker with a name like Esmerelda Sanchez. I glanced at Lucinda, laying out sandwiches and flirting lightly with one of the crew who'd decided to get a head start on lunch. With her perfect olive skin, dark eyes, long black hair, and lush figure, Lucinda would have suited the part better than the skinny, blond Rebecca, who'd have been better cast in a California surfing movie.

Everyone said Elias had been a perfectionist. Why would he have cast the unsuitable Rebecca for this part?

Gary continued shouting. "Don't you cry. Don't you dare cry. I have no time to waste while you have your makeup fixed."

Gloria got to her feet and marched onto the set. "Will you be quiet, Gary. You are not helping." She put her arms around Rebecca, who was fighting to hold back the tears. "There, there, dear. Never mind him. Some men need to overcompensate when they step into another man's position. It's difficult filming in this heat, but there's a nice breeze today, and that helps, doesn't it? Can someone bring us a glass of water, please?"

Gary looked like he was about to argue, but Mary-Alice, who'd moved to stand next to him, caught his eye. He grumbled and stalked back to his chair.

I ran for the catering table, grabbed a jug of water, poured a glassful, and took it to Rebecca. She accepted it in shaking hands and drank deeply.

"Thank you," she mumbled.

"Take your time," Mary-Alice said. "We'll try again when you're ready. Gary's not the same director Elias was, and he prefers understated to overly dramatic. Do you understand?"

"Yes," Rebecca mumbled. She handed me the empty glass with a shy smile. I carried it back to the table, and Gloria followed me. I hadn't seen Matthew and Freemont arrive, but they were now studying the lunch offerings.

"What's going on?" Matthew said. "Don't tell me Gary's having histrionics already."

"He doesn't care for Rebecca's acting style," Gloria said. "A better actor would be able to help her, but not Todd. He's a hack. Did you know Elias was considering replacing him?"

"Where'd you hear that?" Freemont said. "Mr. T. figured Mr. Thompson was perfect for the part. He was excited to get him."

"Doesn't matter if he was or not," Matthew said. "Too late now to replace anyone. This picture is going to be a mess."

"Places, everyone," Gary yelled. "And we'll give it one more try."

Velvet and I stayed for an hour, watching the filming as well as helping Lucinda and the Haggerman's staff serve the starving moviemakers.

"Good thing you told me to make a lot," Lucinda said. "I thought our customers at the diner were big eaters."

"Can't beat free food," Velvet said, helping herself to a ham sandwich and putting it on a plate next to a scoop of Jell-O salad packed full of canned fruit. "You did a great job with no notice."

"Tony helped out," Lucinda said, referring to her fiancé. "He's no cook, but even he can put together a sandwich, if I tell him what to use. He did that while Mom and I made the cakes and cookies. He and I packed everything up and then cleaned the kitchen so Mom could go home and get some sleep. The diner was busier than normal yesterday, what with all those reporters in town for the mayor's press conference, and I'm worried how Mom's going to manage today, but the money was too much to resist. As my dad always said, Catskills people have all winter to sleep."

Gloria and Rebecca didn't line up at the trestle tables for lunch. Instead, they walked down to the lake and sat close together on a dilapidated bench while gaping holiday families kept a respectful distance. Mary-Alice joined them a short time later, bringing a bottle of Coke for each of the women. Todd wolfed down a handful of sandwiches and, accompanied by a director's assistant and a security guard, waded into the crowd of onlookers to talk to kids, smile at squealing teenage girls, and sign autographs.

Velvet and I needed to get back to work, but this movie business was just so interesting.

Lunch break over, Gary called everyone into position.

After the berating from the director, Rebecca managed to pull herself together. Her acting still seemed overly dramatic to me, but she did less of the wide eyes and theatrical chest clutching.

They did three more takes, and then Gary said it would do, "probably." Rebecca fled into the trailer that served as her dressing room.

"We'd better go," I said to Velvet. "We both have work to get back to."

"Sadly, yes."

"I'll tell Olivia she'll have to find a ride home if she wants to stay longer."

While crew hands adjusted the porch furniture to make it look as though the next scene was in a different location, Olivia, Gloria, and Judy chatted. They were joined by Nancy Littlejohn, dressed and made up and ready to step in front of the camera.

"We're leaving," I said to Olivia.

"I'm going to stay a while longer," she said. "I'll make my own way home. How did you ladies get here?"

"We called a cab," Judy said. "I'm sure we can get one when we're ready to leave. There must be a telephone around here somewhere. Do you see anything resembling an office in this horrible place, Gloria?"

"Gary will make arrangements for us."

"I'll see you back at Haggerman's later, then," I said to my mother.

"What's going to happen in this scene?" Velvet asked Nancy. "Are you in it?"

"I am. This is my major scene in the entire movie. I play Rebecca's boss at the factory, and I've come to the Catskills to try to convince the young woman to forget about her"— she made quotation marks in the air—"'true love,' as he can't be trusted to do the right thing by her. When I don't convince her, I confront Todd, and that's what we're going to shoot next."

"So dramatic," Velvet said with a delighted shiver.

Nancy snorted. "If it was up to me, I'd rewrite the script."

"In what way?" I asked.

"I'd tell the fool of a girl to take him for all he's worth. He wants to set her up in a fancy apartment in Manhattan, let him. Make herself comfortable, enjoy the good times, start building a nice nest egg for herself out of the trinkets he buys for her. Play the field while he's off trying to be a hero."

"Sounds okay to me," Judy said.

"Good thing," Gloria said, "you're not writing the script, then, isn't it, Nancy?"

"Come on, Gloria," Nancy said with a laugh, "you and I've both been around the block a few times. Love and romance is fine and good, but as long as it's a man's world I say we women need to take them for all we can. And we know there's only one way to do that. You agree with me, don't you, Olivia?"

Olivia raised one sculpted eyebrow as only she could. "My daughter and I believe in making our own way in our world."

I refrained from saying, *Are you kidding?* Olivia had been married three times. Her third husband had stolen all her money. She'd only been saved from penury by the unexpected death of a male admirer.

Olivia turned to me with a smile. "Elizabeth, at any rate, is making her own way." She actually looked proud of me, and I felt an unexpected tightness in my chest. My mother and I had never been close, physically or emotionally. Maybe now, in this place so strange to both of us, we could start making up for some of what we'd missed.

Velvet touched my arm. "We both are."

"On that note," I said. "We're off to make our own ways in the world. Bye, all."

"Where's Todd?" Gary bellowed. "I haven't got all day here!"

As Velvet and I walked away from the set, I said, "Matthew told me we'll be needed again tomorrow. Let me make sure that's okay with Lucinda."

All the sandwiches and salads, pies and cakes had been scooped up, and not many cookies were left. My gardener's assistant, Francis, stood to attention behind the table, feet apart, hands clasped behind his back, looking straight ahead as though he were back in the army, ready to pour drinks for anyone who wanted one.

"Good job, Francis," I called, and he gave me a huge smile in return. "Where's Lucinda?"

"C-ch-checking the truck." He fought to control his stammer.

"You go ahead," I said to Velvet. "I'll meet you at the car after I check in with Lucinda."

Velvet gave me a wave and trotted off, and I headed for the truck.

"You could be in the movies, you know," Todd was saying as I came in earshot.

"Not the life for me," Lucinda replied.

I stopped walking.

"You've got the looks. That's all that matters. I can introduce you to a few people, take you around."

"I'm engaged," she said.

"I don't—"

"Everything okay here?" I stepped around the truck.

Lucinda's back was pressed up against the open door.

Todd stood close to her. Too close, I thought, smiling into her face. At the sound of my voice he took a step back. Lucinda threw me a grateful smile. "Elizabeth. We're fine. What's up?"

"I'm leaving. I wanted to check that we're okay to do the same tomorrow. Todd, Gary's calling for you, and he doesn't sound happy about it."

"Gary's never happy. Think about what I said," he said to Lucinda. He looked at me but didn't give me that famous smile before he walked away.

"You okay?" I asked Lucinda.

She laughed. "Perfectly fine. Guys like that come into the diner all the time. Maybe not quite so handsome, and definitely not so famous, but the same. They think they're God's gift to women. I can handle them, even him. It's all just a game to them. I could tell his heart wasn't in it."

"Fun and games until someone gets hurt or their life's ruined," I said.

She touched the small engagement ring on her left hand. The happiness on her face made her look so very beautiful. "I'm well grounded, Elizabeth. By my mom, by Tony. By the Catskills. I'm loved for myself, just the way I am, and I know that."

Chapter 18

"THAT WAS SO MUCH FUN, WASN'T IT?" VELVET SAID AS WE drove back to Haggerman's.

I didn't know about fun, but it was interesting watching the movie being made. Although I didn't like the way Gary bullied Rebecca, and I said so.

"It's not bullying. It's about trying to get the best performance out of her that he can."

"She did better after a quiet chat with Gloria and Mary-Alice than after Gary yelling at her."

"I suppose you're right."

"What do you think of Todd?"

I took a deep breath. Now was the time. Time for me to tell her precisely what I thought of Todd. I had to be honest, even though she might never speak to me again. The best of way of being honest, I realized, was to tell her about my own experience. The words came out in a rush, as I kept my eyes firmly on the road ahead. "I'm sorry Ron Grady died,

I truly am. I'm sorry for his sake and for his mother's, but not for mine."

Velvet twisted in her seat. "What are you saying, Elizabeth?"

"I never told you—I was too ashamed, I guess—but things were never good between us. Not after the first rush of what I can only call infatuation. Infatuation on my part and, I now understand, a need to have someone to control on his. He wasn't a good man. I didn't give myself long enough to come to understand that."

"He was going to war."

"Yes. And I should have waited until he came back. But everyone else was rushing into marriage, and I got swept up in the drama of it all. Ron was . . . not a nice man, Velvet, and once that ring was on my finger he didn't pretend to be anymore. All I'm saying is, if I'd waited a bit longer I would have come to realize that." I fought back the tears as I remembered smashed furniture and broken china, the smell of cheap booze and even cheaper perfume on him, the insults and the threats, and my wages gone missing from my pocketbook.

Velvet touched my arm as I put my foot on the brake to slow as the turnoff to Haggerman's approached. "Elizabeth. I'm so sorry, I never knew. You have nothing to be ashamed of, but maybe I do. That I didn't realize what you were going through. I guess, when I think about it, Ron was just so charming and handsome, even I was caught up by it. I thought you were so lucky. I'm glad you told me, I am, but I don't understand why you've brought it up now. If this is about Todd—"

She didn't get any further. I made the turn, and a hotel security guard waved me down. I pulled to a stop, and he stuck his head in the open window. "Afternoon, Miz Grady. I figured you'd want to know that those newspaper folks have been back. I sent them off with a flea in their ear, but I don't trust them not to try to get in the back way."

"Did they say what they wanted? Were there any new developments today?"

"State police came by earlier for the second time today. Left about an hour or so ago. The newspaper people showed up not long after that."

"Were the police alone when they left?" I was asking if they'd arrested anyone—like Luke and Nick Timmins.

"Just them."

"Thank you." I threw the car into gear, and we drove up the hill. "Pests," I said. "I bet the state police said something to a reporter that had them all scurrying out from under their rocks and rushing back here."

"If it does turn out that the mob sent someone to kill Elias," Velvet said, "maybe you can find out who that person is and hire him to knock off a few reporters."

"Don't tempt me," I said.

We reached the top of the hill. The big welcoming hotel, sparking white in the sun, spread out in front of us, the emerald lawn, the colorful flower beds, the cool clear lake dotted with canoes and paddleboats, people on the beach relaxing in the sun or resting in the shade of colorful umbrellas, the green hills rising in the distance.

"You know," Velvet said. "This is a nice place to work. We work hard, you in particular, but not as hard as women in a noisy factory or a crowded office in the city, and at the end of the day we can grab some time to appreciate being in this lovely place."

"That's surprisingly deep, coming from you," I said.

She laughed her bright, infectious laugh and punched me on the arm. "Come on, Elizabeth. Admit I'm right. You can't always be the dark serious one."

"You're right."

The moment for me to tell her what I knew about Todd had passed, but I hoped she'd understood what I'd tried to say.

* * *

BUT I WAS THE DARK SERIOUS ONE, AND TRY AS I MIGHT, I couldn't put my mind to much more than the death of Elias Theropodous, and what—or most important, who—brought that about. I phoned the *New York Times* and left a message for Jim Westenham to contact me, and then I called the police station to be told Chief Dawson was not in. Neither of them returned my call.

I had more luck at Kennelwood, and Richard came to the phone. The fire damage, he told me, was being cleaned up, and they should be able to return to full service tomorrow. "Thank you for stepping in at the last minute, Elizabeth."

"Don't thank me, thank Lucinda and Mrs. McGreevy."

"I'll leave word at the concierge desk to tell anyone who's looking for a recommendation of where to eat in town to try the Red Spot."

"That would be good of you. I'm calling for another reason."

"To say you'll have dinner with me tomorrow night?"

"What? Oh, gosh, did you—"

"No, I didn't ask you. But I'm asking now. Let's go into town. I'll make a reservation at someplace nice."

I didn't want to get into a relationship. Not with Richard Kennelwood, not with anyone. I had no time for frivolities; I needed to concentrate on running the hotel. But, I said to myself, he wasn't asking me to marry him, just to have a nice dinner. Even I should be allowed a night out now and again. I answered before I could change my mind.

"I'd like that."

"I'll pick you up at seven tomorrow, then."

"Seven it is." I hung up. Then I realized I'd forgotten to ask what I'd called to ask him and had to phone him back. But he had no news about the progress of the police investigation into Elias's murder. "As far as I know, no one from the Summervale police or the state police were here today, and if there was any news I haven't had the radio on. I did hear that the autopsy said he'd drunk whatever . . . made him sick, not much more than a couple of hours before he died. So that takes Kennelwood out of the picture."

"And places Haggerman's firmly in it. Thanks, Richard."

"Until tomorrow," he said.

I was chewing on my pencil, gazing out the window, when Rosemary knocked on my office door. "Elizabeth?"

"Sorry. Come on in. What time is it?"

"It's a few minutes before six. I'm on my way to the cocktail party, but something's happened you need to know about."

"What?"

"One of the waiters told me a guest said he'd been approached by a woman when he was walking in the woods. She asked him if he felt safe here."

"What on earth!" I threw down my pencil.

"Yup. The waiter was coming on shift, and the man stopped him on the path. He's quite elderly, and he was upset by the encounter. The waiter thought I'd want to know. Which I do. And I thought you'd want to know."

"Which I do. Could the guest describe the woman?"

"Tall, thin, dressed in what he called city clothes."

Jane Donaldson, almost certainly. "The guard at the gate told me the newspaper people had come back earlier, and he chased them off."

"Plenty of ways to get onto the property on foot," Rosemary said. "We're not exactly walled off in here."

"When did this happen?"

"Not much more than fifteen minutes ago."

I stood up. "Did the guest say where?"

"Near the end of the path by the service dock and boat sheds."

I stormed out of my office. The state police had been

here earlier, talking to the kitchen and waitstaff. They must have then blabbed to the ladies and gentlemen of the press, and once again the blasted reporters were trying to stir up trouble by implying that Haggerman's food was deadly.

If I caught that Jane Donaldson on my property, I'd give her deadly.

Not many people were in the lake or the pool, and grounds staff were washing down tables, bringing in the cushions, and rearranging the lounge chairs. A game of chess was underway by the tennis courts. Well-dressed couples walked up the path from the cabins, heading for the cocktail party or predinner drinks on the veranda. A harried hotel nanny passed me, herding four children in front of her. She might as well have been trying to herd Winston to the cabin he shares with Aunt Tatiana, by all the success she was having.

I reached the end of the public path and carried on through the trees. It hadn't rained for several days, and the level of the creek was low. I skipped lightly across the line of rocks in the water and made it to the other side without incident. Outdoor-recreation staff were bringing paddleboats in, and others getting rowboats ready for evening fishing expeditions. I called to a young man laden with life jackets.

"Evening, Mrs. Grady."

"Good evening. I'm looking for a woman I've been told is hanging about. She's quite tall, taller than me." I lifted my arm to indicate. "And very thin. Early thirties. Dressed in a city suit."

"Yeah. I saw someone like that. Maybe ten, twenty minutes ago. Harry spoke to her. Harry! Got a minute? Mrs. Grady's looking for someone."

Harry, seventy if he was a day, lumbered over. He wore a cloth cap and touched the brim respectfully. Once again I described Jane Donaldson.

"Yeah, I spoke to her," he said. "Told her this area's off-limits to guests, and the sign says so. Couldn't she read?"

I didn't bother to say he could have been a bit more polite if he'd thought she was a guest. "Did she leave?"

He shrugged. "She walked away. I didn't pay her no more mind."

"Thanks. If you see this person again, call security immediately. Tell the others the same. She is not a guest and she is not welcome here."

Two sets of eyebrows rose.

I turned and headed back. I was about to step over the creek when the woman in question popped out from behind a tree. "Looking for me, Elizabeth?"

"As it happens, I am. This is private property, and you've been asked to leave."

Jane had twigs stuck in her hair, mud on her shoes, a run in her stocking, sweat stains on her blouse, and a thin trail of drying blood dripping down her right cheek. A mosquito landed on her hand and she swatted furiously at it. "I hate the wilderness."

"This isn't exactly the wilderness, but there's an easy solution to your problem. Leave."

"I would, gladly, but I'm in pursuit of an important story. The people have a right to know."

"The people have a right not be bothered while they're enjoying their vacation."

"You won't give me an interview. No one on your staff will talk to me. I must say, Elizabeth, you've put the fear of God into them. I couldn't even get anyone to talk to me off the record."

"Glad to hear it."

"I have to get the facts somewhere."

"Don't give me that nonsense. You're not looking for facts. You're looking for muck, and the deeper you can spread it the better."

"You've been quick enough to talk to the *New York Times*."

"The *New York Times* is a respectable newspaper."

Jane showed me her teeth. "Unlike the paper owned by Brian Klockenham. *Uncle Bry.* Your little blond friend's quick, I'll give her that. It's not easy to catch me off guard."

In the woods dead leaves rustled and a twig broke under an animal's weight. Jane shrieked and swung around, her face a picture of abject terror. I laughed out loud as Winston burst out of the trees, ears up, stubby tail wagging, tongue lolling.

The reporter growled at him as Winston sniffed her shoes. "I hate dogs."

"Why is that not a surprise? If you don't go now, I'll have you thrown off the property."

"Don't bother. I'm ready to leave. Never mind your terrorized staff, your guests are surprisingly loyal. Did you know that? One old lady threatened to bash me over the head with her cane. I might sue."

"You do that." I stood my ground, waiting.

She forced out a smile. "Help me out here, Elizabeth. Someone killed Elias Theropodous. He was poisoned here, at your hotel, and the state police say so. It's to your advantage if I present your hotel in a favorable light."

"No one, least of all the police, is claiming that anyone associated with Haggerman's killed him or that our kitchen is anything less than perfectly sanitary and all our drinks and meals prepared to the highest of standards. As well as being delicious and nutritious. Mr. Theropodous was targeted by someone from outside. Regardless of what unfortunate events befell him, it had nothing to do with us."

Bored, Winston wandered away, nose snuffling along the ground.

"Whatever." Jane moved as though to turn and walk away, but then she abruptly spun around and lunged for me. I squealed, threw up my hands, and leapt back, landing with both feet in the cold waters of the creek. I slipped on a wet rock, and my arms windmilled in an attempt to keep me upright. I managed to save myself and didn't fall, bottom first, into the creek. Winston returned, barking furiously.

Jane laughed. "You shouldn't be so jumpy, Lizzie. I'm going, but I'll be back if there are any more developments. Count on it." She disappeared into the woods, hopefully going to wherever she'd left her car. Winston made as though to follow her, but I called to him, and for once he did as he'd been told. I heard the woman's heavy footsteps, accompanied by the snapping of branches and her constant griping, for a long time.

When all was quiet again, I looked down. Water was washing over the top of my shoes, and my stockings were soaked.

I didn't have a spare pair of pumps in Velvet's room. I intended to go to the hotel to check in at the kitchen and then show my face in the lobby and on the veranda as people gathered before dinner. If Jane had bothered any more of our guests, or if anyone had concerns about the reporter sneaking around in the bushes, I needed to be nearby to hear them and reassure my guests I had everything under control.

Grumbling, I headed to the house I share with Olivia while Winston ran on ahead. Olivia had told me earlier Gloria was planning to join Gary, Matthew, and some of the other cast and crew at Kennelwood for a casual dinner after looking over the footage they'd taken the last few days. They'd then decide what steps needed to be taken before they packed up their equipment and left the Catskills.

I climbed the steps to the porch and opened the screen door. The inner door was open to let in the air, and Winston ran ahead of me.

"Only me," I called. "I have to change my—" I froze, the sentence dying in my throat.

My mother lay on the carpet next to the dining room table, facedown, arms outstretched. A dinner plate was on the table, next to an unfinished glass of wine and her book. A shattered water glass lay on the floor next to her.

I screamed and ran toward her. I dropped to my knees while Winston tried to lick the side of her face. "Olivia!" I shoved the dog aside and turned my mother over. Her eyes were closed and she did not move.

Chapter 19

"I NEED AN AMBULANCE. I NEED A DOCTOR. I NEED . . . help!" I screamed into the phone.

"Calling the ambulance service now, Mrs. Grady," the switchboard operator said, her voice perfectly calm. "Dr. Fife is staying at the hotel. I'll have him paged."

"Hurry. Please tell them to hurry."

I threw the receiver onto the cradle and ran back to my mother. Her eyelashes fluttered, and I was so relieved I burst into tears. "It's okay. I'm here. It's going to be okay."

Winston whined and pushed his muzzle into her side, telling her to get up. Her chest rose and fell, slowly but at least it was moving. "Elizabeth." The gigantic dark eyes flicked open, and I could read the fear in them. Winston licked her face. I grabbed the dog by his collar, dragged him into my room, and slammed the door on his protests.

I dropped to my knees next to Olivia and cradled her hand in mine. "I'm here, Mom. I'm here."

It was probably only a few minutes, but it felt like hours

until Winston's steady whine turned to a bark, and I heard pounding footsteps hitting the steps and the creak of the porch floorboards.

Velvet and Randy ran into the house. They hadn't yet dressed for this evening's dancing and were in their casual clothes. Velvet wrapped her arms around me and guided me to my feet, while Randy took my place. "It's okay," Velvet said. "Dr. Fife's gone to his room for his bag and a bellhop's with him to bring him here. The funeral home's sending their ambulance."

"Miss Peters," Randy said. "Lie still. Help's on the way."

"I . . . I . . . ," she said.

"Whoa!" Randy yelled. I pulled myself away from Velvet in time to see Randy scrambling backward and my mother rolling onto her side and vomiting onto the carpet.

"It's okay." Randy's voice was steady and calm. "It's going to be okay, Miss Peters. You lie still and let us take care of everything. That's good," he called over his shoulder to me, "that she's been sick. Get it all up."

Olivia moaned and fell back again. Her face was pale, her eyes dark pools in a stark white face, her lips colorless.

More footsteps and the screen door crashed open again. The doctor who'd helped me with Elias on Monday night ran in, carrying his black medical bag. My aunt Tatiana was right behind him. A bellhop hovered in the doorway.

Randy got up to let the doctor work.

"Lie still, Miss Peters," Dr. Fife said. "You're going to be perfectly fine. We'll get you to the hospital and have you checked out just to be safe."

Velvet led me to the couch and pushed me down. Aunt Tatiana stood behind the doctor, wringing her hands. "What is it, Doctor? What's the matter?"

"Was she conscious when you found her?" he called over his shoulder to me.

"No. yes. Maybe. I turned her over, but she didn't move,

so I ran for the phone. When I got back her eyes were open and she was breathing."

He pulled Olivia's eyelids up and peered into her eyes and then he felt behind her ears. "Some color's returning, and that's good. This"—he indicated the mess on the floor—"when did this happen?"

"A minute or two before you got here," Randy said.

"She brought it up and then immediately started getting better?"

"Yeah. Looks like it."

"I suggest you call the police, Mrs. Grady," the doctor said. "The last time I saw this, it was as we were about to take Mr. Theropodous to the hospital."

Y

"SORRY ABOUT THE BUSMAN'S HOLIDAY," I SAID TO THE doctor.

He gave me a warm smile. "I've never been one for relaxing on vacation. To my wife's continual despair. As I'm not needed here anymore, I'll be off."

"Thank you."

"I'll be available if the police need to talk to me," Dr. Fife said.

Olivia had brought up the remainder of the contents of her stomach as she was being loaded onto the stretcher to be taken to the ambulance, and the doctor had been hopeful that was the last of it.

Whatever it was.

Randy had called Dave Dawson, and the chief had been waiting at the hospital when Velvet, Aunt Tatiana, and I arrived. After Olivia had been checked out and admitted, Dr. Higgins and the chief of police huddled together, talking in low voices for a long time.

Chief Dawson dropped into the badly sprung chair across from the badly sprung couch where Velvet, Tatiana, and I huddled together. "You can go up to the ward and see

Miss Peters shortly. The doctor assures me she's going to be fine, but she needs rest and watching over tonight."

Aunt Tatiana muttered in Russian.

"Looks as though something she ate made her sick," Dave said. "Does Miss Peters prepare her own meals in your house?"

I shook my head firmly. "Never. We make tea and coffee, maybe toast now and again, but neither of us cook. My mother never learned, and although I like to cook, I simply don't have the time these days. We always have our meals brought up from the hotel kitchen. A room-service tray was on the dining room table and the remains of her dinner on room-service plates. I saw an unfinished glass of wine, but that most likely came out of our cupboard."

"I'll send one of my officers to collect them."

"Before you continue with this line of questioning," I said. "I called the hotel after we got here and they say that, once again, not one other person has shown any signs of illness, not even the slightest."

"Once again," Velvet repeated. "You think this has something to do with Elias Theropodous?"

"It has to," I said. "The coincidence is too much."

"Elias took sick hours after he ate," Velvet said. "Olivia didn't even finish her dinner."

I looked at Chief Dawson. He gave me a slight nod, telling me to continue.

"First, we don't know exactly when Elias was given the poison. *Up to* a couple of hours, the autopsy said. It might have been sooner than that. Second, Olivia is a very slow eater, as you know. Her book was on the table next to her plate. If she'd been reading over her meal she might have been there for some time."

"Dosage matters," the chief said. "As does the size of the person ingesting it. If Miss Peters, who's substantially smaller than Mr. Theropodous, had received a larger dose, it might have taken effect quicker. Ironically, the stronger dose might have saved her life. Her stomach rebelled instantly."

"That and the fact that Elizabeth found her when she did," Velvet said.

I shuddered. If Jane Donaldson hadn't startled me into stepping into the creek, I wouldn't have gone home for dry shoes. Olivia might have been okay if I hadn't discovered her, but that was by no means certain. I wouldn't thank Jane for saving my mother's life, but I'd think it.

"I see no reason this should get into the press," Dave said. "A woman took ill and was admitted to the hospital. It's a private matter."

"Thank you," I said.

"As long as no one else at Haggerman's shows up at this hospital tonight, that is. I'll have the contents of your mother's plate and glass analyzed, but that'll take a few days."

A nurse, a picture of efficiency in her crisp white cap and dress with a watch pinned to the shoulder, wide black belt, white stockings, and heavy white shoes, came into the waiting room. "Miss Peters is settled in her room. She can have visitors, but only for a couple of minutes and only her daughter and Chief Dawson. Doctor's orders."

"I am sister!" Tatiana rose to her feet. My mother and her sister had been born and educated in America but when she was stressed, which wasn't often, Tatiana fell into her own mother's speech patterns.

"Doctor's orders," the nurse repeated. Her look was so severe, her tone so firm, even Aunt Tatiana was intimidated. She resumed her seat.

"We'll wait here," Velvet said.

Chief Dawson and I found my mother propped up in bed, dressed in a tattered, many-times-washed, yellowing hospital gown, clutching the bedcovers. She was fully conscious, although frighteningly pale and shaky. Her face had been scrubbed clean and her hair tied back into a rough bun. She gave me a weak smile, and I took her hand in mine. It felt so thin, so fragile.

"How are you feeling?"

"Sick. Dreadful. The doctor assures me I'll be better tomorrow."

"Can you tell me what happened this evening, Miss Peters?" Dave said.

"I scarcely know."

"The doctor believes you ate something that . . . disagreed with you."

Her eyes opened wide. "You think . . . poison?"

"It's a possibility," I said. "What did you have for dinner?"

"The broccoli soup followed by a ham and cheese sandwich and a salad. Nothing special. It came from the kitchen. I had a glass of wine with it, but I poured the wine from a bottle I opened myself."

"Who brought the tray to you?" I asked.

"I don't know."

"You don't know? Can you describe him?"

"That's the point, Elizabeth. I didn't see who brought it."

That took me aback. "How is that possible?"

"What are you saying?" Dave asked. "Tell me how it works."

"I phone the kitchen some time over the afternoon and let them know if I'm eating in, if Elizabeth or anyone else will be joining me, and what I would like," Olivia said. "I instruct them as to what time to bring it."

"Do they prepare your food individually or as part of the regular hotel menu?"

"I never ask for anything special, unless I'm entertaining, which was not the case today. The kitchen tells me what's available and I order. A room-service waiter or a busboy brings a tray to the house at the desired time."

"But you didn't see who brought it tonight," I said.

Olivia leaned back against her pillows. She closed her eyes.

"You need to think," I said. "This could be important."

"I am thinking," she said. "If you will only stop talking."

Dave suppressed a chuckle.

"Gloria, Judy, and I returned from the film shoot around three. Gloria and I came directly to the house. Judy said she was going to her room for a nap, as she has a performance tonight. I made Gloria and me a cup of tea, and she went to her room to write letters. She was planning to go to Kennelwood later, to see the rushes and have dinner there, so I called the kitchen to arrange to have something sent to me. I had not had anything for lunch, so I asked them to bring my dinner early, at five. Thus I had a sandwich, as the main courses would not be ready yet. I then went for a nap of my own." Her voice trailed off.

"And . . . ," I prompted.

She opened her eyes. "I woke around four thirty, had a bath, and refreshed my appearance, because I'd decided to go to the ballroom later to hear Judy, as it's her last night with us. At five thirty, I realized my dinner had not arrived, although I'd requested it for five. I phoned the kitchen, and they assured me it had been sent. I checked the porch, and a room-service tray was on the table. I hadn't heard the waiter arrive."

Dave and I exchanged glances. My mother's food had been left on the porch for as long as half an hour.

"I need to talk to whoever brought it," I said. "They aren't supposed to leave food sitting outside, for heaven's sake. The porch at our house isn't enclosed, and a cloche won't keep out an inquisitive, not to mention hungry, raccoon. It won't even keep out Winston."

"Winston?" Dave asked.

"My aunt Tatiana's dog." I turned back to my mother. "Olivia, do you know—?"

She was asleep, snoring softly.

I brushed my lips against the paper-thin, almost translucent skin of her cheek, and Dave and I left the room.

"She had a salad with her supper," I said when we were outside in the corridor. "I haven't forgotten that my salad-man is Elias Theropodous's brother. Did you find anything out about that?"

"The staties talked to him. He admits that he and Elias met on Saturday morning, as you told me. The old resentments boiled over almost instantly, and they started arguing. Nick stormed out of the diner, and he claims not to have seen or spoken to his brother since. He says he heard at the same time as everyone else in the hotel that Elias had died, and he was sorry they hadn't reconciled but, according to him, that was Elias's fault. Not his."

"Did they ask him if he paid someone to kill his brother?"

"Not in so many words. I'll keep my eye on him, but I can't do much more than that."

"I asked Luke, the waiter, about the car. Turns out it's not his; he's using it while his friend's away. All that means is he didn't buy a car, not that he might not have been paid off by Nick Timmins, or someone else."

"Luke was interviewed extensively after Elias's death, and he claims to have observed nothing untoward at the dinner, or later in the ballroom. I specifically asked if he'd seen anyone potentially interfering with Elias's food or drink and he said no. I asked him if he himself had added anything, even accidentally, and again he said no. I know what you're thinking, Elizabeth, but there's no indication, so far, that Nick Timmins wanted to kill his brother, or that your waiter helped him do it."

WHEN DAVE AND I RETURNED TO THE WAITING ROOM, WE found not only Aunt Tatiana and Velvet but Mary-Alice Renzetti and Richard Kennelwood also.

Richard leapt to his feet when we came in. "How is she?"

"She's sleeping now. She'll be fine," I said. "Thank you for coming. How did you hear?"

"I called him," Velvet said. "Gloria needs to know Olivia's in the hospital, so she doesn't worry when she gets back from Kennelwood and sees the state we left your house in and Olivia gone."

"Thanks," I said to her.

"Matthew asked me to come on his behalf," Mary-Alice said. "I was happy to do so."

"Where's Gloria?" I asked.

"Freemont drove us, and we dropped her at your hotel on the way here," Mary-Alice said. "We'd finished viewing the rushes when Richard found us to deliver the news, so Gloria decided to head back without having dinner. We—I mean Gary isn't happy with the scene between Roger and Todd that was filmed at Haggerman's on Monday morning, so he wants to go back tomorrow and redo it. I hope that's okay?"

"Elizabeth and Lucinda have arranged to cater at the bungalow colony tomorrow," Velvet said.

"It'll work. We need the early-morning light for the scene on the dock with Todd and Roger, and then we can head over to the bungalow colony for the rest of the day."

"Whatever you need," I said.

"I'm sorry," Mary-Alice said. "I'm sure you don't want to talk about moviemaking troubles right now."

"Elizabeth?" Velvet said. "What do you want to do?"

"I need to get back to the hotel. There's no point in me staying here. They've given Olivia something so she'll sleep the night through." I became aware of Dave, standing slightly outside our circle, watching and listening. "Chief, do you need me any more tonight?"

"No. You go home. I want to have another word with the doctor and then go to Haggerman's to talk to this room-service waiter."

"What room-service waiter?" Velvet asked.

He didn't answer.

"Where are the state police?" I asked him.

"They went out for dinner. I haven't seen them since. They don't seem to be all that good at checking in with the station."

"I'll drive you," Richard said to me. "Or rather, Freemont will drive you."

"We came in my car," I said.

"You go with Richard," Velvet said. "I'll bring your car back, and Tatiana can come with me."

🍸

NIGHT HAD FALLEN WHILE WE'D BEEN AT THE HOSPITAL. Freemont steered the powerful car down the dark roads. Richard was in the front passenger seat, and I sat in the back with Mary-Alice.

As we'd separated in the hospital parking lot, Velvet and Aunt Tatiana had wrapped me in enormous hugs. "You must be exhausted, *lastachka*," my aunt said. "You get some sleep. All will be well tomorrow."

I was not exhausted. Not in the least. Instead, I was energized. I had not the slightest doubt someone had attempted to kill my mother, and I wasn't going to rest until I found out who that was.

I hadn't been expected to drop into the house in the late afternoon. It was only by chance that I needed to change my shoes. *If I hadn't found her . . .* It didn't bear thinking about.

I thought about it. Perhaps the dose hadn't been intended to kill Olivia. She did bring most of it up almost right away. Did the person who gave it to her know that would happen?

I couldn't think of any reason someone would want to kill Olivia or even make her sick. She'd told me stories over the years of the lengths to which dancers in competition for an important role could go. Up to and including putting something in a rival's food so she couldn't make it through the audition.

But Olivia wasn't competing with anyone for anything these days.

Elias Theropodous had been poisoned at Haggerman's Catskills Resort. A few days later, the hotel owner had suffered the same fate, although fortunately not fatal in her case. The two instances had to be related, but Olivia and Elias had nothing at all in common other than a handful of previous acquaintances. Nothing I knew about, at any rate. Elias's killer might have wanted to get rid of Olivia if she knew what had happened to Elias, but she hadn't been asking questions about that, or even speculating. As far as I knew. Olivia would have confided in me if she'd come to any conclusions.

Richard and Freemont talked in low voices, mainly about cars. Mary-Alice stared out into the passing night. I thought.

Olivia hadn't been asking questions about the death of Elias. I had.

If my mother had died, all my focus would be on my grief and on how I was going to be able to keep the hotel running. Even if she hadn't died but had taken seriously ill, I would have been spending all my spare time at the hospital.

I'd been asking questions about Elias's death, because I needed to save the reputation of my resort. I needed to get the police and pesky journalists off my property and away from my guests.

I tried to think who I'd asked questions of and if anyone had seemed particularly annoyed at my interference. I tried to remember everything I'd observed among the movie people. I turned to Mary-Alice. "You were the force behind Elias's success, weren't you?"

"What makes you say that?" she said calmly.

"Simple observation. You whispered in Elias's ear when he was giving instructions, and then he changed what he was saying. Gary obviously relies on you for advice, but I suspect it's more that you out-and-out tell him what to do. Gloria knows. She told you she wants changes made to her role. She wouldn't tell the director's secretary that. But most of all, I know because you told me just now. You said 'we' when you mentioned that you weren't satisfied with the rushes, but you quickly backtracked and said Gary wasn't happy."

Richard twisted around in his seat.

"I'm right, aren't I, Mr. Freemont?" I said.

The chauffeur didn't reply.

"Elias," Mary-Alice said, "had been a good director. Once. He had potential, and the studio saw that potential. He could have been a great director but didn't have the focus. He didn't have the drive or the imagination. He fell in love with his own image of what he could be, and he believed what they were saying about him was enough. It wasn't. So he came to rely more and more on me for advice. He and my father had worked closely together for a number of years. My father could have been a truly great director, but he died far too young. He'd talked all his movies over with me, bouncing ideas off me, asking my advice. Taking my advice. When he died, Elias hired me, supposedly to be his secretary, but what he really wanted was for me to tell him what my father would have done. Eventually, I gave Elias far more than advice. I told him what to do. I was, in truth, the director of *Catskill Dreams* and most of his other movies."

"Why didn't you say something?" I asked. "Why not tell the producers what your part had been? Make them recognize your contribution?"

"Really, Elizabeth. I can't believe you're that naive. A woman, even a daughter of Julian Renzetti, directing an Oscar-winning movie? It would destroy their world."

"So you killed him."

She let out a bark of laughter. "You think I killed Elias? Why would I do that? His death isn't going to get me my director's credits. More likely, I'll be tossed out on my ear. I'm just a secretary, remember. The studio has no role for me anymore. Gary's listening to me. Now. That has a lot to do with Gloria's influence, but once we're back in the studio, he'll forget it was me who made his picture and he'll pretend, to himself most of all, he did it all by himself." She settled back in her seat with a sigh. "That's the way it always works. You're thinking whoever killed Elias tried to kill your mother, and I think you're right. But I was nowhere near Haggerman's this afternoon. We filmed at Sparkling Waters until shortly before four, and then I went directly back to Kennelwood. Gary and Matthew met to go over the budget, and I sat in. A few minutes after five, the others joined us to watch the rushes."

It was taking a long time to get to the hotel. I looked out the window and realized we were going in circles. Freemont wanted to give me time to talk to Mary-Alice.

"If not you, then—"

"Then who? I don't know, Elizabeth. I've been thinking about it. We all have. No one liked Elias, and no one is terribly sorry that he died, but every one of us, from Mick the gaffer to Matthew the producer was dependent on Elias staying alive to finish this picture. Once he died, there was no guarantee the studio would continue with Gary."

"What about Gary himself?"

"As I said, no guarantee. Gary's benefited from taking on this picture, sure, but he'll have other chances to make his mark without taking the risk of killing a man. The studio has their eye on him, and with my help he can be a big name. Up to him if he'll want any more of my help, but that's still to come. You're stretching, Elizabeth. None of us killed Elias; we had no reason to. To tell you the truth, some of us had plenty of reasons to, but not here and now. Someone at your hotel killed Elias, and that person poisoned your mother. You've got a nutter either on your staff or as a guest, and you'd better find out who that is before they do it again.

Freemont, are you lost? It's taking an awful long time to get to the hotels."

"Just being careful on the night roads, Miss Renzetti. Plenty of deer around. They jump out sometimes, straight into the path of a car."

I slumped back in my seat. Maybe Mary-Alice was right. Maybe I was trying to find a killer among the movie people so I wouldn't have to admit I had a "nutter" at my hotel.

We'd been lucky this time. There was no reason the papers would pick up on Olivia's condition or make anything out of it. But if another person took ill eating at Haggerman's? And then another?

We'd be driven out of business. "I don't suppose your father was at my place this afternoon," I said to Richard.

He chuckled. "'Fraid not. He's been feeling better the last few days, so he put in a few rounds of golf this afternoon. He came back early, as the heat and exercise took more out of him than he expected. He's hoping to watch some of the filming tomorrow, so he planned to take it easy for the rest of the day today."

"What did you think of it?" Mary-Alice said to me. "The making of a movie is pretty boring in itself. A heck of a lot of standing around."

"It was interesting," I said. "The people are interesting."

"I suppose as a hotelier you're interested in people."

Freemont made a U-turn on a quiet country road and headed toward Haggerman's.

"Not particularly. I'm not even a hotelier. I'm a bookkeeper. I like numbers far more than I like people. If I may say, I don't think Rebecca's right for the part. I thought a character named Esmerelda should have more . . . I don't know . . . passion?"

"Elias and I disagreed about that, and for once he would not back down. He wanted Rebecca Marsden and that was that. I went on to fight other battles."

"You mean casting Todd?"

"Todd? That was no battle. We both wanted Todd from the beginning."

"Gloria said Elias wanted to get rid of Todd."

"She's wrong," Freemont said. "I don't know why Miss Grant keeps telling people that." The big car slowed and pulled into the road to Haggerman's. I asked Freemont to stop while I had a quick word with the security guard.

No sign of any reporters, no police since earlier today, he told me.

"Chief Dawson will be here shortly," I said. "Can you tell him I'll be on the veranda, and I'd like to speak to him as soon as he arrives."

"Yes, ma'am."

"Mary-Alice," I said when the lights of the hotel came into view, "before I go, can you tell me what you remember about where everyone was today? After leaving the bungalow colony, I mean? Please, it might be important. Who came to the rushes meeting, and when?"

"You're barking up the wrong tree here, Elizabeth."

"Humor her," Richard said. "Humor us."

"Okay." Mary-Alice had a director's eye for detail. She described what she knew of who was where and when.

I'd like to say I had a burst of insight, but nothing became any clearer to me.

When Freemont pulled up to the front of the hotel, Richard said, "Take Miss Renzetti to Kennelwood. I'll grab a cab later."

"You don't—" I began.

"I do." He got out of the car. Freemont held open my door, and I did the same.

Richard and I climbed the steps. The sound of Judy Rae's rich voice drifted down from the ballroom above our heads. Elegantly dressed men and women were gathered on the veranda, enjoying a cigarette or sipping cocktails. A card game was underway in a far corner. The night air was hot but thankfully not too dreadfully sticky with humidity and the breeze off the lake blew light and fresh.

I dropped into a chair close to the door.

"Are you okay, Elizabeth?" Richard asked.

"My mother's going to be fine and that's all that matters."

"That and finding out what happened. I assume that's why you're waiting for Dave."

"It is." I started to get to my feet, but Richard put his hand up. "What do you want? I'll get it."

"I have to tell the desk I'm back."

"I'll do that. You sit."

I smiled at him and settled gratefully back down. "Thank you."

No one paid much attention to me. A few people nodded politely as they came and went. They didn't seem overly concerned that a poisoner was running amuck at Haggerman's, and that was definitely a good thing as far as I was concerned.

Richard was soon back, and at that moment a Summervale police car pulled up and parked half on the lawn. People glanced up at the car's arrival, but as Dave was alone and he didn't seem in any sort of hurry, they returned their attention to their own business.

"If you're going to speak to my staff," I said when Dave had joined us, "I need to be there."

"Okay," he said.

I led the way across the lobby, through the door beneath the stairs, and down the long dimly lit corridor toward the kitchen. The business offices were all closed, and the lights switched off. No sound came from the switchboard room. I peeked into the kitchen office as we passed and saw Chef Leonardo working at his order sheets in the dim light of a desk lamp.

Dinner was finished, but preparation of the evening dessert buffet was underway in the kitchen. Nick Timmins was bent over a towering chiffon cake, slathering on rose-colored icing and shouting instructions while his assistants assembled colorful Jell-O molds and a gorgeous baked Alaska, stirred the ingredients for individual bowls of rice pudding, or chopped maraschino cherries for the decorations. The sound of dishes and pots being washed and put away came from the room off the main kitchen area and a dishwasher carried out a stack of small plates and put them on a cart to be taken upstairs for the buffet.

I clapped my hands. "Everyone, please. Listen up." The cacophony of a busy kitchen died. Heads popped around corners and out of alcoves. "Miss Peters's dinner was taken to her at her house at around five this afternoon. I need to speak to the person who delivered it."

The staff exchanged glances. They shrugged. Eyes flicked toward Richard Kennelwood and Dave Dawson standing beside me.

"Does anyone know who that was?" I asked.

Chef Leonardo stepped into the kitchen, still holding his pen. "Speak up!" he bellowed. "Who took Miss Peters her dinner?"

A busboy slowly put up his hand and stepped hesitantly forward. Color flared in his cheeks. "I . . . I . . . did, Mrs. Grady. Is something wrong?" He tried to avoid looking at the chef or the policeman.

"Chief Dawson and I would like to talk to you. Won't take long. Chef Leonardo, can we use your office?"

"No."

"Oh. Uh . . . please?"

Dave didn't wait for an answer. He jerked his head toward the busboy, indicated the office, and said, "In here."

"Now that's over, what do you lot think you're doing?" Nick Timmins roared. "Do we have the night off? Back to work. You, Leon, if you've nothing better to do, check that pan of butter isn't burning."

"Nothing better to do!" the chef yelled back. "You think this hotel will last a day if I don't get my orders in?"

Dave and the busboy went into the kitchen office. Richard and I slipped in behind them, and I shut the door. No one took a seat. The busboy, who was close to fifty, shifted from one foot to the other and twisted his hands together. Dave gave me a slight nod, telling me to go ahead.

"What's your name?" I asked the busboy.

"Al. Al Gerough."

"Al, thank you. This is Chief Dawson and Mr. Kennelwood. Please rest assured, you're not in any trouble. We have a couple of questions, that's all. You took Miss Peters her supper. Who asked you to do that?"

"Miss Sullivan. I don't mean she asked me particular, like, but the regular room-service waiter wasn't around and so she shouted for some help. I wasn't busy 'cause we'd caught up on the dishes, so I said I'd do it."

"Was the meal ready when you got it? I mean served and on the tray?"

He nodded and told me he'd checked the room-service order with instructions as to where the tray was to be taken, and he had done so.

"You didn't see Miss Peters herself?"

"No. Her note said she wasn't to be disturbed and to leave the tray on the porch table."

"Her note?"

"Yup. The note stuck to the door."

"Did you keep this note?" Dave asked.

Al blinked rapidly. "Keep it? No. I threw it in the trash when I got back."

I hated to think of the amount of garbage that would have been generated in this kitchen between five o'clock and now.

"Did you see anyone at Miss Peters's house?" Dave asked.

"Nope."

"Maybe on the path or in the woods nearby?" I said.

"Nope."

Dave gave me a nod, and I said, "Thank you, Al. You can go back to work now. I'd appreciate it if you don't discuss what we talked about with anyone."

"What?"

"She means," Richard said, "that if you tell anyone, anyone at all, including the chef or saladman what we asked you, you'll be fired on the spot."

Al blanched, and then he ducked his head and scurried away.

"That was a mite harsh," I said when the door had closed behind him.

"Although necessary if you don't want everyone speculating what had been in this dinner when word gets around that Olivia's in the hospital. Speculating further, that is."

"It might not," I said. "Get around, I mean. She has little or nothing to do with the staff on a regular basis, and it's not unusual for her not to be seen for a day or two."

"Word always gets around," Richard said. "Trust me."

"Which is beside the point," Dave said. "What do you conclude by what he had to say, Elizabeth?"

"My mother didn't write any such note. That means the food wasn't poisoned in the kitchen, which doesn't bear thinking about, and it wasn't a matter of someone passing and deciding to play a mean joke. It had been planned ahead of time."

Chapter 20

RICHARD AND I WALKED DAVE TO HIS CAR.

"Bad business," Richard said as we watched the lights of the police car disappear over the hill.

I let out a long sigh. "Most of our suspects are staying at your hotel. Have you noticed anyone acting . . . suspiciously, shall we say?"

"I don't even know what *suspiciously* means, but I can't say I've noticed anything out of the ordinary, no. Or what passes for ordinary with a bunch like that. On the whole they're polite to the other guests, but they keep their distance. The actors don't sit down and join in a round of bridge or anything, but they sign autographs when asked and pose for pictures."

"I suppose they come and go as they like, and no one clocks their movements when they're not on set."

"Not that I've noticed. They've got a couple more days of filming scheduled, and then the whole thing will be wrapped up and they'll be gone. It'll be hard for Dave to continue his investigation when they're scattered across the country. Let's hope your problem, our problem, leaves with them."

"I hate the idea of never knowing what happened," I said.

"So do I."

A man tripped on the stairs; saved himself by clutching a potted plant; said, "Excuse me"; and burped. He then staggered off into the night. A woman ran after him.

"Can I buy you a nightcap?" Richard asked me.

"That would be lovely, but not tonight, I think. May I have a rain check? It's been an emotional day."

"I understand, and you most certainly can have a rain check. If you need anything, anything at all, feel free to call me. I mean that, Elizabeth."

"Thank you," I said.

The smile faded from his face. He rubbed at his jaw. Dark stubble was coming in fast, and his eyes were full of tiredness and worry. "As for our dinner plans tomorrow, I'll understand if you need to cancel if there are any developments with your mother."

"Why don't I call you in the afternoon and check in? Would that be too late?"

"No. Not at all. Good night, Elizabeth." He hesitated, and for the briefest of moments I wondered if—hoped?—he was going to kiss me. But whether he wanted to or not, too many people were around. He hailed a bellhop. "Can you get me a cab, please? Kennelwood Hotel."

"Yes, sir."

"Good night," I said.

The bellhop put his fingers in his mouth and whistled, and the lights of a cab parked in the approach to the entrance came on.

Y

IT HAD BEEN AN EMOTIONAL DAY, BUT I WASN'T READY for bed. Instead, I went into the hotel. I wasn't dressed for the ballroom, but I decided not to worry about that. I came in as Judy Rae was finishing her set to enthusiastic applause. The band struck up "Pennsylvania 6-5000" as the singer descended the set of stairs at the side of the stage. A man was waiting for her at the bottom. He bowed deeply, and she gave him a radiant smile. "May I get you a drink, Miss Rae?" he asked.

"That would be delightful, thank you. I'll have a martini."

"That song was beautiful, Judy," I said.

"Thank you," she said as her admirer bustled off, intent on his errand.

"Did you enjoy watching the filming earlier today?" I asked her.

"Only in that it reminded me, not that I needed reminding, that I made the right decision when I left Hollywood and an acting career behind me."

"Did you see my mother after you got back here?"

"No, I didn't. We separated at the steps of the hotel, and I went to my room and had a nap. I don't want to complain, Elizabeth, but now that we're on the topic, the rooms the Concord provides for the top-ranked entertainers have private bathrooms."

"Good for them, but we're not on the topic of entertainers' accommodation. I hope you don't mind my asking, but you told me you and Elias Theropodous had a relationship at one time."

"Thank you so much." She smiled at her admirer as he presented her with a perfectly crafted martini. He opened his mouth, probably intending to ask her for a dance. He glanced at my scowling face, thought better of the idea, and retreated.

"It never quite came to that, and the less said about that the better," Judy said.

"Essentially, he ran you out of Hollywood." I'd had enough of beating about the bush with these people. As had been mentioned, the movie shoot would be finished soon and they'd be on their way. Tonight was Judy's last night with us.

Tomorrow a comedian would take center stage. Time was running out if I was going to find out what happened to Elias Theropodous and, not incidentally, to my mother.

Olivia and I had an unusual relationship. She was my mother, but she'd never mothered me. Aunt Tatiana had taken that role while Olivia had always been more like an indulgent aunt. Dropping by occasionally, bearing lavish gifts; her clothes, her jewelry, her fame, making her the talk of our working-class Brooklyn neighborhood and, I had to admit, making me the envy of my circle of friends.

Did Olivia ever regret the years we hadn't had together? I don't know. When she inherited Haggerman's and decided to make a go of it, she'd called immediately to ask me to come with her. Was that because she'd hoped we could, at last, have a mother-daughter relationship? Or because she needed someone to run her hotel for her and I came cheap?

I didn't know.

It didn't matter, not really. I was here, and we were slowly building a relationship that suited each of us.

That someone would casually attempt to destroy that newfound bond for their own ends made my blood boil.

"*Run me out* is a harsh way of putting it." Judy sipped her drink. Her dark eyes watched me over the rim of her glass. I said nothing, and she shrugged. "Although accurate. I didn't want to have an affair with him, and he got his revenge by making sure I never landed a part again. Not, I'm sorry to say, an unusual situation in Hollywood. You're asking me if I carried a grudge toward the miserable man. It is absolutely none of your business, but as his death happened in your hotel, I suppose you think that makes it your business, so I'll answer. I would have happily strangled him at one time, but that was long ago. I say *strangled* because I would have wanted to see the fear in his eyes as he died and him to know I was responsible. I'd not have administered something as remote as poison. Fortunately, for my own peace of mind, I've been lucky, and I was able to move on. I had a singing career to fall back on." She lifted both arms, one hand still holding her glass, and indicated her surroundings. Music played, well-dressed couples swung past us, lights shone, and people laughed.

"Luck, plus a heck of a lot of hard work, and I got over Elias Theropodous and his manipulations. When I heard he was going to be here at the same time I was, I realized I hadn't spared a thought for him in a long time. If you're looking for his killer, Elizabeth, you'll have to find someone he wronged more recently. That won't be difficult. Now, if you have nothing more to accuse me of, I've finished this drink and I'm sure I can find a gentleman to buy me another." She pushed her way past me.

I hadn't expected Judy to break down and tearfully confess to poisoning Elias. That didn't mean I didn't think she could have done it. I suspected she wasn't quite as blasé about the ruins of her acting career as she put on. As we talked, I'd been watching for signs of some curiosity on her part concerning Olivia's condition. If Judy had poisoned Olivia I didn't think she'd have been able to keep her curiosity in check. She'd need to know how Olivia was doing. She'd showed no interest in my mother's well-being or her whereabouts.

That didn't mean she hadn't been responsible. Maybe Judy Raé was a better actress than anyone gave her credit for, but I decided to give her the benefit of the doubt, and I left the ballroom.

THE NOTE ATTACHED TO OUR DOOR MEANT SOMEONE had added the poison to Olivia's food after it had been prepared, dished up, and brought to the house by Al the busboy. Between five o'clock, when the tray was delivered, and five thirty, when Olivia brought it in, someone had been at our house.

Who was the question. Who, and why.

The why I thought I knew. To stop me from poking my nose into the police investigation.

I was getting absolutely nowhere, but did Elias's killer think I knew more than I did?

The lights of the hotel fell behind me as I walked to the staff quarters. The waters of the lake lapped softly at the shore, and from somewhere in the darkness a loon called.

Undergrowth rustled and Winston stepped onto the path. Before leaving the house to take Olivia to the hospital, I'd asked a bellhop to free him from my bedroom. I crouched down, and he ran to me, ears up, rear end wiggling. I scratched his head. "Silly dog. Let's take you home."

I headed away from the lake and walked up the narrow path running parallel to the woods as the dog trotted beside me. I glanced through the trees in the direction of our house as I passed. All the lights were off, so Gloria must have gone to bed.

Our house is located after the sign that reads STAFF ONLY, but more than one guest has decided that doesn't apply to them. The house itself is a few steps off the path, tucked against the edge of several acres of untouched woodland. We have no plans to expand the hotel, but if the popularity of the Catskills keeps growing by leaps and bounds, the way it has since the war, we might consider it someday.

A handful of trees provides some degree of privacy, but it's obvious to anyone passing that a house is situated there. The porch itself isn't big, only large enough for a small table and a few armchairs. The living room's at the front, facing the porch and the path, with Olivia's bedroom next to it, and mine tucked in at the back, against the solid line of the forest.

I shivered as I thought of someone watching our house, crouching beneath the trees, waiting for the chance to attack Olivia. Had they come with the intention of poisoning her food? They must have. No one wanders around with a bag of . . . whatever it had been . . . in their pocket.

Or maybe they do.

How long had this person been waiting for the opportunity to act? All day? Or did he know what time to arrive? Five o'clock's early for anyone to have supper. Had he, or she, been listening under the windows and heard Olivia call the hotel and tell them what time to bring her tray?

That had to be it. This person knew what time to come back and set the trap with a note stuck to the door.

I'd check with Olivia first thing tomorrow and ask if she'd noticed anyone hanging around our house, paying it any particular attention.

The other alternative, of course, was that the person responsible had overheard Olivia from the other end. Meaning, they'd been in the kitchen when she called. If a guest, anyone from the movie crew, or one of the entertainers, such as Judy Rae, had been in the kitchen, they would have been noticed. Noticed and evicted instantly, with much fuss and a lot of attention. Everyone within earshot would have remembered.

I looked down at the dog, trotting happily beside me. "You're no help," I said. "If you'd seen someone creeping around our house, you should have chased him off, or at least warned Olivia." I wondered if we should get ourselves a guard dog.

Winston lifted his hind leg and peed against a scruffy old pine tree.

Aunt Tatiana lives by herself, along with Winston, in a two-room cabin not far from the female employees' main residence. The roof sags on the eastern side, the windows don't quite fit into their frames, and the walls lean toward one another like drunken sailors in Times Square on a Saturday night, but she's made it homely and cheerful with the use of a lot of cleaning supplies and a lifetime of things she brought from Brooklyn when she arrived to take over housekeeping at her sister's resort. The cabin's not insulated or heated, and in the fall Tatiana moves into one of the guest cabins closer to the hotel.

Lights burned in the living room window, so I knew my aunt was still up. I knocked on the door, and it opened immediately. Winston ran inside and headed straight for his dishes in the small alcove that contains her samovar as well as a hot plate, kettle, toaster, and ancient icebox.

"*Lastachka*, is everything all right?" My aunt was ready for bed in a tattered, belted housecoat, slippers, and a head covered in pink rollers. A mug of tea, still emitting steam, sat next to a thick hard-covered book on the side table near her chair. The chair had been Uncle Rudolph's. The one he sat in every night after they closed the store downstairs and he settled down with his pipe to listen to the increasingly bad news from Europe on the radio while Aunt Tatiana bustled about in the small kitchen making borscht or *syrniki* and I bent over my homework on the kitchen table.

I smiled softly at the memory before bringing myself back to the here and now. "If you mean with Olivia, I haven't heard anything more. I brought Winston back."

"You needn't have," my aunt said. "Winston knows his way home."

"So he does, but I was out for a walk, thinking over everything that happened."

"Would you like a cup of tea? Kettle's hot."

"No tea, but I'll come in for a few minutes. I want to ask you a favor." She stepped back and invited me to have a seat. "You told me your friend who's the head housekeeper at Kennelwood said something about the movie people sneaking between rooms. I'm wondering if she meant anyone in particular."

"You have to leave Velvet to make her own mistakes," Aunt Tatiana said.

"You always were a mind reader," I replied. "But in this case, you're off base. I'm worried about Velvet, yes. I know it's none of my business, but she's totally enamored of this moviemaking, not to mention Todd Thompson, who, I've been reliably informed, is a cad. But that's not why I'm asking. I'm trying to get a feel for the people involved in this and who's sneaking around with who might give me a clue." As I'd walked and thought earlier, I remembered Richard saying he hadn't observed anything untoward on the part of the movie crew. Then again, unless they paraded their peccadillos and indiscretions in public, management wouldn't be any the wiser.

The source of all knowledge in a hotel, as in most other things in life, is the cleaning staff.

"You want me to ask Irena?" Tatiana said.

"Please?"

"Is late, *lastachka*."

"Not all that late. You're still up. Does she have a telephone in her room?"

"She doesn't live at the hotel. She lives in town with her husband. Yes, she has a telephone." Aunt Tatiana's cabin might be falling down around her ears, but it had a fully functioning mini kitchen and a telephone. She went to the little phone table and flicked through her address book. She dialed. Her friend picked up almost immediately, so I didn't feel too bad about disturbing her.

Aunt Tatiana and my mother had grown up in a Russian-speaking home, but once they started school, their parents had insisted they speak English to each other and to their friends. Tatiana and her husband, Rudolph, also a child of Russian immigrants, spoke only English in their house, and my mother never uttered another word of Russian once she started to dance professionally. On visits to my grandparents when I was a child, they spoke to me in heavily accented, broken English. To my continual regret, my Russian is poor to nonexistent. After Aunt Tatiana greeted her friend, I didn't understand another word.

They didn't talk for long, and soon Aunt Tatiana put the phone down. "The movie people are the talk of the hotel, so there's no shortage of gossip. The chambermaids say the young woman, the blond one, has her own room, but she does not sleep alone. The evidence is there for anyone to see in the morning."

"Todd Thompson. The rat." It had to be Todd sneaking into Rebecca's room. I hadn't been trying to find out anything that affected Velvet and the feelings she was developing for Todd, but now I had to worry about whether I should tell her that as well as what I knew about his marital situation and his flirting with Lucinda.

Aunt Tatiana shook her head in disapproval. "The old man. The one who died."

"Elias?"

"She doesn't know the name, but that's the man who died, right? He was not trying to pretend he wasn't in her room. He left things behind. His things."

So Elias was visiting Rebecca in the night. *Naughty, naughty.*

My mind whirled. I thought back to the Monday dinner. Rebecca had not been happy that evening, not at all. She hadn't smiled at Elias as though they were lovers, or as if she even liked him. She'd barely looked at him. He'd told her he wanted to go over her lines with her later. She'd pulled a face, and he'd snapped at her.

I guess "go over her lines" meant something different to him than it does to everyone else.

Rebecca had every opportunity to put the poison in Elias's food or drink. Certainly she had as much opportunity as anyone else there that night.

Did she hate him that much? She could have asked the hotel for another room; she could have locked her door and refused to open it when he came knocking.

If she'd done that, or taken any other measures, such as telling him she wasn't interested in him, would he have fired her? The way he fired Judy Rae all those years ago? What had Judy said to me earlier? *Not an unusual situation in Hollywood.*

Whether he would have fired Rebecca or not doesn't matter. Not if she thought he would.

"*Lastachka?*" Aunt Tatiana said.

"Sorry. I'm thinking it all over."

"You think the young actress killed the old man?"

"It's possible."

"More likely her husband or boyfriend."

"Yes, that's true. Except that there's no husband or boyfriend on the scene. I haven't noticed anyone paying any particular attention to Rebecca, and I can't see Rebecca trying to kill my mother."

"Someone tried to kill O!" Tatiana shrieked.

I grimaced. "Gosh, I'm sorry. I shouldn't have said that out loud." I'd decided not to tell Tatiana that we suspected Olivia had been poisoned, not until—or even if—I got to the bottom of it. I didn't want my aunt to worry. And now I'd blurted it out. "Her dinner tonight was poisoned, the doctor's sure of it. We believe she was given the same substance that killed Elias."

"Who is we?"

"Chief Dawson, Richard Kennelwood, and I."

Aunt Tatiana dropped into her chair. "I thought an upset stomach, maybe a touch of the flu . . ."

"I suppose it's possible Rebecca did it." I spoke slowly. "Almost anything's possible." When Rebecca finished her scenes with Todd at the bungalow colony, she'd gone directly to her trailer. I hadn't seen her again. I thought over what Mary-Alice had told me about everyone's movements this afternoon. She hadn't mentioned Rebecca. Rebecca hadn't gone to the viewing of the rushes.

Had she been creeping around in the woods outside my house, waiting for the opportunity to kill my mother?

That would be a dangerous thing for her to do. She was a beautiful woman; she had a recognizable face. Rebecca hadn't done any filming here, but plenty of people at Haggerman's, guests and staff, had seen her Monday evening and knew who she was. Olivia had been poisoned in the middle of the day; if Rebecca had been here she would have been noticed. She would have risked being followed by eager autograph hunters. Tomorrow, I might have a word with young Lacy. She was a curious and observant girl and interested in the activities of the movie people. She'd been about to approach Gloria and Judy at one time, she'd told me, but her father had called her away. She might have seen Rebecca or one of the other actors or crew where they shouldn't have been.

I thought back to Monday night, and then I remembered something else. Rebecca had flirted openly with Luke, the waiter. Elias had been angry about that. I knew now he'd been angry because he wanted Rebecca for himself. Had Rebecca killed Elias and then convinced Luke to poison Olivia?

Luke had explained where that fancy car came from. Didn't mean he wasn't ready and willing to do Rebecca's bidding.

"What are you thinking?" Tatiana said.

"I'm thinking it's late and you're tired. As am I."

"Are you going to the hospital in the morning?"

"Yes, I'd like to go first thing. Do you want to come with me?"

She nodded. I bent over her chair and gave her a kiss, called my good night to Winston, and left.

As I picked my way down the dark path, I was conscious of the whisper of the wind in the trees and the movement of every small night creature.

I needed to tell Dave Dawson what I knew. What I'd guessed, at any rate. I reminded myself that I knew nothing much at all. I'd leapt to a heck of a lot of conclusions. I didn't have his home phone number. I could leave a message with the police dispatcher, but they might not call him tonight. And even if they did, there was no telephone in Velvet's building, so he'd have to call the hotel and they'd send a sleepy page for me.

I decided to go to bed. Let everyone sleep. Olivia was safe in the hospital. I'd be safe in Velvet's room.

Maybe during the night I'd think of something more concrete to take to the police.

❖

I FOUND VELVET SITTING UP IN BED READING. SHE PUT the book aside when I came in. "Everything okay?"

"If you mean with Olivia, I haven't heard from the hospital, and they'd call me if there'd been any change."

"You're late. I was getting worried."

I sat on the edge of her bed. Her face was scrubbed clean, her blue eyes clear, her hair tied in a long golden braid. "I didn't hear what the doctor said to you, but I'm guessing whatever happened to Olivia wasn't an accident," she said.

"Doesn't look like it. Richard and I have been asking some questions, trying to do what we can to help Chief Dawson, particularly as he doesn't seem to be getting any help from the state police, because we're both trying to protect the reputation of our businesses, but—"

"You think that's why Richard Kennelwood's helping you?"

I looked at her. "You suspect he has another reason?"

"Yes, Elizabeth, he has a totally other reason. It has nothing to do with him covering up a crime, so don't worry about that. You can be so naive sometimes."

That was the second time today someone had called me naive. Maybe I'm not as worldly as I like to think I am. "I'll ask you what that means tomorrow. As I was saying, this attack on Olivia has made it more than a hotel matter. It's personal."

"They'll be wrapping up filming here in the morning, and at the bungalow colony in another day or two. Meaning they'll be finished and out of your hair. And then you'll be out of my hair and back in your own bed." She stretched out her arms. "Such bliss. I can't wait for a good night's sleep. Do you know you snore dreadfully?"

"I do not!"

"Yes, you do. The first night, I thought the mountainside was caving in." She grinned at me.

"As for them all leaving . . ." I hesitated before blurting out what was on my mind. "Have you made any plans around that?"

Her eyes narrowed, and her noise crinkled in a question. "Plans? What does the end of the movie filming have to do with me?"

"You're not thinking of . . . going with them?"

"Good heavens, Elizabeth, why would you—?" She burst out laughing. "You didn't think . . . Surely not . . . You think I'm planning to run away with Todd? How delicious is that?" The smile died and she took my hand in hers. "Is that why you told me about . . . about Ron?"

I swallowed.

"I'm honored you shared your secret with me, Elizabeth, truly I am. You did it because you care about me, and I love you even more for that. But I have no plans to go anywhere."

"But . . . but . . . you talked about being in movies. You said it was all so glamorous. You and Todd . . . You seem to be getting on really well. You had a date with him the other night."

"You are so naive, Elizabeth, and I mean that in a good way. Truly. Todd is utterly charming and so much fun to be with. He knows how to give a girl a good time and make her feel special. The problem with Todd, and all the other guys like him, is that they know how to make *every* woman feel special." She put her arm around me. "You need me here. I wouldn't leave you in the lurch."

"Sure you would."

"Okay, I would. I know I can't act, and that means out in Hollywood, if ever I did arrive all sweet and innocent, they'd want me for one thing, and that one thing, by which I mean my stunningly lovely good looks, won't last for long. Not by their standards anyway. I heard how they talk about Rebecca; you saw Gary screaming at her today. *Respect* isn't the word any of them use. She's lucky she has Gloria to intervene on her behalf. Can't always count on that."

"Gloria. What do you mean?"

"When Gary was having a go at Rebecca today, Gloria told him to back off. The other night when we were in the ballroom after the dinner, Gloria had a few quiet words with Rebecca after Elias got mad at her."

Gloria.

I jumped up. "I gotta check something out. Won't be long."

"What?"

"I'll be back."

I charged out of the room and down the stairs. It was after midnight, and the women who danced in the ballroom were staggering in, bleary-eyed, dresses rumpled, shoes in hand, laughing too loudly.

I ran to the hotel, past guests out for a stroll before turning in or heading to their cabins. The veranda and lobby were crowded with people not wanting the evening to end.

The bellhop assigned to watch over the main entrance opened the door for me with a respectful nod.

"Were you here late this afternoon?" I asked him. "Say, between four thirty and six?"

He blinked at the urgency in my tone but had the sense not to ask any foolish questions. "Yes, Mrs. Grady. I was. I went for my dinner break promptly at eight."

"Do you know who Miss Gloria Grant is? The woman staying at Miss Peters's house."

"Sure. The movie star. Nice lady. She gave me an autograph for my wife. My wife was thrilled."

"Did you see Miss Grant leave the hotel this afternoon?"

His face crunched in thought. "I remember. She and Miss Peters and the singer were dropped off here around four. Miss Grant left again a bit later, this time by herself."

"Did she take a cab? It would have picked her up outside."

"Yeah, she did. Can't say for sure what time though, sorry, although it was before folks went in for dinner. Before the cocktail hour, as people were still wearing bathing suits and their outdoor clothes and the like."

"Tell me what you noticed about her movements around that time. Please."

"Nothing worth noting. She came down the path and went directly to the taxi stand. She didn't speak to anyone, not that I saw. She got in a cab and left. If you need to speak to the cabbie, it was Karl Hurwitz."

"The cab was waiting at the taxi stand when Miss Grant arrived?"

"Yeah. Not a lot of call for taxis at that time of day. Early to go into town for dinner, late for lunch, and folks leaving have checked out long before."

"Thank you."

"Why do you want to know? Has something happened?"

"Everything's fine."

He touched his cap. "Have a nice night, Mrs. Grady."

I turned to leave, but the young man behind the reception desk was waving at me and I went over. "Yes?"

"Is Miss Peters all right? We heard she's in the hospital, and everyone's concerned."

I'd been hoping the news wouldn't get around the hotel, but I'd been naive—that word again—to think Olivia's whereabouts could be kept secret. "She's suffering from an upset tummy, that's all. Thank you for asking."

"I'll let the staff know. I was surprised her guest's checking out early, but I guess it's okay if Miss Peters isn't too sick."

"Her guest? You mean Miss Grant?"

"She called me a short while ago and asked what time the morning train for New York City leaves Monticello. I've made a note for the day staff to have a taxi called and a bellhop to go to the house to collect her bags in time for her to catch it."

"Okay. Thanks." I walked back to Velvet's room full of thought.

Gloria Grant had poisoned my mother, I was almost sure of it. She, unlike the rest of them, was a regular fixture of the hotel. She'd been here for almost a week and hadn't confined herself to the house. She'd eaten in the dining room, danced in the ballroom, lounged around the pool, had drinks on the veranda, and strolled freely around the property. She chatted to people, staff as well as guests, and signed autographs. Lacy had seen her talking to the gardeners. No one would have cause to wonder why she was hanging around Olivia's house in the afternoon. At the time Olivia phoned the kitchen and asked for her dinner to be brought at five o'clock, Gloria was in her room—i.e. my room—supposedly writing letters.

Gloria had been due at Kennelwood at five to join the others in watching the rushes. She'd been late; Mary-Alice had told me that in the car on the way back from the hospital. Gloria had apologized, saying she hadn't been able to get a cab.

But the cabbie had been sitting in the hotel driveway at that time waiting for a fare.

Gloria had poisoned Olivia and that had to mean she killed Elias Theropodous. I thought I knew why.

I had absolutely no way of proving it.

Chapter 21

"EVERYTHING OKAY?" VELVET LOOKED UP FROM HER book when I came in.

"Yes. No. But it will be. You said you're not interested in going to Hollywood with Todd."

"Yeah."

"You've changed your mind."

"I have?"

"You have."

I sat on her bed and told her everything.

WE WERE BOTH UP EARLY, BUT WE WEREN'T ANY EARLIER than the movie people. Our parking lot was full of trucks and trailers, and early-rising guests were watching the crew setting up their equipment down by the dock when I ran past. Pale light was spreading across the hills to the east, and the lake was a smooth sheet of shimmering blue glass.

Gary was waving his hands at the cameramen while

Mary-Alice hovered at his elbow. Todd, today dressed not in his army uniform but in the white blazer and navy blue slacks, sipped at a cup of coffee, chatting to Matthew Oswald and Richard Kennelwood. The makeup woman fussed over Roger. No sign of Rebecca or of Nancy Littlejohn, but they wouldn't be needed for these scenes.

From my office I called the hospital with a message for my mother to tell her I'd been delayed and would be in to see her later, and I sent a page in search of Aunt Tatiana to say I'd be going to the hospital later than originally planned. I called the police dispatch number and left an urgent message for Dave Dawson, asking him to come to Haggerman's as soon as he could. Judging by the tone of the voice of the man on the other end of the line, he didn't regard my message as more important than any other.

Messages sent, I headed to my house. I left my office by the back door, deliberately avoiding the main path and the movie crew. I didn't want anyone to stop me and attempt to engage me in conversation.

I found Velvet waiting, as instructed, behind a tree.

"This is a stupid idea, Elizabeth," she said. "As I recall you tried this the last time, and it didn't work. Call Chief Dawson, and let him know what you're up to. What we're up to."

"This time," I said, "I can be sure my listener will be in place, because that person will be me. Gloria's planning to leave shortly. If I can't get Dave before the train departs, she'll be out of his reach. We have to do this now. I'm hoping we can trick her into confessing, and when she knows I know, the game will be up and I can have security hold her here until the police arrive."

"Okay, say I buy that. Which I don't but never mind. Why is it up to you to trap her?"

"If what I think happened, happened, I can't let Gloria simply walk away, to go back to her normal life. I might have been able to do that—to leave it to the police, I mean— if not for the attack on Olivia. On my mother. That I can't forget, or forgive. Nor can I hope the police will be able to prove their case. They might not be able to. I have no proof, and they don't either."

"Okay," Velvet said. "You're the boss." She put her hands under her chin, cocked her head, blinked rapidly, and showed her teeth. "It's time for my close-up."

I gave her arm a squeeze and what I hoped was an encouraging smile, and I slipped away.

The lights were on in the house, and the drapes were pulled across the living room windows, open to let in the cool night breezes. I crept, slowly and carefully, up the steps. I tiptoed across the porch, scarcely breathing, and leaned against the wall next to the open window.

Velvet waited until I was in place, and then she clomped up the stairs and rapped loudly on the door. "Helloooo! Anyone at home? It's me, Velvet."

The door opened. "Good morning," Gloria said. "It's early, dear. Is everything okay? Olivia's not here. I got a notice that she'd taken ill last night and had been admitted to the hospital. Did you hear?"

"Yes, I did. Elizabeth's gone to the hospital already. I hope you don't mind me bothering you, but I couldn't sleep. It's you I want to talk to, not Olivia."

"That sounds intriguing. Come in."

Velvet stepped inside. "Oh," my friend said, "It looks as though you're packed and ready to go."

I didn't care for the unnaturally high tone of her voice. Hopefully Gloria wouldn't know Velvet well enough to recognize that she was trying to project.

"I hate to leave when poor Olivia's in the hospital, but I have appointments in New York City I can't miss. I'll send flowers to thank her and her daughter for their hospitality. I don't have a great deal of time, my taxi will be here shortly. What can I do for you?"

"I . . . I want your advice. You've been in Hollywood for a long time."

"I like to think it's not been that long."

"Sorry."

"Quite all right. It has been a long time."

"Do you think . . . I mean . . . do you think a girl like me can make it in the movies?"

"Why are you asking me that? I seem to recall we discussed that very thing at dinner the other night, and I advised you against it. Has something changed?"

"Todd wants me to come with him. To Hollywood. It would mean leaving Haggerman's, but I don't mind that. I don't like it here much anyway, and Elizabeth can be such a . . . never mind what Elizabeth can be. I want to be with Todd." Velvet squealed in a very un-Velvet-like way. "He's *sooooo* fabulous, but I don't know about moving to Hollywood if I can't get work. I mean, Todd'll help me get set up and do all he can to introduce me to people and such, but I thought maybe you'd be willing to help me too."

"Todd Thompson asked you to come with him?" Gloria's voice had turned to steel. "To Hollywood?"

Velvet sighed dreamily. "Yes. Isn't it marvelous?"

"*Marvelous* is not the word I'd have chosen. Are you not aware that Todd is married?"

"Married? He is? I mean, yeah, he told me about that."

Maybe Velvet wasn't such a poor actor after all: she'd adapted quickly to that surprising piece of information. "They're getting a divorce; his wife doesn't understand how important acting is to him. He'll help me with my career. Like Elias helped you."

"You think Elias Theropodous helped me?" Gloria snapped. "You think Todd Thompson wants to help you? Don't be a fool."

Winston waddled out of the woods and climbed the stairs. He saw me crouching beside the open window and woofed in greeting. He sniffed my shoes.

"There's that horrid dog again," Gloria said. "I simply cannot understand why Olivia puts up with it. Then again,

perhaps I can. Being out of show business has softened her.
That life makes a woman hard, Velvet. You seem like a
nice girl. Take my word for it, you don't want to turn hard.
As for Elias and his help . . ." The floorboards creaked as
she began to pace. "I was young and innocent, much like
you. I was flattered by the attentions of the important man,
much like you are. He spun a web around me, and I allowed
myself to be trapped in it. It wasn't long before he moved
on to fresher pastures, and I was discarded. All those roles
I thought I got because I was talented, all the attention at
parties, the fuss from the studio executives . . . gone in an
instant. Elias was a user, and if Todd's telling you the same,
then he's a user too."

"But . . . he loves me."

Gloria's laugh was bitter. "Maybe he does. Today. You're
pretty enough, but there will always be someone prettier.
Someone more talented, more desperate. Greedier."

"You mean like Rebecca?" Velvet said.

I held my breath. Winston barked, asking me what I was
doing out here. I waved my hands in the air, trying to shoo
him away. He did not want to be shooed.

"Rebecca," Gloria said. "She's much like you, Velvet, an
innocent. At least she was at one time. She comes from
Iowa, the same town as I do. I knew her family when I was
growing up, and so I wanted to help her. I tried to keep an
eye on her when she first arrived in Hollywood, guide her
away from all the traps, but I went to New York for several
months to take a role in a play. When I got back . . . Rebecca was Elias's newest protégé."

"What's wrong with that?" Velvet said. "I don't understand. Rebecca's the hottest new thing in Hollywood. She's
starring opposite Todd Thompson in a movie that has Oscar buzz. Hundreds of girls, thousands, would kill for a
chance at that."

"And she's a miserable, nervous wreck, drinking too
much, popping pills to help her sleep, not eating for fear of

putting on weight. You think a young protégé only has to *act* for her mentor? You are naive. Even more than Rebecca was. The price of fame is a hard one for a young woman. Elias wasn't even directing her properly. All that rubbish about clutching her chest and gasping in shock. That picture was going to bomb with Elias directing it, despite all Mary-Alice's attempts to save it, and I can guarantee he wouldn't have been blamed for Rebecca's poor performance. She would never have been cast again, by anyone, not even so much as a walk-on part."

"You didn't want to see that happen," Velvet said.

"I did not. And so I ensured it didn't."

"What does that mean?"

Seeing as to how I wasn't about to drop to my knees and play, Winston abandoned me and scratched on the door.

"You might be naive," Gloria said, "but you're not stupid. What do you think it means?"

I just about jumped out of my skin when a loud voice called, "Elizabeth, there you are. We've been looking for you."

I spun around to see Richard Kennelwood and Jim Westenham heading my way. I put a finger to my lips. Winston barked a greeting.

"What was that?" Gloria said. "Is someone out there? You told me Elizabeth went to the hospital. Wasn't that true? I thought I managed to get that stupid girl to get her nose out of other people's business."

"Whatever happened between you and Elias doesn't have anything to do with me. With me and Todd." Velvet spoke quickly, almost shouting. "Todd's not Elias. Todd says—"

"Is that Velvet?" Richard said. "Who's she talking to?"

"Wait, Gloria, please," Velvet said. "What should I tell Todd? He loves me and I love him and we want to be together forever."

The door flew open, and Gloria stood there. She was dressed for traveling in a pale blue suit and practical shoes. She saw Richard and Jim, standing at the bottom of the steps, looking baffled. She turned her head and saw me, trying to look nonchalant and innocent. "You!"

"Hi," I said, putting on my best hotelier smile. "It's a nice morning. I was about to knock. I thought you'd like to know that my mother's going to live. No thanks to you."

Before my very eyes Gloria's beautiful face turned ugly. Her eyes darkened and narrowed, her brows tightened, her lips twisted into a snarl.

Winston whimpered and crept down the stairs, keeping low to the ground, tail between his legs.

"Miss Grant," Richard said. "Is everything okay here? Can I help?"

Gloria turned on him. "Help! You think you're going to help!"

He lifted his hands. "Whoa! We don't mean to interfere."

Velvet came out of the house, and Gloria's face changed again. Now it was just sad. Sad and old and tired. "You poor, stupid girl. Look what he's done to you. What they've all done to you. To you and to me and to all of us."

She ran down the steps, past Richard and Jim without giving them another glance, and headed down the hill. The two men looked at me. They looked at Velvet.

"We have to stop her." I made for the stairs.

Winston had decided this looked like a good game, and he ran up the stairs, reaching the top step at the exact moment I did. To avoid kicking him or tripping over him, I instinctively pulled back my foot, throwing myself off-balance. I stumbled backward, crashed into the table, bounced off it, grabbed wildly at the arm of a chair, missed, and slid to the ground in a tumble of arms and legs. Velvet yelled. Winston barked. Jim and Richard, dodging the dog, reached my side, and Richard dropped to his knees next to me.

"Elizabeth, are you all right? Do you need to go to the hospital?" His thickly lashed dark eyes, full of concern, stared into mine. Velvet and Jim peered over his shoulder.

I took an instant inventory of all my body parts. "I . . . I'm okay. I'm okay. Help me up. We have to go after her."

"Will someone tell me what's going on," Jim said.

"Don't try to get up," Richard said to me. "Rest for a few minutes."

"What are you two doing here?" Velvet asked.

"I heard Olivia's in the hospital, and I was coming to ask Elizabeth how she's doing," Jim said. "Matthew Oswald invited the press to watch the filming this morning, and the actors are going to give interviews after. He's trying to make nice so they'll drop the angle about Elias being murdered by the studio because his picture was going to be an expensive flop."

"No one asked me if that was okay," I said. "I am supposed to be in charge here. Never mind that now." I held out my hand. "Help me up. I have to go after Gloria. She killed Elias and tried to kill Olivia."

"You can't be serious," Jim said.

Richard gripped my hand and hauled me to my feet. My head spun, but I decided I'd worry about that later.

I jumped off the porch and sprinted down the path. Winston streaked past me.

Chapter 22

"GLORIA! WAIT!" I CALLED BUT EITHER SHE DIDN'T HEAR
me or didn't care. She was a good deal older than I, but
she'd had a head start, and she was powered by anger and
hate.

The sun had risen behind the hills on the far side of the
lake. Paddleboats moved lazily across the surface of the water. Movie technicians smoked cigarettes in the shade and
chatted among themselves. Excited guests stood on the hill
watching the activity. Gary was giving instructions to the
actors, while Randy, dressed in his bathing suit, paced
nervously behind the camera, ready to walk across the fore-
ground as the scene began.

Richard reached me. I kept running. I could hear pounding
footsteps behind us as Velvet and Jim tried to catch up, Jim
still demanding to know what was going on.

Gloria pushed her way through the onlookers. Everyone
moved politely out of the way, and many gave her curious
glances.

"Excuse me," I said. "Please excuse me."

"Hi, Mrs. Grady," Lacy called. "Are you going to be in the movie too?"

"I'm sorry, madam," Richard said, "was that your foot?"

"Are those people movie stars, Mommy?" a child asked.

Some of my staff saw me heading their way and either hurried away or hastened to look as though they were hard at work, doing . . . something. Anything.

Without a moment's hesitation, Gloria sprinted across the lawn toward the dock. A section of her hair had come out of its pins and streamed behind her. Gary, Roger, and Todd were facing the lake and hadn't yet seen us coming. Mary-Alice heard the commotion as she straightened Todd's collar and looked up in surprise. Todd threw his cigarette into the water, and then he and Roger walked to the edge of the dock. They took their positions and assumed argumentative expressions.

"Quiet, everyone," Gary shouted as he took himself out of camera range. "Annnnd action!" The clapper board clapped.

Matthew was standing in a circle of media people who'd been allowed to get close to the scene. I spotted Jane Donaldson, still in her dull brown city suit. Gloria ran past them without a glance or a moment's hesitation. She skirted the camera and sound equipment, ducked under a lamp, and ran onto the dock. Winston galloped along beside her, barking at the top of his voice.

"What the heck?" Gary yelled. "Cut! Gloria what are you doing! You've ruined the shot. Someone, get that dog out of there."

Gloria paid the director no attention. She stopped running when her feet touched the wooden planks and she walked, slowly and deliberately, toward the two actors. Her fists were clenched, and her chest heaved with exercise and fury.

"Gloria," Roger said, "is something the matter?"

My feet hit the boards of the dock, Richard's a moment behind me.

"Get out of the way!" Gary bellowed. "Where's security!"

"Will you shut up," Mary-Alice said. "Something's obviously wrong."

Gloria walked up to Todd and stopped. She stood directly in front of him, filling his space, staring up into his face, not saying a word. Winston sensed her anger, and he whined.

"Gloria?" Todd said. "Are you all right?"

Roger threw me a question. I jerked my head toward the shoreline, and he stepped to one side and slipped away.

"I'm perfectly fine," Gloria said. "But you, Todd, are not. None of you are. You're all the same. You, Elias, the whole lot of you."

"I don't know what you're talking about," Todd said.

"I lied," Velvet called. "Gloria, I lied. Todd never asked me to go to Hollywood with him."

"What the heck?" Todd's face was a picture of confusion. "Why would you say that?"

Behind me, I heard Mary-Alice's low voice say, probably to the security guard, "Stay back until I tell you to move." Otherwise all was quiet. Everyone—staff, hotel guests, movie crew, journalists—watched.

Gloria let out one enormous scream, releasing years of pure, pent-up rage. She pulled back her right arm and slapped Todd across the face with enough force the younger man staggered. He lifted his hand to his cheek and stared at her through wide, shocked eyes. Then he shook his head and said, "You've finally gone nuts, old lady."

With a roar of fury, Gloria leapt toward him. She screamed and screamed and pummeled his chest and his face while Todd scrambled to try to grab hold of her flailing hands.

Richard reached for her, but he was unsure of how much force to use on the older woman, and she shook him off easily. I wasn't so chivalrous, and I grabbed Gloria's right arm and pulled hard, dragging her away from Todd.

"It's okay, Gloria. It's okay. Let's go up to the hotel and have a cup of tea. Have you had breakfast?" Beneath my fingers, I could feel some of the fight begin to drain out of her.

Todd yelled at her. "You crazy old woman. I've no idea what you're so mad about."

That didn't help. Gloria stiffened and she shoved me, hard. I staggered backward and collided with Richard. He lost his footing and fell so hard onto the dock I felt the planks shudder beneath my feet. Velvet cried out. A woman screamed. Winston began barking again.

"They're ruining the shot!" Gary bellowed. "We're losing the light. Someone, do something."

Gloria did something. With one final, long piercing scream she threw her entire body against Todd. He was knocked off-balance and fell back, his arms windmilling to keep himself upright.

I spun around, keeping my eyes on Gloria in case she attacked again, but Mary-Alice had arrived.

She laid her hand lightly on Gloria's arm. "It's okay, Miss Grant. It's all going to be okay. Why don't you come with me, and we can talk." She gently turned the other woman so she was looking directly into her eyes.

"He was going to ruin her," Gloria said, her voice surprisingly calm. "That lovely young girl, Velvet. The way Elias ruined me. The way Elias was ruining Rebecca. I can't allow that to happen again."

"You're absolutely right, Miss Grant." Mary-Alice put her arm around Gloria's shoulders and led her away, murmuring soft words of encouragement.

A camera bulb flashed. The newspaper people started shouting questions. Gary bellowed for everyone to resume their positions. No one paid him the slightest bit of attention.

"Take Miss Grant to the hotel," I called to Mary-Alice. "Velvet, show them to my office."

Randy stepped onto the dock. "What can I do?"

"Go with Velvet," I said. "Keep people away from them. Call Chief Dawson and tell him he's needed here."

Richard pushed himself to his feet and gave his head a shake. "I'll try to help control the press."

"Come on, ladies," Randy said, his voice calm and in control. "Let's find a place to sit down."

Everyone organized, I turned to speak to Todd. "You need to . . . Todd? Todd!"

Winston stood at the edge of the dock, leaning over, barking down at the clear fresh water. I peered over the edge in time to see the dark curls of Todd Thompson, Hollywood's next big star, slip silently beneath the surface.

Chapter 23

IN ALL THE EXCITEMENT EVERYONE HAD BEEN WATCHING
Gloria and hadn't noticed Todd, unable to regain his footing, lose his balance, and fall. We were only a few yards
from shore, but the water at the end of the dock was deeper
than a man's head, and I remembered being told Todd
couldn't swim.

My uncle Rudolph had been an enthusiastic proponent
of regular exercise, and over the winters he'd often take me
with him to the Bedford-Stuyvesant Y. I'm not a strong
swimmer, but I can keep myself afloat and even make some
headway if the waves aren't too high.

I screamed for help as I leapt off the dock. A blur of
white and tan flew past me, and Winston landed with an
enormous splash. The water was cool but not cold, and
once I'd struggled to the surface I swam away from the
dock. In two long strokes, I reached the spot where I'd last
seen Todd. I thrashed about, trying to locate him. Fortunately the water was clear, and he was wearing a white

blazer. I took a deep breath and dove. I could see the edges of the cloth drifting a few feet below me. I kicked down, trying to force myself deeper, but my shoes didn't help. I stretched my arm out as far as I could and grabbed for Todd's hand. I managed to touch it, but before I could get a good grip it slipped away. My lungs burned, and I was beginning to panic. I kicked furiously and tried to force my body farther down.

And then someone was beside me. A face peered into mine, an index finger pointed to the surface. I flipped my body and used my legs to propel myself toward the light, as Randy dove deeper. My head broke the surface, and I could hear shouted questions and people screaming. Winston swam in circles through the swirling water. I sucked in sweet fresh air, and took another deep breath, ready to submerge again in case Randy needed help. Two heads, one dark, one blond, popped to the surface. Randy's right arm was wrapped around Todd's upper body, and he used his left to pull them both steadily toward shore. I paddled alongside them, and Winston followed. Todd's eyes were closed, and I couldn't tell if he was breathing.

Hands reached out to grab the unmoving man. Todd was hauled out of the water, and Randy crawled after him. My head lifeguard dropped to his knees, lifted Todd's chin, put his lips on the other man's, and began breathing for him.

I staggered ashore, gasping for my own breath, spitting out water. I collapsed and lay on my back, staring up into the blue sky, coughing and trying to get gulps of fresh air. Winston shook the lake off him, spraying me with water. Golden hair fell over my face, and Velvet's blue eyes peered into mine. "Elizabeth? Do you need help?"

"I'm fine." I coughed. "I mean, I'll be fine. Soon. Where's Gloria?"

"I got a bellhop to take her and Mary-Alice to your office and make sure they stay there. Security went with them, and Richard's calling the police. Jim's gone into full newspaperman mode and is trying to get a statement from Matthew."

We heard a loud gasp and looked over in time to see Todd rolling over and bringing up a substantial amount of Delayed Lake.

The crowd cheered. Lacy, who'd pushed herself to the front row of onlookers, clapped her hands, and her sister, Carol, standing next to her, burst into tears.

"Perhaps it's time for a short break," Gary said.

"You okay there, young fellow?" Roger leaned over Todd. Todd gasped and coughed and nodded.

"In that case, I'd say it's time for a good stiff drink," Roger said. "Never mind the blasted scene."

"You sure you're all right, Elizabeth?" Velvet said to me.

"I'll live."

"Good." She straightened up and ran to help Randy to his feet.

"You." Jane Donaldson pushed herself through the excited crowd to address Randy. "What does it feel like to save a man's life?"

"All in a day's work at Haggerman's Catskills Resort," Randy said modestly. He smiled at Velvet. Her face glowed as she looked at him.

My aunt Tatiana was next to step forward, followed by one of her chambermaids, their arms laden with hotel towels. She plucked one off the top and threw it to Todd, then another to Randy, and finally one to me. "Dry off," she ordered, "or you'll catch your death, the lot of you."

A light bulb flashed and a camera shutter clicked.

Chapter 24

🍸

"CHIEF DAWSON'S ON HIS WAY," RICHARD SAID.

I had a towel thrown over my shoulders, my dress was soaked, the outline of my bra showed through the wet fabric, my girdle and stockings were sticking to my legs, my shoes sloshed when I walked, strands of water weeds were stuck in my hair, and my once-stylish poodle cut looked like a sheepdog emerging from a bath.

I turned my head quickly away from the mirror behind the reception desk. I'd staggered up to the hotel with Velvet and Randy. A movie security guard walked with Todd. Gary yelled after us, telling Todd to hurry up and get into dry clothes, he was losing the morning light. Half the reporters rushed Matthew, asking if this would be the end of *Catskill Dreams*. The other half ran after Todd, shouting questions and demanding the actor make a statement.

Todd said nothing; he kept his eyes on the ground and his lips pursed tightly together. Young Lacy fell into step beside him, and no one shooed her away. Her sister, Carol, along with several other teenage girls, ignored Todd and whispered excitedly as Randy passed.

"*Soooo* heroic," I heard one of them say.

"*Soooo* handsome," sighed another.

We climbed the stairs to the veranda. The two couples playing bridge in a quiet corner paid us no attention, but they were the only ones. Everyone else stopped what they were doing to stare.

"I want no reporters inside," I said to the bellhop as we walked through the doors.

"Yes, ma'am." He planted himself in the entrance, feet apart, arms crossed over his chest, formidable expression on his face.

Richard had slipped up to me and spoke quietly. "I got Chief Dawson. He's on his way."

"Good." I stopped in the center of the lobby, dripping lake water on the carpet. Receptionists watched me from behind the long mahogany counter, office clerks and cook's assistants clustered around the stairs, bellhops filled the doorway, a press of guests behind them, and more guests peered over the second-floor railing or gaped at me from the depths of the comfortable chairs. The hairdresser stood in the hallway, still holding her scissors, and two of her clients had leapt up from under the dryers without bothering to cover the rollers in their hair. Breakfasters huddled in the dining room doorway, clutching slices of half-eaten toast or glasses of juice. Luke hadn't bothered to put down his full tray before coming to see what was going on. No one said a word.

"That was so cool," Lacy shouted. "You should have seen it. Mrs. Grady saved Todd. She's a hero."

I didn't feel much like a hero. "Richard," I said, "can you show Mr. Thompson to the men's room? You"—I pointed at a hotel security guard, standing around uselessly—"see that Mr. Thompson is not disturbed. Randy, get yourself dried off and dressed. You're about Todd's size. Can you grab him some clothes when you come back?"

"Sure," Randy said.

"I'll go with him," Gordon the bellhop said, "and get the clothes for the other guy. Save some time."

"Thank you," I said. It was summer, and even though it was early in the day, it was hot. People walked around in wet bathing suits all the time, but Todd had had a shock and he needed to get dry and warm fast.

Velvet walked with Randy and Gordon. She and Randy spoke softly, exchanged smiles, and then the two men slipped through the crowd and disappeared.

"If you are an employee of Haggerman's," I said in a loud voice, "I am wondering why you have nothing to do. Has the hotel gone out of business? Luke Robinson, is breakfast service over?"

"What? I mean, no. I mean, no, Mrs. Grady."

"Glad to hear it. Please return to your duties everyone." Staff scurried away.

"Ladies and gentlemen," I said, "it looks as though it's going to be another fabulous Catskills day. Please don't let us keep you from getting out there and enjoying it."

No one actually left, but they pretended to be returning to whatever they'd been doing.

"You need dry clothes too, Elizabeth," Velvet said.

"I've got a sweater in my office. That'll do."

Behind me, a herd of stampeding elephants hit the planks of the veranda and burst through the hotel doors. Not elephants as I'd first assumed, but stampeding newspaper reporters. They swarmed around the bellhop trying vainly to keep them out and ran through the lobby, almost shoving our guests out of the way in their rush for the writing room to be first to hit the phones.

"Elizabeth!" Jim Westenham shouted from the middle of the pack. "Can I use the phone in the office?"

"No," I said. "You're on your own from now on."

Jim shoved aside the reporter from the *Chicago Tribune*. I led the way to the staff hallway and the business offices. The clerks scattered as I approached and settled themselves behind their desks, pretending to be fully occupied. "Tell the switchboard, I want no calls," I shouted.

My own office door was shut. I gave Velvet a look, she nodded, and I threw open the door.

"There you are," Mary-Alice said cheerfully. "Oh, it's you, Elizabeth. I asked one of your clerks to get us some tea. It seems to be taking a long time."

"I'll see to that." Velvet stuck her head out the door and bellowed. "Where's that tea!"

When she pulled her head back into my office, Dave Dawson and Richard Kennelwood came with her. "Todd's drying himself off, and two security guards are on the men's room door," Richard said.

Gloria Grant sat behind my desk. Her face was composed, her hands folded in her lap. She'd tucked her hair neatly into its pins. She got slowly, almost regally, to her feet. "Good morning, Chief Dawson. I assume you are here for me."

"Yes, ma'am," he said. "I hear there's been some trouble. You can tell me about it at the Summervale police station."

To my considerable surprise Gloria turned to me with a smile. "You're very clever, Elizabeth. I shouldn't be surprised. You take after your mother, although you conceal the steel beneath that smiling womanly exterior better than she does. Perhaps that's because you're not in show business. All the better for you." She looked at Velvet. "And you. You're not a good actress, not at all, but you managed to fool me for long enough. Todd never asked you to run away with him. No matter. If not you, and not now, another sweet young thing will come along soon enough once he starts feeling his power." She smiled. "I hope I've put a stop to that. Make him think twice before he strays from his marriage vows."

Suddenly, out of nowhere, I was angry. All the gracious charm and flattery in the world couldn't cover up the fact that this woman had killed a man and almost killed my mother. My mother, who'd done nothing to her but offer friendship and hospitality. "Olivia was your friend," I spat. "Does friendship count for nothing to you?"

"It counts for a great deal," Gloria said. "Oftentimes the friendship of women is all we have in our later years. I had no intention of killing her. It was the middle of the day, plenty of people around. I judged the dose carefully, knowing Olivia would be sick almost immediately and help would arrive."

"Rubbish. You couldn't have known I'd come home when I did. She might not have been found until it was"—I swallowed—"too late."

"If it makes you feel any better, dear, I planned to excuse myself from dinner with Gary and the others, and come back to check on her."

"It doesn't."

She shrugged, not much caring. "I considered that a chance worth taking. You were getting close to discovering the truth, and I had to try to put a stop to that. I wanted to add a little something to your food, but you have a highly irregular mealtime schedule and people are around you all the time. I simply couldn't see how to manage that."

Dave Dawson hadn't said a word since he suggested going to the police station. He stood still and quiet, not shifting his feet or adjusting his shoulders, his hat in his hands, his beige uniform blending into the office walls. He was letting Gloria talk it all out, to confess.

A light tap sounded at the door, and Velvet opened it to accept the tea tray. They'd gone to the trouble to serve the tea properly in the china we use for afternoon tea on the veranda—a pretty green-and-pink teapot with two delicate cups and saucers in the same pattern, and small white containers of milk and sugar. Velvet put the tray on top of my stack of budget papers. Mary-Alice glanced at Dave Dawson. He gave her a nod, and she poured and handed a cup to Gloria.

"Thank you." Gloria sat down and accepted it.

"You added a little something to Olivia's food on the room service tray," I said. "Something you stole from our gardening shed."

Gloria sipped her tea and nodded. "You should have your staff keep that door locked at all times. Plenty of children running around, you know. Who knows what things children get up to when they're unsupervised. Some of your nannies don't pay the attention to their charges that they should, never mind the mothers!"

"I'll get straight on that," I said dryly. "You went into the shed, and you didn't shut the door properly when you left. You were searching for something you could give to Elias. You knew what would work, didn't you? I noticed you like plants. You'd admired our flowers, and you were seen in conversation with one of our gardeners. We've had an attack of moles this year."

"Moles are such a pest. They can totally destroy a lovely flower bed or patch of lawn. Is that what gave me away, dear? My gardening knowledge?"

"Partly. That plus the fact that you kept telling people Elias didn't want Todd to get the part in this movie, but everyone said that simply wasn't true. You were trying to throw suspicion away from yourself, and you don't like Todd anyway, so might as well put the suspicion on him. You stood up for Rebecca; you tried to protect her from Elias, but you knew you were failing. Same with Mary-Alice. You knew she was the force behind Elias's success. I think you believed that if Elias was gone Mary-Alice would be able to openly influence Gary."

"I didn't—" Mary-Alice protested.

"I know you didn't, dear," Gloria said. "Unlike Elizabeth here, you don't have the gumption to stick up for yourself."

Mary-Alice opened her mouth to protest. She closed it again.

"Your father and I were great friends, did you know that? Probably not, but it's of no consequence now. He would have betrayed me, eventually, when I started aging, as all the rest of them did. I will confess I wasn't acting entirely altruistically. This movie would be better, much better, if it has a scene in which the character of the grandmother directly confronts the girlfriend. Two women on the opposite ends of the social spectrum, head to head. The contrast between the older woman—elegant, rich, powerful—and the young one with nothing but her beauty and her sweet innocence. *That* is the stuff Academy Award–winning movies are made of. But, as long as I was cast in the role of grandmother, Elias couldn't see it. He wouldn't see it. He wouldn't give me a chance to once again prove my acting chops, not even if you, Mary-Alice, told him to."

Gloria put down her teacup and stood in one elegant wave. "What is done is done. Chief Dawson, my fate is in your hands."

He stepped forward.

"For now," Gloria added. She turned to me with a smile. "I am not without influence or means. No one is mourning Elias, and your mother is unharmed. I'll look forward to returning to your lovely resort once my lawyers finish clearing up this little mess."

"You will not be welcome," I said.

Dave took Gloria's arm. "I'll be back later for a statement from you, Elizabeth," he said.

He threw open the door, and a cluster of shame-faced clerks fell back and rushed to their desks. Matthew Oswald and a deputy were waiting in the outer room.

Dave and Gloria left; the deputy followed them. Matthew came into my office, shaking his head.

"Goodness," Mary-Alice said.

"You could run the refrigerators in this place on that woman's emotions," Velvet said. "Do you really believe she killed Elias for Rebecca's sake?"

"I believe she believes she did. But she couldn't keep herself from saying she wanted a bigger part in the movie."

"It wouldn't have worked," Mary-Alice said. "This is Todd's character's movie. Not his grandmother's. I tried to tell Gloria that, but Gloria doesn't listen to anything Gloria doesn't want to hear."

We stood silently, all of us lost in our own thoughts and swirling emotions. We started at a voice.

"What on earth is going on here? Has everyone lost their minds? Guests are huddled in corners whispering, no one is doing a lick of work, and newspapermen are crawling out of the woodwork." Olivia stood in the doorway, dressed in yesterday's stained and badly wrinkled clothes. She wore no makeup, and her hair was stuffed into a lopsided lump at the back of her head. "Elizabeth, I tried to get someone to call you, but the hotel switchboard told the nurse they wouldn't put her call through. I never! I had to get a taxi to bring me home from the hospital. As soon as I stepped out of the cab, I was waylaid by reporters shouting for a state-ment. I had absolutely no idea what nonsense they were on about." She patted her hair. "I must look a dreadful mess. You could have warned me they'd be taking my picture."

"For once, Olivia," I said, "I don't think you need to worry about it being your picture in the papers."

Chapter 25

ONCE EVERYONE HAD LEFT MY OFFICE, I'D GONE TO THE house to change into dry clothes and tuck Olivia—shocked into silence at the news that her longtime friend had been arrested for trying to murder her—into bed for the remainder of the day. She didn't need to rest, she told me, but Aunt Tatiana and I insisted.

With Olivia settled and me changed, I returned to the hotel to try to get some work done. The movie crew had packed up all their stuff and cleared out without finishing the scene between Todd and Roger. The last of the journalists had been evicted from the property, and they stampeded into town to try to get a statement out of Dave. *Good luck with that*, I thought.

Francis Monahan nodded politely to me as he weeded flower beds. I spent a few moments watching Velvet giving a tennis lesson and saw Randy sitting high over the pool in his lifeguard's chair, while giggling teenage girls paraded and preened under his ever-watchful eye. Despite Lacy telling everyone who'd listen, and many who didn't want to, that I'd saved Todd, it seemed as though the role of hero-of-the-hour had been assigned to Randy.

I was fine with that. About all I'd done was thrash around in the water.

I went into the hotel through the rear entrance. In the kitchen Chef Leonardo and Saladman Nick were screaming at each other. I kept on walking.

"I can take you for a ride after work, if you like," Luke was saying to a young and pretty cook's helper as I passed the room where we stored dishes, cutlery, and linens.

As I walked through the business office, I told the clerks, "I'll be in for the rest of the day if anyone needs to speak to me." I went through to my small, cramped, dark office. I left the door open, dropped into the chair behind my desk, picked up my pencil, plucked the first message slip off the top of the stack, and picked up the phone.

I worked straight through, only looking up when a kitchen helper brought me coffee and cookies and later my lunch. I was highly relieved to see I hadn't been given a tuna fish sandwich today.

Dave Dawson phoned to say Gloria had been formally charged with the murder of Elias T. Theropodous and the attempted murder of Olga Petrovia Montgomery. (My mother, I feared, would not be happy at having her real name in the official paperwork.)

Late in the afternoon, Mary-Alice called to fill me in on what was happening with the movie. "Matthew and the studio have agreed to continue with the picture. Gloria's scenes are finished, but they're going to be scrubbed entirely and we're rushing a younger actress up from the city to play Todd's mother instead. She'll mostly stand in the background and wring her hands while Todd and Roger argue. Matthew has asked me to check if we can use your property to reshoot the scenes without Gloria. Shouldn't need more than a couple of days at most."

I sighed heavily and spun my pencil on my desk. "I don't know, Mary-Alice. We've gone to a heck of a lot of trouble and inconvenience having you lot here." Not to mention my mother almost being murdered and me almost drowning trying to save their star. I waited.

"I understand," Mary-Alice said at last. "I'm authorized to double your fee."

"That'll do it."

She chucked. "I figured it would. Before I let you get back to work, I have some news of my own. Matthew has asked me to direct the new scenes."

"That's great!"

"He seems to think I have a better understanding of the dynamics between Todd and his family and between Todd and Rebecca than Gary does. Gary is, needless to say, not happy, but he's been promised he can still direct the scenes when Todd supposedly goes off to the war, so that's mollified him. Somewhat."

"Perhaps that'll be the start of something for you," I said. "And you'll get the recognition you deserve."

"That might be taking things too far, but I can hope. The director's credits are going to be so long in this movie, they probably think they can sneak my name in and no one will notice. We'll be back first thing tomorrow. We'll be filming the dock scenes and still need that morning light."

🍸

EVERYONE HAD GONE HOME, AND ALL WAS QUIET IN THE outer office. I heard the door to the corridor open and footsteps cross the floor and then a light tap on my open door.

"Dinnertime!" Richard Kennelwood's head popped around the corner.

I glanced at my watch. Seven thirty. "Our dinner! I'm so sorry, Richard." I gave my head a shake. "I forgot. It's been—"

"It's been a rough day," he said. "Don't worry about it. Can I come in?"

"Of course." I tried not to pat my hair. I'd done what I could to fix it when I'd changed earlier, but I hadn't been to the hairdresser so she could put it right again.

Richard carried a huge wicker basket covered with a red-and-white-checked cloth. My eyebrows rose.

"I figured you wouldn't feel much like getting changed and going out for dinner. I don't feel much like it myself. I called your house, and your mother told me you were still at the office."

"With all that's been happening, I've fallen so far behind."

"May I?" he indicated a side table, piled high with hotel brochures, local advertising material, and telephone directories.

"Feel free," I said.

He swept it all onto the floor and put his basket on the table. "Ta da!" With a flourish he removed the cover and began taking out bread and cheeses and a length of salami, individual meat pies, and a platter of shrimp with a bowl of cocktail sauce on the side. He pulled out a bottle of champagne and two coupe glasses, and last of all two small plates and two fresh linen napkins.

"A veritable feast," I said, delighted.

He deftly popped the cork, poured the champagne, passed me a glass, and then he lifted his in salute. "To a job well done, Elizabeth. You saved both our hotels."

I saluted him back and sipped. The bubbles danced on my tongue. This was definitely the good stuff. Probably taken straight from Richard's father's private stock. "An exaggeration. The news cycle was moving on."

"Perhaps, but an unsolved murder hanging over the hotels wouldn't have been good for business. Speaking of the news cycle moving on, I heard you were on the CBS Television News at six."

"I was what?"

He grinned at me. "Yup. I got a call from a friend in the city who has a television. He said the top story was the saving of Todd Thompson from drowning. Your name was mentioned, as was Haggerman's. Along with footage of the"—he made quotation marks in the air with his fingers—"'dramatic rescue.' The movie cameras kept shooting the entire time. A bit of clever editing managed to make Delayed Lake on a summer's morning look like the North Atlantic in a tempest."

"They're not going to use it in the movie, are they?" I was horrified.

"No. They won't want to pay you and Randy, for one thing. Besides, it doesn't suit the plot to have their lead actor dragged out of the water half-drowned by a lifeguard and a lady hotel manager."

"I'm glad I didn't see it. Do you think they'll show it again?"

"Probably not. The second item on the news was the arrest of Gloria—which was, fortunately, either not caught on film or Matthew managed to destroy it before it could be slipped to the media outlets. Gloria's lawyer's arrived in Summervale, and he announced he'll be making a statement in the morning. He's giving the TV news cameras time to get up here. Once they have that footage, and can dig up some old film clips of Gloria, your dramatic rescue will be forgotten."

"Good. I know they say any publicity is good publicity, but I don't want that sort of attention focused on Haggerman's. This is, after all, a family-friendly resort, the perfect place for your relaxing summer vacation, far from the worries of the city. Not a place where murder, attempted murder, and 'dramatic rescues' happen."

"Cheese?"

"Thank you."

He prepared me a plate of food, and then one for himself. We sipped champagne, munched on snacks, and smiled at each other across my desk. I was sitting in my hard, stiff-backed office chair, my desk was piled high with papers, the lamps were all on, someone shouted out in the corridor.

It might have been the most romantic thing I had ever experienced. I felt myself coloring at the thought, and I ducked my head.

"Despite Gary screaming at everyone to get back into position after Gloria had been taken away," Richard said, "Matthew shut the set down. He went back to my place and spent the rest of the morning on the phone to Los Angeles. When he finally emerged, he told me he managed to talk the studio into continuing with the shoot."

"I spoke to Mary-Alice earlier. They'll be back here tomorrow to carry on as though nothing happened."

"I . . . uh . . . saw Jim Westenham hanging around my place. When the press couldn't get anything out of Dave Dawson about what would happen next, and no pictures of Gloria Grant in chains or behind bars were forthcoming, they rushed to Kennelwood to speak to Gary or Matthew. Gary refused to appear, but Matthew gave a short statement about continuing the filming. I believe he might have even said 'the show must go on' and something about the movie being a tribute to Elias. He also, by the way, told them the set would be closed to the press from now on."

"Thank heavens for that. What does that have to do with Jim?"

"Nothing really. I was just . . . uh . . . wondering if he'd come back here?"

I shook my head. "I haven't seen him. He must have a long story to file."

"That's good," Richard said.

"Why is it good?"

"No reason." He bit into a flaky pastry. "Nice pies these."

We drank our champagne, ate our picnic supper, and changed the topic. Neither of us wanted to think any more about the nastier side of show business. Instead, Richard had me roaring with laughter over his stories about being a curious little boy growing up in a Catskills resort, and I told him about my divided childhood. One part spent with Aunt Tatiana and Uncle Rudolph in their tiny apartment above a corner store in Brooklyn, and the other part being whisked off to the Russian Tea Room for lunch with Olivia or putting on an overly starched frilly party dress to attend a matinee and meet her fellow performers after the show, and then being sent home alone in a cab loaded down with highly impractical presents.

He poured the last drops out of the bottle into my glass, and to my surprise, I realized that outside my window night had fallen.

"It's late." Richard got to his feet. "And it's been a heck of a long day." He started putting the picnic debris into the basket. "Are you ready to go home?"

"Yes, I think I am. Anything else can wait until tomorrow. I hope it can wait until tomorrow." I stood up, grabbed my purse and key chain, switched off the fan and the lights, and we left through the dark and quiet main office. The lobby was crowded with guests heading back to their cabins after dinner or coming in for the evening's dancing. No one paid any attention to us except for the bellhop who held the door with a nod and a polite "Evening, Mrs. Grady. Sir."

Richard and I walked up the path together, going slowly and not talking, enjoying the peace of the evening and each other's company.

Chapter 26

"FRONT PAGE OF TODAY'S *NEW YORK TIMES*."

"I don't want to look," I said.

Olivia snatched the paper out of Velvet's hand and stared at the front page. "You're right," she said, folding the paper. "You don't want to look."

"Now I have to." I held out my hand.

"Don't say I didn't warn you." Olivia reluctantly passed it to me.

I shrieked.

It was the morning after the dramatic events down by the dock. Last night, Richard had walked me to the house I share with Olivia. We said good night on the porch, as insects darted around the light above our heads. He didn't kiss me, and I didn't know how I felt about that. I expected Olivia to waylay me the moment I stepped through the door, demanding to hear why I was with Richard, but instead she had something more important on her mind.

"You were on the television news! The telephone hasn't

stopped ringing since with calls from my New York friends who have televisions and others who heard about it. It was, they say, very exciting. Todd Thompson saved from certain death by the fast actions of a hotel lifeguard and . . . an un-named woman."

"Thank heavens, I am unnamed," I said. "Enjoy it tonight, Olivia. I bet that footage will be destroyed mighty fast. The studio will see to that. It doesn't show Todd Thompson, all-American hero, in a particularly good light."

"We should buy a television."

"We can't afford one. We don't need one. I won't be on again."

"We need to keep up with what's happening in the world," Olivia said.

"We have a radio."

"A radio is adequate, but we must move with the times, Elizabeth. We'll get a television," my mother said in that voice that put an end to any chance of discussion. She reached for the phone, but I put my hand on her arm. "Never mind what's been on television, are *you* all right?"

"Me? I'm fine, dear. Right as rain. I had a long nap this afternoon and a light soup for my supper. The doctor assured me the poison will have cleared my system by now." She gave me a stiff smile.

I did not smile back. "I don't mean that. I mean emotion-ally. Your friend tried to kill you. Okay, she says she didn't intend to actually kill you, just make you sick, but it could have turned out that way, and I don't imagine she particu-larly cared if it did. That has to be hard to deal with."

She stared into my eyes, and then she lifted one hand and stroked my cheek. "Hard. Yes, it is hard. I don't have a lot left to me, and thus I value the continuing friendship of old acquaintances. That is—was—important to me. Glo-ria's betrayal is hard to take indeed."

I put my hand over hers and felt its warmth. "Olivia, you have a great deal left to you. You have this marvelous resort, this beautiful place to live. You have the adoration of legions of fans. You have your health. You have your sister, as loyal as only an older sister can be. You have . . ." I swallowed. "You have me."

This time her smile had lit up her entire face. "You're right, dear. I have so very much. You, most of all."

Now I stared at the front page of the *New York Times* in shock. The movie studio might be able to have the footage of Randy and me rescuing Todd destroyed, but plenty of newspaper cameras had been on the scene.

The photograph filled the entire top of the paper, above the fold. It showed Randy, looking terribly handsome and muscular in his bathing suit, swimming to shore with his powerful arms wrapped around Todd Thompson. Todd, on the other hand, didn't look at all handsome nor muscular in his sodden white blazer. A figure resembling a drowned rat with red hair treaded water behind them. That drowned rat, I realized, was me.

The caption read, "Randy Fontaine and Elizabeth Grady of Haggerman's Catskills Resort are credited with saving the life of Hollywood star Todd Thompson." The accompanying article was bylined Jim Westenham. It was a long piece and continued on page A2.

"Nice photo, Elizabeth," Velvet chuckled.

"No one in the Catskills reads the *Times*, do they?" I said. "How'd you get this anyway?"

"George brought the papers up from town. He knew I'd want to see this one."

"The lake looks nice," Olivia said.

The background of the photo had a gorgeous view of the wide expanse of Delayed Lake, a couple of paddleboats bobbing on the calm water, and the treed hills rising beyond.

"Randy looks nice," Velvet said. "There'll be no living with him now."

I shoved the newspaper at Velvet. "Take this and burn it."

"Can't burn all the copies, Elizabeth. George said the newspaper rack at the store was overflowing."

Out on the porch Winston barked to be let in, but before I could do so, the door opened and Aunt Tatiana came in. She dropped an armload of newspapers onto the table.

"What on earth . . . ," I said.

"George bought up a copy of every paper at the store in town," Tatiana said.

"The presses must have been churning and trucks rolling all night." Velvet flicked through them.

"These are only the early morning editions from the East Coast," Tatiana said. "The other papers will be arriving this afternoon."

I stared at them. All the papers had some version of a shot with me in the water or crawling, gasping, onto the shore.

"Oh, look," Velvet said dryly. "I think that's my hand there. My moment of fame."

The phone rang, and I hurried to get it, glad of the interruption. In every single picture I looked absolutely dreadful.

"Hi, Mrs. Grady. It's Darlene here. I'm sorry to bother you at home when you said you'd be in late this morning. It's not anything urgent, but I thought you'd want to know."

"Know what? I'm not giving statements to reporters."

"It's not that. We're overwhelmed here. Every booking agency we've ever dealt with, and some we haven't, have been calling asking to make reservations since the moment the office opened. Plenty of individuals are phoning directly. If we can't give them the week they want, they're taking anything. We're already almost full at Christmas."

"Christmas?"

"And New Year's."

"New Year's?"

"People are clamoring to stay here. Haggerman's is suddenly the hottest thing in the Catskills, if not the entire state of New York. If I were you, Mrs. Grady, I'd think of upping our prices."

"Goodness." I put the phone down in a daze.

Aunt Tatiana, Velvet, and Olivia stared at me.

"What is it?" Velvet said. "Has the kitchen burned down at last?"

I picked up one of the papers once more and studied it. The background did look good. Randy looked good, like a lifeguard you'd trust to watch over your children. I didn't look good, but that didn't matter in the grand scheme of things.

"What do you know," I said. "As they say in show business, any publicity is good publicity, and it would appear our fame is spreading. Now it's time we all get back to work."

"The doctor told me I'm to take things easy for a few days," Olivia said. "I need to retire to my room. Elizabeth, can you ask the kitchen to send me my breakfast. I'll have the summertime omelet this morning."

I linked one arm through Velvet's and one through Aunt Tatiana's and led the way to the porch. We walked down the path to the hotel, while Winston ran on ahead, barking at squirrels to get out of his way.

ACKNOWLEDGMENTS

In the spring of 2021, I was once again unable to travel to the Catskills to do the sort of location research I wanted because of pandemic travel restrictions, but I got a lot of help from books and online sources, which I hope helped to maintain veracity about the times and the places. The memories of those who grew up in the Catskills or summered there every year are strong.

Many thanks to my dear friend Cheryl Freedman for helping iron out problems in the early draft. As always, Cheryl's friendship combined with her keen professional editor's eye proved invaluable.

Thanks to Kim Lionetti, agent extraordinaire, and Miranda Hill, editor also extraordinaire, for loving the concept and for their help in bringing Elizabeth and Haggerman's Catskills Resort to life.

And most of all, my sincere thanks to all the cozy lovers out there for reading my books and for helping to spread the word. Cozy readers really are the best.

THE TIPS OF THE TALL TURQUOISE AND GREEN HATS bobbed in the lightly falling snow as the elves weaved through crowds of painted dolls, toy soldiers, shepherds with their sheep, reindeer, poultry, clowns, sugarplums, gingerbread people, and candy canes.

"I feel like an idiot," Jackie grumbled. "If Kyle dumps me because he sees me in this ridiculous getup, it'll be on your head, Merry Wilkinson."

I paid her no attention. Jackie always grumbled; it was her natural state. I could only imagine the level of grumbling if she'd been left out of our group. She wore a knee-length tunic of gold, turquoise, and forest green over black leggings. Her hat was a foot-high turquoise triangle with a green pom-pom bouncing on the end. Papier-mâché formed into hornlike appendages and then covered with green felt had been attached to the front of her high-heeled, calf-high boots. Turquoise triangles, outlined in gold glitter, were painted on her cheeks, and her eye shadow was a

matching shade of turquoise. I thought the playful makeup
brought out my shop assistant's natural beauty much better
than the overly applied stuff she normally wore. I kept that
opinion to myself.

"Shouldn't you . . . ah . . . be helping?" I nodded to the
line disappearing into the crowd. One of the littlest of the
elves was in great danger of wandering off, so enchanted
was he by everything going on around him.

"If I must." She sighed heavily, but hurried to take the boy's
hand and, with a soft word, guide him back into the line.

My mother marched at the front, leading the group toward
our float. She was singing scales, and even if the children
couldn't see over the crowd they should have been able to follow the sound of her voice. My mother had been a diva at the
Metropolitan Opera. She knew how to make herself heard.

I adjusted my mobcap and retied the strings of my apron.

It was December first and we were assembling for the
Santa Claus parade, the biggest event of the year in Rudolph,
New York, otherwise known as Christmas Town. If there's
one thing we know how to do in Rudolph, it's Christmas.

I checked behind me for stragglers and then hurried to
catch up. The children were from my mom's vocal classes.
The youngest ones would sit on the decorated flatbed while
the teenagers marched beside, singing carols. They were all
dressed in the same colors and style as Jackie, in varying
degrees of quality depending on their parents' sewing skills.
They were elves, and I was Mrs. Claus.

Jackie had argued for considerably more décolletage
in her elf costume and a much shorter tunic. I'd put my foot
firmly down on that. Then she stubbornly refused to let her
mother make the costume roomy enough to fit over her
winter coat. I let her win that one. Jackie could freeze if she
wanted to. The children's costumes had been made large
enough to fit over winter coats and snowsuits. I wore two
wool sweaters under my dress, a pair of thick tights, and
heavy socks, all of which added about thirty pounds to my

frame. I didn't need thirty pounds, but it was Christmas and if I was going to be Mrs. Claus, I wanted to dress the part.

Up ahead, I saw Mom climb onto the float. Small children scrambled up after her. The teenagers took their positions and immediately pulled out their smartphones while waiting to begin. Parents milled about snapping pictures.

"Ho, ho, ho," Santa Claus boomed, waving greetings left and right as he walked through the crowd, heading for his own float.

The youngest children squealed in delight; the teenagers rolled their eyes and continued texting, while the parents clapped their hands and tried to look thrilled.

It was, of course, not Santa but my dad, the appropriately named Noel. Dad's round stomach was real, as was his thick white beard and the shock of white curls only slightly tinged with gray even though he was coming up on sixty. He totally looked the part in the traditional Santa costume of red suit with white fur cuffs, red and white hat, wide black belt, and high black boots.

I was the last one onto my float. I grabbed my long skirts in one hand; Jackie took the other and hauled me up with as much grace as if she were landing a pike through a hole in the ice.

"Everyone ready?" I called. The children cheered. It seemed like we might actually be able to pull this off. This was the first year I owned my own shop in Rudolph, and thus was responsible for my own float, but in the past I'd always tried to get home to help with the parade. Other years, we'd used a handful of the younger kids from Mom's classes to sit on the float, but this year—without consulting me first—she decided to make the parade the focus of their fall program. All told, there were thirty children, aged five to seventeen.

I'd decorated the float so it looked like Santa's workshop. It had bales of hay for the elves to sit on, a couple of battered old wooden tables as workbenches, whatever I could scrounge in the way of hammers for tools, and some

broken toys that looked like they were still being assembled. It was, I thought proudly, just great. George Mann, a
crusty old farmer who'd been roped into helping by my dad,
provided the tractor that would pull the float. I'd tried to get
George to dress in costume, but he'd looked me in the eye
and said, "No." I doubted George owned anything but
muddy boots, brown overalls, and faded flannel shirts anyway. If anyone asked who he was supposed to be, I'd say the
farmer in charge of the reindeer.

I had high hopes for my float. My goal was nothing less
than the best in parade trophy.

One thing we didn't have to concern ourselves with was
creating a north pole–like atmosphere. Here on the southern
shores of Lake Ontario we get snow. A lot of snow. It was
falling now, big fat fluffy flakes. The temperature hovered
just below the freezing point and there was no wind; people
would be comfortable standing on the sidewalk or sitting on
blankets spread out on the curb while waiting for the parade.
All the shops, including mine, Mrs. Claus's Treasures, were
closed this morning so everyone could participate in the fes-
tivities, but the business development office had set up stands
at regular intervals to serve hot drinks and baked goods.

The semiannual Santa Claus parade is the highlight of
the tourist year in Rudolph. People come from hundreds of
miles away to see it. When I'd walked through town this
morning, going to check that the float had survived the
night, I'd noticed that all the hotels and B&Bs had "No
Vacancy" signs outside. That would make everyone happy.
I say semiannual parade, because we have one in July also.
What the heck, gotta get those marks, I mean tourists, to
town somehow.

The parade assembly area was in the parking lot behind
the town's community center. This morning the lot was a
churning mass of adults and children in costume, marching
bands, flags, floats, some definitely better than others, and
tractors to pull them.

"Hey, kids, give us a smile," a voice called out. Russ Durham, editor in chief of the *Rudolph Gazette*, lifted his camera, and the giggling children struck a pose. Jackie, supposedly embarrassed to be seen in her costume, leapt to her feet and cocked a hip as the camera clicked.

At an unseen signal, engines at the front of the line roared to life. Marchers stamped their feet. Trumpeters and French horn players blew into their instruments. Children applauded and the high school cheerleaders did cartwheels.

Nothing, however, seemed to be happening at the front of my float. I clambered up onto a bale of hay and peered through the plastic-wrap windows. George was in the tractor's seat, where he should be.

"Let's get going," I called.

He shrugged, not bothering to turn around. He might have said something but I couldn't hear over the noise of the parade starting. Then, to my horror, George got out of his seat and jumped to the ground. He opened the flap at the front of the tractor and his head disappeared into its mysterious depths.

My heart dropped into my stomach. I made my way through jabbering kids and climbed off the back of the float.

Russ had gone to see what George was up to. When I reached the engine, the two men were scratching their heads.

"Your kids look great," Russ said to me. His accent was slow and sexy, full of the color and spice of Louisiana.

"They sure do."

"So do you." He gave me a smile full of dancing hazel eyes and straight white teeth.

"I do not. I look like a harassed old lady." I peered at him through my spectacles. The frames contained nothing but plain glass, part of the costume. I'd stuffed my black hair inside the red-and-white-checked mobcap that came complete with attached white curls.

"A beautiful harassed old lady, then," he said. I felt my color rise. Hopefully Russ would think the red cheeks were part of the costume.

But I had more important things to worry about right then than how I looked. "Please, please don't tell me there's a problem," I begged George.

"Darn thing won't start," the old farmer replied.

"It has to start!"

"What's the holdup there?" someone called.

The floats near the beginning of the parade, where we were, represented a toymaker's front window, a candy store, a turkey farm, a groaning dinner table, and the stable in Bethlehem. The quilters' guild had red and green quilts arranged on their laps, and the high school marching band members were grinches. The book clubbers wore long skirts and bonnets and were led by Ralph Dickerson, wearing a nightgown and cap and carrying a candlestick. The role of Scrooge definitely suited Ralph, the town's budget chief.

It all looked like total chaos, but the town had been doing this for almost twenty years and they had it down pat.

"Why don't you try it again?" Russ helpfully suggested.

"Been tryin'," George replied.

A man vaulted over the bar at the back of the toymaker's float, the one directly in front of mine, and landed lightly on his feet, his movements a considerable contrast to his appearance. He looked to be about ninety years old with his enormous gray mustache and sideburns, nose accented by a lump of putty holding up his glasses, and an outfit of woolen jacket, knee-length breeches, and shoes with buckles, but I knew he was a thirty-year-old by the name of Alan Anderson; occupation, toymaker. Alan was the second-most popular man in Rudolph, after Santa, but only when wearing his toymaker regalia. He was tall and handsome with blond hair that curled around the back of his neck, sparkling blue eyes, and a ready laugh, but he could be quite shy, and he preferred to go incognito, so to speak.

Alan and I had dated for a short while in high school. It didn't last after graduation. He'd been happy to remain in Rudolph, learning woodworking from his father and making beautiful things, slowly and carefully. I had stars in my eyes as I planned a fast-paced life in the hectic, exciting magazine world of Manhattan. We'd each got what we wanted, but one of us—me—had given up the dream and returned to Rudolph.

I'd wondered briefly if the old spark might be rekindled, but December in Christmas Town was not a time to be courting. We were all too darn busy.

Ready to find
your next great read?

Let us help.

Visit prh.com/nextread

Penguin
Random
House